Ruby's
Misadventures With Reality

AN EMERALD CITY MYSTERY

SAMANTHA BOHRMAN

Entangled Publishing, LLC
2614 South Timberline Road
Suite 109
Fort Collins, CO 80525
Visit our website at www.entangledpublishing.com.

Select Suspense is an imprint of Entangled Publishing, LLC.

Edited by Alycia Tornetta
Cover design by Dana Lamothe at Designs by Dana
Cover art from Dollar Photo Club

Manufactured in the United States of America

First Edition July 2015

To Justin, Mike, and Tamika, but mostly Wendy.

Chapter One

Dorothy and the Dollar Store Rubbers

Wearing nothing but a borrowed bathrobe, Ruby stood in Noel West's high-end prefab kitchen and leaned against the granite countertop while smiling like an actress in a refrigerator commercial. Noel looked like he might speak, but he took a farm boy-sized bite of his blueberry Pop-Tart instead. She willed him to say something to explain last night—anything would do—but all he managed was a disappointing, "If you're thirsty, the water from the fridge dispenser is ice cold."

"Gee. Thanks," she said, and they went back to smiling and sipping coffee like two wayward Old Navy mannequins. It was everything she'd ever wanted, if only she knew how she'd gotten here.

She remembered speaking in front of the Zoning Commission yesterday. She had been wearing her best approximation of a power suit while giving a local developer hell. Then, it all went fuzzy until this morning when she'd woken up in Noel's Ethan Allen-inspired bedroom in serious need of a toothbrush and a shower. Under her borrowed bathrobe, her skin was covered in fine purple grit, as if she'd run through a sprinkler and then rolled in grape-flavored Pop Rocks. Waking up at the zoning commissioner's house covered in what she could only assume was purple sex paste with a smooshed party hat under her pillow—it just didn't add up, not for a temp attorney who spent most nights Facebooking in front of *The Bachelor*.

Ruby gave him a coy look and giggled self-consciously. "Is it just me or are you purple, too?"

He arched an eyebrow and chuckled, but he didn't answer. Just her apparently.

She shouldn't have been surprised. Noel didn't look like the kind of guy who would paint himself purple and roll around in the sheets, or admit to it, anyway. In his crisp white button-down shirt and flawlessly tailored slacks, he looked like money, like his weekend accessories might be a leggy model and a tennis racket. But he wasn't snobby. Noel wore his fortune and looks as comfortably as Ruby might wear a leopard-print bikini and a fashion turban.

Of course she was thrilled that she probably, might have, almost certainly *did* sleep with Emerald City's most attractive zoning commissioner, but her uncertainty stopped her from breaking into a touchdown dance in front of his fridge. She'd been lusting after Noel from across the room for years. She'd been waiting for the perfect moment to get to know him, the moment when her hair looked great and she knew exactly what to say. Waking up with him was almost too good to be true. Almost. It wasn't like Noel was a shelf from IKEA—looked good in the store, but didn't come with directions or any of the necessary parts and would never fit in her living room. She was pretty sure that they had a fabulous time last night. It took all her restraint not to continue probing about last night, but she decided to play it cool for another five minutes.

A crumb fell unnoticed from Noel's lips. "When do you need to get to work, Ruby?" He'd said her name too deliberately, as if to remind himself of who she was. "You didn't mention what time you needed to wake up…you know, last night after…"

After what? Was he hoping she would fill in the details or did he lose his train of thought? She pulled the corners of her mouth into a premeditated smile. "Mind if I grab some more coffee?"

"Of course. Let me." Like a perfect host, he refilled her cup. "I've got a Pop-Tart in the toaster for you, too."

She smiled graciously, playing Emily Post to his Prince Charming—Pop-Tarts and purple sex paste notwithstanding.

When he handed her the coffee cup, his hand brushed hers and all thoughts of gracious decorum evaporated. Her nerves stood on end and her fingers tingled where they had touched.

If Noel's fingers tingled, she couldn't tell. His face was inscrutable. "Sorry to leave you so soon, but I've gotta run. I have a hearing in an hour." He glanced at the time. "I'd be happy to give you a ride, though. If you need one."

"No, I'll be fine." As she said this, she realized she didn't even know where his house was or how she'd gotten there. All she knew was that she needed a shower. "Mind if I stay and use your shower? That must have been a pretty wild night!" She gave him a wide-eyed "Please, tell me something about anything" look. The desperation must have radiated off her a little too strongly.

He shifted on his feet awkwardly and said, "Thanks for agreeing to keep it professional. It's so important to remain impartial in zoning decisions."

Ruby nodded, wondering if this was how he ended all his dates. She also wondered when the professional and impartial zoning decisions conversation had taken place. If she wasn't mistaken, there had been *two* crumpled party hats in that bed.

With the uncomfortable zoning bias issue out of the way—he really did look relieved—Noel took her hand. He started to give it a squeeze, but must have thought better of it. He pulled her into an embrace instead.

With his thick butterscotch hair and chambray eyes, Noel looked like her vision of Prince Charming. He could have passed for Prince William, except he was even better looking, with a more outdoorsy vibe. More royal. More charming and probably even more daring when it came to helicopter rescue and such. When he took her in his arms, she didn't want to be anywhere else ever. She tilted her chin up to meet his eyes and her heart began to race. The space between them sizzled with desire. Ruby stood on her toes and closed the distance. When she pressed herself against him, his breath hitched. Issues of zoning bias aside, when their lips met he reciprocated in a very un-business-like way. The kiss he had meant to be a good-bye felt more like a reason to climb back into bed and let the variance applications wait for another half an hour, at least to Ruby.

In a husky voice that made her wonder why they had to "keep it professional," he said, "I'll see you at work, Ruby

O'Deare."

She nodded. She'd like to try this scene again, maybe when her head felt better and she'd combed her hair. But Noel headed for the door.

Left alone in his stainless steel kitchen with nothing but the hum of the refrigerator, Ruby felt like she'd been picked up by a twister, spun around, and dropped in Oz. And it was only Wednesday.

After showering, she found yesterday's clothes in a pile on the floor. She looked at herself in the mirror and immediately wished she hadn't. The way her glossy coat of auburn hair dye contrasted with her hung-over pallor made her look life-like, but not quite alive, which was exactly how she felt. With a deep breath, she thought, *I can do this. I just have to make it until five.* But first she needed a ride. She dialed Ming, her best friend and roommate, but some guy named Todd answered instead. "Is Ming there?"

"Nope. I'm answering her phone today."

"If you see her, ask her to call Ruby right away. I need a ride." She had no clue where her car was, but it wasn't at Noel West's house.

"RUUUBY!" he yelled into the phone, as if greeting a drinking buddy at the local bar. "Where you at, girl?"

"Do I know you?"

He laughed uproariously, as if it was a funny question.

"Seriously, do I know you?"

"I'm crashing on your couch for a while."

"Okay, I guess." Ruby gave him Noel's address, which she found on a piece of mail in the entryway, and told him she'd meet him at a nearby bus stop.

She hobbled down the street to the stop in her four-inch

heels, where she sat on the only portion of the bench not occupied by one of Emerald's latest art installations, a cluster
of Norman Rockwell-inspired bronze statues. This one fea-
tured a woman and two toddlers sporting cheesy grins and
holding lollipops. It was an attempt to boost Emerald's snob
cred with "real" art. To save money on bronze, the statues
were less than life-sized. The end result—munchkins awkwardly lurking at bus stops and on street corners.

As she reached the stop, a bus pulled up. When she
didn't move to get on, the driver asked, "You getting on?"

"Um, no I'm waiting for a ride. A different one." As if
that made any sense.

The driver shook his head. "Whatever, lady."

Ruby felt the sting of tears behind her eyes when the
bus drove away, but she took a deep breath and reminded
herself that she had probably had the night of her life. Hopefully, Noel would explain everything and they'd have a good
laugh. Hopefully.

In her blue-checkered blouse and a pair of black sun-
glasses, Ruby sat next to the munchkins. She regarded them
with mild disdain and fished through her purse for lipstick in
the hopes of looking less like a wax figure of Judy Garland.
She came across a receipt from the Dollar Store—not somewhere she normally went. To her knowledge, she had never
been to the Dollar Store. The receipt said otherwise. It was
dated yesterday and the purchased products gave hints about
what might have transpired during last night's debauchery.
At eleven p.m. she'd purchased one box of Night Light Condoms and a Pepsi. The question was: Had Noel been with her
at the time of purchase, or had she arrived on his doorstep
unannounced with a Pepsi and glow-in-the-dark condoms?

Chapter Two

OVER THE RAINBOW, PANTYHOSE REQUIRED

For once, Ruby felt relieved to be back at work. Her fifteen-minute ride with Todd, who inexplicably introduced himself as her new roommate, only added to her sense of displacement. At least at work she recognized everyone and knew the rules: no open-toed shoes, pantyhose required, 1,300 billable hours a month minimum. For once, she took comfort in this clarity.

Smith, Dworkin, and LeBlue provided nothing, if not clarity. When they'd hired her last month, they'd been very clear about her role. Her supervisor, a woman unapologetically named Destinee Childs, had told her, "The job will last nine months. Tops. Don't expect an invitation to the Christmas party."

Ruby sat down at her desk, started up her computer, and surveyed her little space. Her glass-topped desk's neatness verged on sterile. She had no family pictures or kid art, only a framed photo of a dog that pre-dated her arrival. A motivational poster hung above her desk. It pictured a businessman riding a dollar bill over a rainbow like a magic carpet. Not long ago, she'd tried to trade her coworker Ted for his soaring eagle "Persevere!" poster, but he wouldn't go for it, so she was stuck with the man on the dollar bill mocking her in 36-point font, "Follow your dreams! Way up high!" As if. She was just staving off the inevitable. At the end of nine months, she expected to be serving jalapeno poppers and mudslides at Applebee's. Such was the fate of a middle-of-the-pack law grad in a tepid economy. Come to think of it, Todd might come in handy if he contributed to the rent.

Before getting down to business, she tried Ming again, hopeful her friend could explain something, how she ended up in Noel West's bed covered in purple grit or anything about Todd. When Ming didn't answer, she checked her email and made a list of things to do: catalogue evidence, file an answer in an insurance case, and call Estelle Harris, a pro bono client assigned by the court. The court must not have realized Ruby was a temp attorney.

Before calling the pro bono client, she picked up the case file. The prosecutor had accused Ms. Harris of robbing a grocery-store branch of the Giddyup Bank. He had charged her with armed robbery, conspiracy to commit robbery, possession of an illegal handgun, and growing a shitload of pot in her basement. From what she could piece together, the prosecutor's office had charged three other people in the same conspiracy: Marcus Johnson, Jermaine Harris, and Trudi O'Kiefe. Ruby read with increasing dismay. Estelle was in deep.

As Ruby stared at the assignment wondering where to even start on a case like this, her supervisor walked in. Just like when you spot a cop and slam on the brakes, Ruby sat up straight and minimized the window on her computer screen. Destinee Childs was a woman as outrageous as her name. She had Anna Nicole's looks and Dick Cheney's demeanor. Ruby wasn't sure who her puppets were, but Destinee was certainly pulling someone's strings. In a frozen tone that iced over her sultry looks, Destinee said, "I saw that you were assigned a pro bono case. If you don't mind, I'd like to take it."

"Really? Why do you want it?" Destinee never so much as made a new pot of coffee when she took the last cup. Whatever was motivating her interest in the case, Ruby assumed it wasn't charity.

"No reason." Her tone said it was no big deal, but Destinee was staring at Ruby with enough intensity to flash-freeze a package of hamburger. Ruby shivered.

"If you don't mind, I think I'll keep it. I really need the experience before I go back on the job market."

Destinee looked puzzled that Ruby hadn't immediately complied with her request. Without a word, she turned and stalked off in the direction from whence she had come. The woman never wasted energy on the little things, like hellos and good-byes, probably to save her voice for harassing her next victim.

More eagerly than she would have fifteen minutes ago, Ruby picked up the phone to dial her new client. Estelle Harris was at home with an ankle bracelet due to overcrowding in the jail and lack of flight risk. After about ten rings, an elderly woman with a wavering voice answered. "Hello."

"My name is Ruby O'Deare. I'm calling for Estelle Harris."

"This is she."

"Hello, Ms. Harris. I'm an attorney with Smith, Dworkin, and LeBlue and I've been assigned by the court to represent you."

"Is that right? Isn't that just wonderful!" She said this as if Ruby were an angel from heaven, rather than an inexperienced, court-appointed attorney.

"Yes. I was wondering if we could schedule a meeting." Ruby started to say that the office secretary, Marvel, handled scheduling and could give Estelle directions to the office when Estelle broke in and said, "Well, I'd be happy to come down and meet with you, but I don't think I can. I don't have a car and my grandson isn't home to give me a ride, not to mention this darn ankle bracelet." Estelle laughed a little when she mentioned the ankle bracelet, as if it was a pretty good joke.

"The ankle bracelet is no problem. You're allowed to meet with your attorney. Would your grandson be able to drive you tomorrow?"

"No, he's in jail. Jermaine is my only family."

"I guess I'll have to come to you. Will three o'clock work?"

"That'd be fine. I appreciate you going out of your way, sweetie."

Ruby got down to her morning business before her meeting with Estelle. After putting in an unspeakably dull morning of billable hours, meaning that she spent only a quarter of her time on Facebook, Petfinder, and Zappos, she gleefully packed up fifteen minutes before she stopped billing. On her way out of the office, she stopped by Marvel's desk. "Heya, Marvel, do you mind if I borrow your car? I need to run out and visit a client."

Marvel looked over the top of a pair of cat-eye glasses that had slid down her nose and said, "Of course! It's parked by the koi pond entrance. It's the blue Geo with a red driver's side door. You can't miss it. Give the door a kick if it won't open."

"Thanks!" Ruby loved Marvel. She dressed like a 1960s fashion plate and knitted scarves at her desk. If her car was anything like she described, Marvel was underpaid.

Smith, Dworkin, and LeBlue, or "Smiddy," as the in-crowd called it, sat on the top floor of Emerald's mall, the Biomall, which happened to be the latest and greatest American mega-mall. Oswald "Oz" Rancka, the mall's developer, made it bigger than the Mall of America and way better. To get hip with the Prius-driving, recycling generation, Oz modeled it after Biosphere II in Arizona. Unlike the Biosphere, which recreated a mangrove wetland and a fog desert, the Biomall created a "shopping biome," basically California without the smog.

On her way out, Ruby walked past the window displays. Some mannequins in knee-length sweater vests, fingerless gloves, and over-sized Russian hats caught her eye. Fur-lined armless swing coats! She was in love.

For a certain population—frequent shoppers and mall walkers—the Biomall's climate-control capabilities made actual Kansas weather completely irrelevant, making apparel like a fur vest with a mini skirt as practical as mittens in Minnesota. Shortly after opening, the Biomall began notching its thermostat up or down to accommodate the latest trends. For girls like Ruby, who only experienced real weather in short bursts between the car and the front door, the mall's thermostat was the only weather to watch. The local news had even taken to reporting on it. The "meteorologist," who probably wanted to kill herself if she had actually attended meteorology school, would report from the koi ponds in the food court. Garbed in a sailor-inspired tank dress, she'd say something like: "Ahoy Matey! Mall shoppers should expect a sharp uptick in temperature. Think Bahamas, ladies! It's summer in Kansas," even though it might actually be late February.

. . .

Ruby stepped onto Estelle's front porch. The open windows seemed to indicate it was of the variety without air conditioning—something Ruby didn't remember encountering outside of TV. Thanks to the Biomall's marketing genius, she found herself dressed more for "today's hottest trend" climate than the actual Kansas weather. And so, she stood in eighty-five degree weather with a seventy-degree dew point dressed in pantyhose and her Dorothy Gale-inspired business attire. The shirt had already adhered to her back with sweat.

Estelle lived in a gentrifying, but mostly shabby, section of town, home to most of Emerald's minority population. It must have been pretty at one time. A spacious wraparound porch brought to mind afternoon tea with strawberry pie and a hand-carved wood door hinted at the house's glory days, now long past if the pile of abandoned furniture on the porch, the chipped exterior paint, and overgrown garden beds were any indication. After a knock on the door and a long wait, a petite black woman answered. She was dressed in a floral housedress, stockings, and a pair of sturdy black shoes. Estelle Harris looked like no armed robber Ruby had ever seen.

"Ms. Harris?"

"Hello. You must be Miss O'Deare." She ushered Ruby in through an entry filled with discarded belongings and old furniture haphazardly organized to create a walking path. "Sorry for the mess, dear. Jermaine has been too busy to help me clean up lately. Let's just go sit down in the kitchen."

Ruby started sweating as much as a lawyer straight from the pages of a John Grisham novel set in Alabama, which made her think she might have to pay attention to the actual weather if she did many more of these pro bono gigs. Estelle Harris didn't seem to notice. She steered Ruby towards the kitchen table, a sunny oasis in the dingy home, where she offered Ruby a cup of coffee and a freshly baked sweet roll.

"Mmm. This roll is amazing."

"I've got a heavy hand with the butter. I'm glad you like it, sweetie."

Ruby felt a twinge of anxiety when she heard Estelle mention butter. As far as she knew she had never ingested butter. She had always stuck to the fat-free trend of the moment, currently a yellow substance advertised as "extract of coco butter flower," actually slag byproduct from the malto-dextrose production that some genius at the ADM plant had dyed yellow and whipped into a frothy spread. After a bite of actual butter, Ruby was starting to think real products might be a good idea.

"So, Mrs. Harris, you've been charged with quite a few things." She trailed off, waiting for Estelle to explain how she could have been charged with robbery.

"Please, call me Estelle." Estelle looked serene considering the heavy-duty charges she faced. Ruby could hardly imagine the police arresting her. She looked like the long-lost black member of the *Golden Girls*, like someone who might have to miss her weekly bridge game to appear in court.

"Well, as I was saying, you've been charged with robbery, conspiracy, and intent to distribute marijuana. Because of the conspiracy charge, you are being held accountable for every bad act, even if you didn't do it. For example, you might not have robbed the bank, but you are being charged with it because the prosecutor thinks you are a member of the conspiracy. Do you understand that?"

Estelle looked as if she preferred a change of subject. "Yes, I understand the charges, but I really don't know what all the fuss is about. I haven't done a thing and neither has my boy." She paused. "Would you like some more coffee, sweetheart, or maybe another roll?"

Ruby accepted both. In between bites she steered the conversation back to the matter at hand. "Mrs. Harris, these charges are very serious. If you don't mind, I think you had better explain to me exactly what happened. I'll interrupt if I have any questions."

"All right, sweetheart. There's really not too much to the story. My grandson, Jermaine, he lives with me. He does business with his girlfriend, Trudi, and his friend, Marcus, mostly at the house. The police decided I must be the ringleader since I own the place." She laughed a little. "Bunch of fools, if you ask me." A look of sadness momentarily disturbed Estelle's placid countenance as she considered the trouble her boy was in.

"I've always encouraged Jermaine to spend time in the house and I like to know his friends, so most nights I cook for them and some mornings I make Jermaine and his friends an omelet, sweet rolls, whatever they want. I like to keep the kitchen stocked."

"That's nice of you," said Ruby. "What kind of business do Marcus and Jermaine talk about?"

"They're both in sales, a couple of regular businessmen. For the most part, I ignore their business talk. I just do the cooking."

"Okay, keep going. I'll try not to interrupt anymore."

"Well, a couple of weeks ago, the police came and pounded on the door. They arrested Jermaine. They said he had robbed the Giddyup Bank at the grocery store down the street, which I can hardly believe. Then, they searched the house and found Jermaine's plants. Jermaine came clean and told me he did grow some marijuana plants, but he said he only grows them for cancer victims and people with glaucoma… I realize it looks bad, but Jermaine really is a good boy."

Ruby doubted it. "So Estelle, you didn't ever drive Jermaine down to the bank?"

"No, I don't drive at all. He drives me to the grocery store now and then, but we never had any business at the bank. We bank at the credit union, not the Giddyup."

"But the grocery store you go to is the same one with the bank that was robbed, correct?"

Estelle nodded.

"What do Jermaine and his friends usually do while you shop for groceries?"

"Most of the time they go over to Little Caesars and pick up a pepperoni pizza and some Crazy Bread while I get the food. Those boys love Crazy Bread. It's no good for them, but what can you do?" Estelle smiled fondly as she contemplated her grandson's habits.

Ruby smiled, as if it was cute. Estelle was obviously in denial.

"Were you at the grocery store the day it was robbed?"

"Yes, I picked up ingredients for an apple pie that afternoon. I remember I was out of butter." Estelle paused for a moment to think. "The boys got a pizza while I shopped, the same as they always do. They were waiting in the car for me with it when I finished shopping. I remember Trudi yelling at Jermaine for getting Crazy Sauce on the seat covers. She was really upset because they were going to need dry cleaning. Very expensive. Anyway, we didn't hear a thing about the robbery until we watched the news that night. My, I was surprised. I was so happy we had missed that excitement. The violence in this neighborhood makes me so nervous. I hate having my boy around it."

With "Denial is a river in Egypt" echoing in her mind, Ruby looked at Estelle politely. It wasn't as if she hadn't been down that river herself, so she wasn't one to judge fellow travelers. She said, "I completely understand. But, I'm still wondering, did you hear Jermaine talking about robbing a bank? Or maybe his friends?"

The reality of the situation was clear to Ruby. Estelle lived in a carefully crafted myth of denial about Jermaine. He had probably robbed the grocery store mini-bank, as the police believed, while Estelle was picking out Granny Smiths.

"Did you carry the groceries out to the car yourself?"

"Oh no. The bag boy helped me out."

Ruby could not believe her ears. The bag boy had loaded Estelle's groceries into the getaway car.

Out of curiosity, Ruby asked, "How many bags did you have?"

"Oh, I think, three, and a gallon of milk."

"Did you see any unusual packages in the car that day?" *Like a giant bag of money.*

"Oh no." She shook her head emphatically.

"Where did the bag boy put the groceries?"

"Marcus had some packages in the trunk so Jermaine helped him slide them in the backseat." Estelle paused. "I understand why Jermaine is in trouble about the marijuana, but I'm sure he shouldn't be in any trouble over a bank robbery."

"One more question, Estelle. The police say you have an illegal handgun. Do you own a gun?"

"Well, yes. Jermaine bought one a while back and put it in the closet. He said he'd feel better about my safety if there was a gun in the house. I've never used it, though. It's been in the closet the whole time."

"Is this the gun the police found when they searched the house?"

"Yes."

"Did they find it in the closet you normally keep it in?"

"Well, I didn't ask."

"Did you tell the police it was your gun when they asked you about it?"

"Of course. It wasn't anybody else's gun."

"Estelle, I'm not sure what evidence the police have

collected against Jermaine, but I'm going to do my best to get your charges dropped."

• • •

Ruby picked up a couple of lattes on the way back to the office. After dropping one of them by Marvel's desk with the car keys, she sat down with Estelle's file. Halfway through her syrupy coffee she still had no clue why the police had bothered to arrest Estelle. Certainly there was no reason for the prosecutor to press charges. By the time she got to the bottom of her latte, her ire was piqued. She flipped through the file to find the prosecutor's name. It was Tyrone Wilcox.

Damn it.

Tyrone was a former football player turned law student, sort of pretentious, but gorgeous. They had dated for a while. She sucked in her ego and dialed.

He answered on the first ring.

With trepidation in her voice, she said, "Tyrone, this is Ruby O'Deare, you remember, from law school."

He laughed. "Of course I remember. Nice to hear from you, Miss O'Deare." He said her name with the same inflection you would say, "Oh, dear!" Her contracts professor had taken to calling her this after one flakey answer the first week of law school. It had stuck. Tyrone used it mercilessly, especially after the break-up.

Setting aside her embarrassment, she said, "I'm calling because I've been assigned to Estelle Harris's defense. I just spoke to Ms. Harris and I can't understand why you slapped her with so many charges."

"There's an obvious conspiracy between Jermaine, Trudi,

Marcus, and probably an unknown bank employee. We have confessions from two of the three. By her own admission, Estelle participated in all of the meetings at which the conspiratorial agreement was formed, provided the weapon, not to mention the fact that she was present at the robbery and a passenger in the getaway car." He let that sink in for a second and said, "We could charge her with everything just for being part of the conspiratorial agreement, but she did far more than that."

Ruby had expected the grandson to leap to Estelle's defense at some point. Apparently, he was taking her down with him. She rearranged the facts in her brain, putting Jermaine in the pile of jerks (next to her contracts professor) and said, "First of all, bringing snacks to a party of conspirators does not make a co-conspirator. You might as well charge the pizza delivery boy. And, she was not part of the robbery. She was grocery shopping."

"Jermaine says she was providing cover for them."

"Cover. Ha. If anything, she drew attention to Jermaine and Marcus because she had the bag boy deliver groceries to the getaway car. That alone should exculpate her."

He answered, "Jermaine claims that was part of the plan. It made the rest of them look innocent."

"You've got to be kidding me. I've never heard such a stupid idea. The bag boy is the one that wrote down the plate number."

"Well, no one accused them of being smart. Ruby, even if Estelle didn't know, the Ostrich Rule applies. Burying her head in the sand does not protect her from charges. She should have known. Should have known is enough to establish *mens rea*. By the way, have you looked at Jermaine's rap sheet? It's a mile long and Estelle has been baking snacks for him through all of it."

"She's his grandmother!"

Ruby returned the phone to the receiver with a little more *oomph* than necessary and looked at the clock. When she saw the time, 5:30, she felt the steam go out of her. It was time to go home and see why her hyper-rational roommate had invited a man who smelled like Fritos to live on the couch, why said stoner was driving her car, and how the hell she had woken up with the too-gorgeous-to-be-real zoning commissioner smeared in purple paint and wearing a party hat.

On her way to the bus, she stopped at a fountain. Like most things at the Biomall, it was over-the-top glitzy. It looked like the Bellagio's fountain had landed in an obscure corner of the mall, in between the bus stop and the entrance to JC Penney's, one of the mall's more unpopular corners, frequented only by old ladies and stoners.

Ruby stood before the fountain and fished through her purse for some change. Just like most people these days, she didn't have any. Suddenly desperate to make a wish, she took out all the receipts out of her purse—about ten from Starbucks, the one from the Dollar Store, a couple from Nordstrom's, some from TJ Max, more receipts than her salary justified by a long shot. She had already given all of her money to the mall so the fountain would just have to take the receipts as evidence of payment.

One by one, she tossed them into the burbling water. After she'd emptied her purse, twenty or so little slips of paper floated on the surface like bleached fall leaves. She looked up to the grand display of water and lights. Thinking of her tenuous job situation and all of the amazing displays of fall clothes she had passed on her way to the fountain, especially that pair of boots at Nordstrom's, she closed her eyes and wished for—she tried to think of something clever or to put words to the unknowable something she was missing, but settled on a trust fund. And Brad Pitt circa *Legends of the Fall.*

Then she walked to the bus because Todd had her car.

Chapter Three

HE'S SO CUTE WITHOUT A BRAIN!

Ruby flung the door open and threw her bag on the floor. Catching sight of Ming, she said, "Ming! I've been trying to get ahold of you all day! What happened last night?"

Ming stood in the kitchen of their shared home, chopping veggies for dinner. The house represented Ming's eclectic decorating tastes, which might be described as Feng Shui techno geek, meaning soft earth tones and careful furniture placement with lots of soul sucking, shiny black screens. The enormous television with accompanying surround-sound equipment negated any sense of peace created by the placement of the couch, particularly since Ming had an obnoxious comedy special cranked at top volume. Ruby did not contribute to the furnishings of the home because Ming didn't let her. Except for the litter box, but that was a necessity. Ming only tolerated Ruby's cats, Tom Cruise and Vera Wang, because they stayed out of the way.

Unlike Ruby, who had only stumbled upon her career because she'd watched *Legally Blonde* too many times and followed the advice of an online quiz (incidentally the same reason as about a quarter of her law school graduating class), Ming had her shit together. By the age of twenty-eight, she'd already racked up two PhDs, one in materials science and one in analytical chemistry, and all of her tattoos were spelled correctly because she knew Mandarin and Cantonese. Yesterday, Ming had celebrated yet another career success. Her latest project, a new *in vivo* biodegradable polymer vessel that functioned as a drug delivery device, had cleared the college's internal review board and was set for use in an experimental drug trial at the medical school. Yesterday's chemistry nerd after-party was probably where Ruby had blacked out. How Noel became involved, she could only imagine.

Ming finished chopping an onion and looked up. "What do you mean? You don't know what happened?" She didn't look as if she'd spent a single minute wondering about Ruby's whereabouts.

"Are you serious? I woke up in *Noel West's* bed this morning. Then he made me a Pop-Tart and broke up with me."

Ming started laughing.

"I don't even know how I got there. Do you?"

"West showed up here around nine or ten, after one of the neighbors called him, probably that uptight guy across the street."

Ruby knew the neighbor—he mowed his lawn five times a week and wore his pants pulled up to his nipples. "Why would Mr. Cuttings call Noel? I don't get it."

Ming looked out from under raised eyebrows. "Seriously, Rubes?"

"What?"

"He's our landlord."

"No way!" Ruby had never cared who the landlord was. Once a month, she wrote a check for her half of the rent to Ming. If only she'd known it was Noel, the zoning commissioner who left her tongue-tied and giggling like an idiot, she would have had something to say to him after planning meetings. For instance, she could have mentioned that the shower didn't drain. Then, they could have talked while he pulled a giant wad of her hair out of the pipe. Or not.

After rolling her eyes, Ming continued, "Yeah, he came in and sat down. I didn't get the impression he cared about the complaint. You sat next to him, drank a beer, and you left together. I didn't ask where you were going."

"Was I sober?"

"Maybe a little tipsy. You looked okay to me, though." With a confused expression, Ming asked, "I don't get how you don't know anything about this guy. Didn't you go to high school together?"

"I wish. His parents shipped him off to prep school. I don't think he came back to Emerald until a year or so ago. He's that guy that everyone knows of, but nobody really knows." Ruby had seen him from time to time at zoning meetings or the grocery store, but she didn't know anything about him, except stuff Marvel told her, plus a few general observations, all of which screamed "out of her league." Marvel thought he owned a yacht and a winery. One time, she'd rhapsodized about his "not-too-hairy chest." Basically, male perfection of the rich, upscale variety.

With a sigh, Ruby decided to let the amnesia issue drop. She would just have to accept the facts—one lost night and a missed opportunity with the hottest guy she'd ever seen at work. If only she had gone for more of a Grace Kelly look. He probably preferred icy blondes. When Ming handed her a glass of wine, Ruby smiled and asked, "Is *The Bachelo*r on?"

It was, so Ruby plopped onto the couch with a plate of stir-fry. She wasn't too surprised to find herself next to Todd who was on the couch, as promised. She didn't even bother to ask. Just filed him away under: 1. "Ming's new assistant," 2. "Crashing on the couch," and 3. "Really cute." Number 3 helped gloss over any other problems she had with Todd. He was like Keanu Reeves or Brendan Frasier in *Encino Man*—goofy, but still capable of making millions of teenage girls swoon. Her only question: where were his clothes?

"Todd," Ming said, "put some clothes on."

"Uh, what?"

"If you want to stay here, you have to wear more than your boxers."

Todd stood up, dished up a plate of food, and returned to the couch still in his boxers, as if he hadn't even heard Ming. Taking in his LL Bean flannel boxers with a fly-fishing motif, Ruby commented, "I didn't really see you as a flannel boxer sort of guy, Todd."

He looked down at his underwear like a woman feeling her ear to see which earrings she's wearing and nodded. "Oh, these? Found 'em at the Suds 'N Duds."

Ming almost choked on a piece of broccoli and Ruby busted out in belly laughs, but Todd just turned up the TV, oblivious. As Ruby watched Todd eat almost all of the stir-fry, she reflected on his new position as Ming's assistant. She could imagine Todd ingesting chemicals, but stepwise synthesis of novel compounds seemed like a stretch. She could see his interview play out in her head: Ming sitting at her work station, bored out of her mind from reading *Polymers Today* while surreptitiously surfing TMZ. Todd walks in. She asks, "What's your GPA?" He says, "1.8." Still blurry from reading journal articles, dazzled by his naturally wavy blond hair, and a little high from the smell of solvents, she says: "You're hired."

Out of the blue, Ming looked up from a medical journal she was reading and asked, "Todd, did you smoke a lot of pot as a kid?"

"Didn't everyone?"

Ming smiled knowingly and passed the journal to Ruby. Pointing out the abstract, she said, "Read that."

The article was about "Disrupted Brain Development and Adolescent Marijuana Use." Ming glanced at Ruby and they shared a moment of amusement. Todd had a brain, but his neurons probably looked more like stunted shrubs than healthy trees. A brain scan for cognitive function would probably show a few random blinking lights—most likely at the video game and remote control stations—and a couple infrequently traveled neuropathways in the basic life skills department like Ramen noodle prep. Ming patted Todd on the back like she would a lost puppy and Ruby knew—they'd just adopted Todd.

Sitting in front of the tube with her best friend and her new permanently stoned puppy, Ruby felt her worries slip away. They all used their laps as tables, let reality TV wash over them, and sipped wine from IKEA juice glasses. For Ruby, it was one of those moments when you can feel the joy of the moment you're living. She was young and free-wheeling and had a brand new pet. She could practically feel the wind whip her hair and lift her from the drudgery of the rest of humanity. She felt like driving a little too fast, playing her music a little too loud, and maybe waking up with her landlord again. If Todd wanted to live on their couch, all the better.

Still, she had a sneaking suspicion that last night's black-out had something to do with Todd. She wouldn't be accepting any pills or brownies or punch glasses from him. Next time, she'd prefer to wake up beside Noel with her wits about her, if there was a next time.

After a while, Ruby's mind drifted back to Estelle. Estelle wouldn't be at home in an ankle bracelet if she had chartered her own course. Instead, she was living with the consequences of Jermaine's decisions.

Ruby could understand how someone could end up in this predicament. She deferred to Ming, her dad, or fate for most of her own decisions. It wasn't like it was turning out all that well. She drove a vehicle that only existed because it was cheaper for Ford to pay settlement costs than redesign what was essentially a Mustang on a Pinto frame. The symbolism was almost as bad as the car payment. But her dad had picked it out.

And her job. For the second time that day, Ruby thought back to the quiz that led her to her law career, a career that currently looked like a brief detour on her way back to her parents' basement. She'd found it on a site called psychic-guru.com. She remembered it clearly, "Are you a career bitch or a house ho?" It had been composed of three equally dumb questions:

1.What do you want to wear to work: a. jeans, b. sexy suits and heels, d. chaps?

2.Would you rather be: a. Meredith Grey, b. Elle Woods, or d. Vivian Ward?

3.Did you ever bite anyone as a child? If so, did you enjoy it?

Even though she noticed that choice "c" was missing and everyone knows that "c" is always the best answer, she decided to become a lawyer when the survey suggested it. It's not like she had options without an advanced degree. Graduating with an undergraduate degree in marine biology didn't open many doors in Kansas. But no one could have talked her out of majoring in dolphins. She had been an exceptionally young eighteen, maturity-wise.

Estelle let her criminal grandson dictate all her choices. Ruby let psychicguru.com dictate hers. Ming suffered from no such problem. Even when she changed course, she did it without looking back, as if one choice naturally led to the next. Take for instance, this very evening, Ming was writing a business plan for her next career move. The plan: to leave the chemistry lab for a career in bra design, for which her materials science background, design aesthetic, and ultimate superiority in everything, made her a perfect fit. Looking up from her planning, Ming asked Ruby, "How would you describe a hybrid fabric that acts as a capacitor, you know for cell phone charging and things, and makes your boobs look perky?"

"What? So you can slide your cell phone between your boobs for charging or something?"

In a matter-of-fact tone, Ming said, "Exactly. No more wires."

Ruby laughed. While Ming revolutionized the bra industry, she would be banking on the Biomall fountain granting her wish. It wouldn't even be luck. She tithed to that fountain, or at least the mall it was located in. Most churches only asked for 10 percent of your income. If the mall was her church, she gave more like 110 percent, and she was ready for a miracle, or at least a reasonable return on her investment.

Chapter Four

Too Sexy for My Job

Ruby decided to work from home the next morning, so she put on a pot of coffee and poured herself a bowl of cereal, mentally giving herself leave to eat something fried for lunch. She was dying for a corn dog—God knows why—probably the Kansas State Fair advertisements.

She located her briefcase, pulled out Estelle's file, and found the police report. It essentially said the same thing Ty had told her. The police had obtained a warrant for Estelle's arrest after Jermaine and Marcus explained the extent of her involvement. Combined with the gun ownership and the bag boy's statement, it had been more than enough for a warrant. It kind of looked like the bastard had tried to cop a deal by handing his grandma over to the cops. She stifled a laugh as she imagined the prosecutor's surprise when they realized who Jermaine had handed over.

She made a call to the arresting officer to get his thoughts on Estelle. "Hello, Officer Peterson. This is Ruby O'Deare, Estelle Harris's attorney."

"Morning."

"I've already read your report and the witness statements, but I was wondering if you had time for a few questions."

"Of course. But the prosecutor's office will want to send someone down to make sure I don't put my foot in my mouth."

"Do you have time to meet this afternoon?"

"That's fine for me. I don't know about the prosecutor."

"I'll call and let him know," said Ruby.

Ruby decided she ought to take a shower and pamper herself, so she deep-conditioned her hair and shaved her legs. She looked smoking hot. She smelled more like how the ocean *should* smell than how it does and glowed hotter than one of those spotlights car dealers aim into space on hot summer nights. She decided to pay Estelle a call on her way to the office, talk settlement, and maybe score a cup of coffee. On the way, she picked up a couple of sandwiches.

Estelle answered the door wearing a colorful fusion of Sun City and urban ghetto, a pink velour tracksuit, support hose pulled tight over her ankle bracelet, and red sequined house slippers with rubber soles. Estelle had carefully applied matching pink eye shadow and coral lipstick.

"You look nice this morning, Estelle," Ruby said truthfully. She really did like Estelle's bold color choice. "I love pink."

Ushering her into the house, Estelle said, "You look lovely, too, this morning, sweetheart. What brings you over here?"

"You like my hair? I bought a bottle of real ocean water. It's supposed to give you a beachy look."

"Well isn't that something!"

"Anyway, I came by for a couple of reasons. First of all, I brought lunch." Ruby pulled out the sandwiches. "Do you like roast beef?"

Estelle pointed to the tightly stretched fabric over her belly. "Can't you tell? I love everything."

"Oh, stop. You look great. But do you have some plates for this?"

Estelle pulled out some plates and glasses of lemonade and indicated Ruby should sit down at the kitchen table. Ruby noticed Estelle lacked a certain spring in her step this morning. In the spaces between her solicitude for Ruby's comfort and her cheerful chatter, Ruby detected a preoccupation. "Estelle, are you worried about something?" Ruby inquired. "I know you're up against some scary-sounding charges, but I'm working on it. I'm pretty sure we can work out some kind of settlement with Tyrone, the prosecutor."

"Oh, it's not that, sweetie. I know you're taking good care of me. I'm more worried about Jermaine than myself, legally that is. He's still a young man."

"How old is Jermaine?"

"Thirty-six."

Ruby considered Estelle's worries for her grandson seriously misplaced, especially given Jermaine's lack of consideration for her. To spare Estelle's feelings, Ruby refrained from informing her that Jermaine had tried to cop a deal by turning her in. "If it's not the charges, what's worrying you?"

Shaking her head, Estelle said, "Jermaine's pressuring me to sell the house."

"Why?" Ruby hadn't seen this problem coming, but that was about par for the course. When did she see anything coming?

Estelle sighed. "Money is a little tight and he says he has a good buyer. Some fancy attorney has been sniffing around the property. She works for Ozcorp."

Ozcorp owned the Biomall and pretty much all of Emerald for that matter. Before Oz had realized his vision for a shopping utopia on the Kansas plains, Emerald had been a two-stoplight town.

"Where would you go if you sold the house?"

"Jermaine said I could move into some new development going up across the street." Estelle said "new development" in the same tone Ruby imagined she would talk about belly-button rings.

"Do you want to?"

Estelle harrumphed. "No. I certainly don't need to move into a fancy condo with a gym and a monorail connection to the Biomall. What would anyone need with all that, especially an old lady?"

Ruby didn't actually know much about negotiating real-estate deals, but she figured she must know more than Estelle. Plus, she didn't trust that Jermaine had Estelle's best interests at heart. He'd already tried to throw her under the bus for the Giddyup robbery. "I'm not a real-estate attorney, but I can help out if you want." Estelle needed someone to defend her interests.

"I would love the help, but you have to know that I can't pay you."

"I don't care. You can pay me in cookies," Ruby said with a smile. She was starting to think of Estelle as her grandma.

Every time she sat down with a caramel roll and Estelle doddered around looking for unnecessary butter patties, she felt unconditional love wash over her. Maybe it was just the butter, though. Butter might feel a lot like love.

"Of course, sweetheart. I made some double-chocolate cookies last night. That attorney said she might drop by today."

Ruby's voice went up an octave in surprise. "You made her cookies?"

"Well, I like to have something to offer company."

Ruby didn't say anything. Estelle might behave like a fairy godmother, but she appeared to be in need of one herself. She doubted that Estelle even needed the money. It was probably Jermaine.

Before she moved on to discussing the Giddyup case, Ruby pulled out one of Smiddy's glossy client brochures. She had brought it along because it contained attorney photos. In her photo, Destinee still looked more like a beauty queen (her former vocation) than a lawyer, especially when pictured next to Mr. Dworkin. Ruby pointed at Destinee's glossy mug and asked, "Do you recognize her?" She really wanted to know why Destinee wanted the case and suspected Estelle might be able to explain.

"Oh, sure. She's the attorney who offered on the house."

Ruby drew her brows together and stared for a second at her boss's picture. She had no clue why Estelle thought Destinee was working for Ozcorp. Whatever the explanation, Ruby doubted it was altruistic. "I don't think you should sell it to her." She would have said more, but she honestly didn't know what to make of it. Destinee never should have tried to take Estelle's case in the first place if she was trying to buy her house. Ruby filed that oddity away for later investigation and moved on to agenda item number two, three if you counted the sandwiches.

"I also want to talk to you about your case. That's the main reason I dropped by. I'm going down to the station later to talk to your arresting officer. I'm thinking there's a good chance the prosecutor will settle. Would you mind pleading out to a lesser charge like possession of an unregistered firearm?"

"I don't care, sweetie. That sounds just fine. How about Jermaine? How is his attorney doing?"

"I don't know, Estelle. But, you really need to worry about yourself right now."

"That's fine, sweetheart. You enjoy your chat with the police. I think you might like that young man who gave me a ride down to the station. He was a real handsome fellow."

Ruby gave Estelle a bemused look, but chalked up the opinion to Estelle's battiness. On her way out the door, she put in a request for more caramel rolls and made her velour-encased friend promise not to talk to any real estate speculators, even if they looked like perfect ladies. Bounding down the front steps, Ruby ran into the mailman, a handsome man who appeared to be approaching retirement age. Ruby glanced back at Estelle and wondered if there might be more to the pink eyeshadow than routine.

• • •

On her way to the police station, Ruby took a route that brought her along the top of a plateau skirting the edge of town. Normally, she barely glanced at Emerald, spread out below like a Christmas village. Today she noticed how the Biomall dwarfed every other structure. Its glass canopy captured the surreal, otherworldly ambience of Biosphere II, rising from the Kansas plains like a crystal castle, reflecting the fields of golden wheat and clear blue sky, serving as both an homage to the nation's bread basket and a protective shield to the even more exciting bounty of spandex pants within.

Ruby had never questioned the Biomall's goodness before. Because her dad was a contractor with only one client, Ozcorp, the company had provided her family's sole source of income. Without Oz, she would have had crooked teeth and off-brand Barbies. She would have missed all of her formative moments (most of which occurred in front of Claire's Boutique). The conversation with Estelle planted a seed of suspicion. What did Ozcorp want with Estelle's house anyway and why did Destinee care?

She pushed aside the thoughts when she pulled into the police station. The police department happened to share a parking lot with the Emerald Zoning Commission, a fact that did not escape her notice this morning. Just in case she ran into Noel, she reapplied her lip-gloss and checked her hair. It looked good enough for prom. The morning after her blackout, she had hoped he'd call with a perfectly reasonable explanation for why he had slept with a drunk girl, apologize, and ask her out again. Now, a few days out, she mostly wanted to prance around and show him what he was missing. With a hair toss and a vehicular exit that showed off a pair of sassy leopard-print tights—technically pantyhose, thank you very much—she sashayed into the building.

A tall tan man with broad shoulders and an air of casual

confidence sidled up to her at the front desk. He looked like a Viking, but smelled like Spain. Ruby had never been to Spain, but he smelled like sun-baked pottery and heady spices. Maybe that was Mexico? Regardless, he smelled good. He gave her an unabashed appreciative once-over and said "Morning, Miss…" pausing to let her fill in her name.

"O'Deare, Ruby O'Deare," she supplied.

"Miss O'Deare," he drawled, "Janet is on her coffee break. Maybe I could help you out instead?" He didn't look like he normally answered phones.

Ruby returned the appreciative glance and parried, "Maybe I should wait for Janet."

"Well, that'd be a shame. Janet takes *long* coffee breaks and I'm right here."

"I think I'll wait." For some reason "I'm Too Sexy" started running through her head—his theme song. Ruby feared that if she stared at him for too long he might begin to grind on something or someone.

He turned out to be right about the coffee breaks. Janet did take inordinately long ones. The song kept playing in her mind, but like a skipped disc she kept repeating the same line in her head over and over again, until thankfully, Too Sexy himself sauntered back in and sat on Janet's desk. He kicked his long legs out and took a sip of coffee. "Are you sure you don't want a little help?"

"Maybe." Really, there was no reason to say no to the man. There were oh-so-many reasons to say yes. He had the kind of muscles that made a girl want to touch.

"I thought you would," he said with too much confidence. "I'd be happy to help you out, but you'll have to let me buy you a drink tonight."

Ruby decided to kill the flirtation before it got off the ground. She hadn't even recovered from her blackout sex with Noel. Plus, she still hoped he'd call. With that in mind, she said, "I'm sort of seeing someone and I'm really busy. I don't think I'll be done until at least eight tonight. I'm very career-focused right now."

"Hmm. Sort of seeing someone… Doesn't sound too serious. How about a quick slice of pie? I assume you still eat dessert?"

She nodded, but didn't say yes, even though she had a sudden impulse to trace the line of his bicep with her index finger.

"Are you married?" He gestured to her naked left hand.

"No."

He raised his eyebrows. "Do you have a boyfriend?"

"I'm not sure," she replied. Hoping to repeat professional misconduct with Noel didn't really fit neatly into any of the normal relationship descriptions, especially given that she didn't even know what happened the first time.

"Sounds like a no to me. What's wrong with dessert?"

He detected her unspoken capitulation as she began to think dessert might be fun.

"Excellent. I'll pick you up at seven. Tell me where you live and I'll help you out with your official police business."

"Make it next week and I'll go," she compromised. She figured that'd give her enough time to rule out all possibility of dating Noel before moving on to the sexy Viking. She caught his eyes and said, "I'm here to question an officer."

At that moment she caught sight of Tyrone. He strutted into the room, still looking more like a football player than a lawyer. She could never remember the name of the position he had played, only that he had looked cute in his uniform. She gave him a hug and said, "Hey, Ty, are you ready for our meeting?"

He smiled and said, "Ruby, good to see you." Ty pointed toward Ruby's new dinner date and said, "I see you've already met Officer Peterson."

Ruby looked at Too Sexy with surprise.

He flashed back a wicked smile and said, "Well, we haven't been formally introduced. I'm Eric." He held out his hand for Ruby.

Ruby's mouth sagged open in a manner hardly less exaggerated than a Warner Bros. cartoon. A date with her client's arresting officer was *not* the shot of professionalism her career needed. And what kind of police officer had shoulder-length blond hair? As she took his hand, she couldn't help but appreciate his big, warm, golden mitt, but she thought, *He should have known better.*

Eric leaned against the info desk in a relaxed, manly way, as if he were leaning against his tool bench with a hammer hefted over his shoulder. Ty said, "Why don't we get this deposition over with?" and pointed down the hall to the meeting room.

On the way into the room, Ruby sidled up to Eric and said, "I'm going to have to skip dessert."

"Mmm. You smell great." He said smelling her hair.

She stepped farther away and said, "Did you hear me? I want to cancel dessert."

In a Rico Suave voice, he said, "Oh, don't do that. Just give me a day. Maybe I can get the case reassigned."

"Doesn't matter. You've already filed the report. You're a potential witness."

Ty took notice of the hushed chitchat and asked, "Do you two know each other?"

Ruby snapped, "No, we just met."

"Okay, well, let's get this meeting started. Ruby, what do you want to ask?"

Ruby introduced herself and noted the date and time for the court reporter. "Hello, my name is Ruby O'Deare. Also present is Ty Wilcox, counsel for Emerald Police. Mr. Peterson, would you please state your full name and occupation for the record?"

"Sure, my name is Eric Thorgaard Peterson. I'm thirty years old, six feet tall, and 190 pounds, mostly muscle. I enjoy sailing and hope to circumnavigate the globe in a two-man, or better yet a one-man, one-woman boat before I'm forty." He nodded to Ruby. "Currently, I'm a detective with the Emerald Police Department, which I will refer to as the EPD henceforth. By the way, Ruby"—he lingered on the word—"is a very pretty name."

Ruby gave him a stunned look and Ty interjected, "Officer Peterson, would you please limit your answers to the pertinent facts."

"Of course, I thought Counselor O'Deare would find my biostats and goals pertinent to her assessment of my performance as an officer, and her, ahem, dinner plans."

"Officer Peterson, please," Ty interjected. "Would you like to meet privately for a moment so I can explain the purpose of this deposition?"

"Oh, I think I understand." If he did understand the basic purpose of the deposition, he didn't appear to care.

Ruby tried her best to continue. She needed to finish this and work on a settlement for Estelle. "Did you arrest

Estelle Harris on August third of this year?"

"Yes."

"Why did you make the arrest?"

"Her grandson, Jermaine, and his associate Marcus confessed to robbing the Giddyup Bank and implicated Estelle Harris as a co-conspirator."

"How did they implicate her?"

"They said she was at the meetings where they planned the robbery and that she provided cover while they completed the actual robbery."

"Did they say whether she was aware of the plan?"

"They implied that she was."

"So they only implied?"

"I'd have to review the transcripts of their interrogations to be sure. I do remember that they said Estelle baked lemon chiffon cake, one of my favorites. Do you like lemon desserts, Counselor O'Deare, or do you prefer chocolate?"

"I'm asking the questions, Officer Peterson. If you would please limit your answers to the scope of the question, this process would be more efficient." Ruby was feeling annoyed, but she also couldn't help but swoon a little at his devil-may-care attitude. Going out with a hedonistic Viking might have some perks. Out of exasperation Ruby looked at Ty, "Could you please control Officer Peterson? I'd hate to call the judge for a talk."

"I'd love to. Eric, can you please quit with the commentary?"

"No problem." Eric looked amused.

After suffering through a few more questions, Ruby called the whole thing off. "I think I've learned everything I can from Officer Peterson." She looked at Eric, "That'll be all. I'd appreciate more cooperation in the future."

Eric gave her a conspiratorial nod that Ruby attempted to ignore and said, "Miss O'Deare. It was a pleasure. I'll look forward to seeing you again. I think you'll find me more cooperative over dinner."

She gave him a look she hoped was mysterious, because she honestly didn't know what type of message she wanted to send the man and said, "See you later."

As Eric left and the court reporter packed up her things, Ty said in an annoyed voice, "It looks like you made quite an impression on Officer Peterson." In a lower tone, he said, "Just so you know, he's in sensitivity training right now. We've had some complaints from the secretarial pool."

Ruby laughed. She suspected that sensitivity training would slide right off Eric's Teflon coating of machismo. "That doesn't surprise me. So, Ty, what did you want to talk about? Are you ready to make a settlement offer?"

"I think we can come to some sort of agreement. You're right about Estelle Harris. I can't talk now, but let's get a settlement done by the end of the day."

Ruby might not have seen Noel on her way into the building, but on her way out, she got her wish. From across the parking lot she watched him hold the door open for a pretty brunette—definitely an attorney. A perfect attorney. She conformed to the cubicle and personal dress rule of thumb: only one personal touch, in her case, a diamond broach shaped like a fleur-de-lis. She dragged a rolling file cabinet stuffed with an obscene number of legal documents.

Ruby's shoulders sagged as she saw Noel gently touch the small of the woman's back, steering her to his car. He gallantly loaded her oversized file box into the trunk, opened the passenger door for her, and drove away. Ruby envisioned them drinking a bottle of Bordeaux and making passionate love right on top of the spilled contents of her rolling file cabinet. She probably even used classy birth control, like an IUD. She sure as hell wouldn't be caught dead with Night Light condoms.

Behind the wheel of her Mustang, Ruby dejectedly turned on the radio and sang, "Don't you wish your girlfriend was hot like me." She tried to own it, but she couldn't sing it with any real feeling so she just changed the channel to a country station, went home, and warmed up some leftovers. She watched *The Bachelor*, which made her cry.

Because Ming and Todd weren't there to stop her—something about an "all-night experiment"—Ruby performed an exhaustive Google search for women in the government center who fit Rolly Bag's description. When she finally found her, Ruby's hopes sank. Rolly Bag went by the name of Moira Hampton.

With her fancy resume and tasteful accessories, Moira was clearly more suited to Noel. Ruby could almost see the couple's future Christmas cards, taken on the top of a ski hill, their cheeks pink from exercise and fresh air, dressed in matching, but not too matchy ski sweaters. Ruby exhaled in defeat. She could never be that girl.

Chapter Five

TRUDI'S A PEACH

Ruby woke up the next morning with a hangover from her neurotic late night Googling. (It took her until two a.m. to finish her investigation of Rolly Bag.) To top that off, she opened the lid of the coffee canister and found it empty, one lonely bean rattling around in the bottom. Bleary-eyed and desperate, she decided to drop by Estelle's house to give her an update, but more importantly, to beg for fresh-baked goodies and coffee like a stray dog.

Estelle answered the door wearing an old-lady nightgown and slipper-socks. "Oh, dear. Would you mind giving me a few minutes to get dressed? I got so caught up watching my morning television I didn't get out of my bedclothes." Ruby could hear a televangelist ranting in the background and Estelle commented, "I have to get my daily dose of Pastor Rick. I *loooove* that man." Estelle's whole face lit up when she mentioned the pastor. The sermon had definitely left her with a spring in her step.

Pastor Rick was Emerald's resident preacher. He had a church in the Biomall's sister mall, the Glass Chapel. Locals called it the Glam Chapel, an appropriate moniker given its location. True to his glam image, he was proselytizing on wealth, "Enjoy your wealth. If God has blessed you, go out and buy yourself a car. Buy a Camaro, whatever makes you happy! This is the U.S.A.! God hates a martyr!" Ruby scratched her head. Not being religious she couldn't be sure, but that sounded a bit off.

Estelle, who was bobbing right at the poverty line with a handful of soggy food stamps, said, "God, I *love* that man. He just feels the spirit."

"You're not the only one," said Ruby. "Do you have any coffee made, or can I start some?"

"Of course I've got coffee, sugar. The morning you find me without a pot of coffee is the day I'll be laid out in the front parlor in my church clothes." Ruby glanced at the so-called front parlor, a dingy room straining to hold yellowing stacks of TV guides, some of Jermaine's grow lights, about three years' worth of recycling, and two stained velveteen sofas.

Estelle followed Ruby's gaze. "Jermaine's been meaning to clean that room up for ages. I just don't know what to do with all that equipment. He has such a green thumb. It's a shame he isn't putting that equipment to better use."

Bullshit! didn't seem to be an appropriate response, so Ruby remarked, "I like your slippers, Estelle."

"Do you, sweetie? You know, I've got more of these things. I bought a whole box in 1985. I figured twelve pairs would do me until I died. I've got two pairs left."

"Oh, I bet you'll make it through two more pairs of slippers, Estelle."

Estelle was already searching for the extra Isotoners. "I don't think so, sweetie, and lord knows, I'm practically psychic." Estelle inspected the rubber tread on her own shoes, "I'm not being morbid. These ones have a few good years left in them."

Determined to bequest Ruby her slippers, Estelle rooted around in the front closet through a pile of random junk until she surfaced with the promised slippers and two Thigh Masters.

"Here you go, dumplin'. I bought a box of these a while back, too," she said, as she held out the Thigh Masters. "They're real good. I used them before I gave up. The springs go out now and then. Your boyfriend will love what it does for you."

"Estelle!" Ruby laughed. As Estelle went off to change, she helped herself to coffee and a muffin and looked at the pile of junk Estelle had collected for her. The woman was a pack rat. A few minutes later, Estelle reemerged in her daily uniform of a velour tracksuit and fussed around the kitchen a little.

"Estelle, I actually came over because I have news about your case. Actually, great news. You are free and clear. I got the DA to drop the charges against you. He was just using them as bargaining chip against Jermaine." Ruby waited expectantly for Estelle to jump up and down or at least look happy.

"Oh, that's wonderful, honey. Thank you so much." Truthfully, Estelle didn't look like she cared that much, most likely because she understood her charges for what they were. She paused for just a moment. "How about Jermaine? Will his charges be dropped, too?"

"No. Since Trudi and Marcus confessed, he's going to have to serve some time. I think he can expect a year." In Ruby's estimation Jermaine deserved what was coming to him. Considering the trouble he routinely dragged her into, Estelle appeared to be better off without him.

"That's hooey. He's such a good boy. If only he'd grown up with a proper family, this never would have happened. A boy needs to learn how to be a man from his daddy. Jermaine just never had that." Estelle stared wistfully in the direction of the living room for a while. "His mama, my daughter, left him with me when he was no more than knee-high. I did my best, but I was always working too much. He had dinner at the diner most nights while I waited tables. By the time he was a teenager I was still waiting tables and he'd taken to running around with Marcus and a bunch of troublemakers. That's no way for a boy to grow up."

"Maybe Jermaine will straighten out after this experience." Ruby gave Estelle a hug on her way out the door and the old lady squeezed her tightly. She didn't believe for one minute that Estelle hadn't given 100 percent to Jermaine.

On the way out, Ruby ran into Trudi, another of the Giddyup hold-up gang. Unlike the boys, Trudi had managed to wriggle out of serving any time by testifying against a cellmate. Trudi had a fine, cat-call-worthy booty, but as a white girl, she hadn't been able to order it up à la carte. This didn't stop Trudi from squeezing herself into a pair of jeggings and a low-cut top.

Ruby offered her hand. "Hi, you must be Trudi."

Trudi observed Ruby's hand suspiciously, as if Ruby planned to spit palm her.

Ruby retracted her hand and tried again, "Um…congratulations." *What was the appropriate thing to say when someone was released from jail?* Congratulations probably didn't capture the moment.

Trudi gave Ruby's armload of Thigh Masters a quick once-over. "You been taking my stuff?"

"Erm. No. Estelle gave me these. Have we met before?"

"Duh. Junior high."

Just when she started to feel like a jerk, Ruby remembered. "Oh, yeah, jazz band. I remember." She and Trudi had played flute for a short stint in ninth grade jazz band. Ruby couldn't remember how she'd ended up in jazz band, but she had a flash of memory, retainers resting on the music stands and loud, off-key flute playing.

"Yep. Jazz band." No matter how important you get in a small town, it all comes back 'round to jazz band most days. With that over, Trudi got to the point. "You need to leave Estelle alone. Me and Jermaine are pretty sick of you filling her head with ideas. This is Jermaine's house. His grandma lives here but he pays the bills. He runs his business out of this house and he's been making improvements. You need to back off. Stop giving her ideas about selling the place."

"I'm not trying to get Estelle to sell anything. I'm helping Estelle with her charges." Ruby was sure that would smooth Trudi's ruffled feathers.

Trudi put her hands on her hips, stuck out her chin, and said, "Jermaine understands just fine. You're a money-grubbing lawyer and you need to back off."

"Oh, I'm working pro bono." Then Ruby clarified, "I'm

helping Estelle for free."

"Pro bono my ass. You're getting something." Trudi stared significantly at the Thigh Masters, as if Ruby was running off with the family china. "Jermaine can get his grandma a lawyer if she needs one. We don't need some stuck-up bitch with a fancy handbag."

Ruby looked down at her purse, a knock-off Chanel. She began to explain, "It's a knock-off," but decided there was no point and turned to leave. Plus, she could swear that Trudi's handbag was real, a brand-spanking new Louis Vuitton. Apparently, robbing banks paid better than temporary legal gigs. As an afterthought, Ruby asked, "What kind of improvement did Jermaine make to the house?"

"Hot tub. Second floor," said Trudi. As she walked into the house she muttered, "I'm calling to complain about you."

Ruby stopped and hollered, "Who are you going to complain to?"

"Your boss."

"Destinee?" Ruby asked.

"Who do you think?" With a slam of the door, Trudi walked into the house, leaving Ruby to wonder why Destinee would take Trudi's word over Ruby's, not that she doubted the truth of the statement. It just didn't make any sense. At this point, all Ruby knew was that: 1. Trudi made more money than her, and 2. Her boss liked Trudi better.

Whatever choice "c" had been on that psychicguru quiz, she should have picked it. Law school had been a *bad* investment.

Everyone knows, "c" is always the best answer.

Chapter Six

Burner on the Fritz (One Month Later)

After settling Estelle's case, the rest of September and most of October blurred into an incoherent string of seemingly identical days at the office punctuated by evenings of forgettable television. Ming was constantly busy and Estelle didn't need help with her property issue. For a full month almost nothing changed, not even Todd's underwear. Every morning Ruby would stumble out of her room to see him sprawled on the couch in a pair of boxers that said "Monday"—an apt metaphor for her life.

Noel never called and she never called him. Depending on her mood, she lamented it as a missed opportunity with Mr. Perfect or good riddance to the zoning commissioner who dumped her over stale Pop-Tarts.

Work wasn't horrible. The traditional eight-to-seven law office workday took the starch out of Ruby and the paycheck barely covered her student loans and credit card bills. After work, she would come home so tired that she would fall asleep in the living room in front of *Law & Order*, a show that made being a lawyer look *so* much better than it actually was.

At one o'clock in the morning she would wake up with a kinked neck and the TV playing some infomercial about 80s rock classics or Brazilian butt workouts. And she would actually watch them, not only because she was too tired to get up and brush her teeth, but because she liked them. She ordered a copy of the *Bum Bum Rapido!* workout that promised to lift her butt in three different ways. Because she was using Todd's bed (the couch) all the time, he had started sleeping in her bedroom, which left her sharing a bedroom with a drifter.

One morning, after a long night of watching the entire hour of *Bum Bum Rapido*, Ruby dragged her un-lifted butt to work. She stared at her computer like a living zombie for two hours before giving up. She sent Destinee an email informing her that she needed to go home because of "female problems" and drove home, supposedly to work from her living room.

. . .

"Shit."

Ruby was trying to light the burner to make coffee, but the stove wasn't working. She tried again, but the igniter didn't work and a smell of rotten eggs began to pool around her, so she cut the gas and walked away. Maybe working from home for the afternoon wasn't such a bright idea. Just as she gave up and sat down all four burners began to emit a *click, click, click, click* synchronously and loudly, as if the first voice in a robotic uprising. She inspected them, but everything appeared to be fine, except for the inexplicable clicking. With no knowledge of appliances and zero mechanical reasoning ability, she ran to look for her phone. If ever there was a time to call the landlord, this was it. If only she hadn't slept with him only to find she was the other woman in a love triangle she hadn't been aware of. *Awkward!* She dialed Ming instead.

"Ming, there's something wrong with the stove. The burners won't stop clicking and I don't know if the gas is on or off. I'm afraid the house is going to explode."

"I doubt it. You're on your own, though. I'm teaching."

"You're standing in front of a class right now?"

"Uh huh. I'm teaching."

Ruby laughed. She could see it clearly. After talking on the phone in front of the class at top volume, Ming would probably berate them for failing to understand the reading or complete their problem sets. Ming didn't get the point of teaching because she didn't need it herself.

Ming finally advised, "Call the landlord." Then, she laughed. "I can't wait to hear about it. Call me back."

For a fraction of a second Ruby considered dialing 911, but she didn't do it—better not to make a complete fool of herself if her cooktop was simply performing a vigorous self-cleaning or something. She did grab the cats, though. She threw Vera and Tom into their kitty carrier against their yowling protests and ran out to wait in the driveway. "Noel. It's Ruby."

"Ruby?"

If she had been sitting, she would have dropped her head to the desk. He didn't even remember her! She reminded him. "Ruby O'Deare. You know, we know each other from planning meetings and…that one night. I don't know if you knew, but I'm also your tenant."

"Of course," he corrected. "I just couldn't hear. Sorry."

She hoped to God he was serious. "I have a problem over at the house. There is something wrong with the stove. It won't stop clicking. I don't think the gas is on, but I still have the feeling that it might explode. Probably not, but it's making me a little nervous."

"I'll be right over. Wait outside." Ruby could hear him shuffling papers and telling his secretary to cancel his next appointment.

He pulled up to Ruby's driveway a few minutes later, jumped out of the car, only briefly pausing to say, "Hi, Ruby" as he hurried into the danger in the manner of a rescuing fireman. He looked just as good as the last time she saw him, maybe even better because he was adorably frazzled about her safety. Though she'd planned to give him the cold shoulder, her pulse fluttered and she couldn't help but smile like an absolute fool. So there she stood, standing in the driveway smiling like a possessed woman (with a box of cats), waiting for her house to explode with Noel in it.

As she watched Noel fulfill all of her sexy fireman fantasies, she couldn't deny that he looked more like the man of her dreams than the date-rapist zoning commissioner she conjured in her darker moments. By the time he emerged from the house, she was convinced—Noel was as good as he looked. He was probably better.

"It's all clear." Then, noticing her struggle with the cat

carrier, he said, "Let me get that for you."

"Is there something wrong with the stove or am I a complete idiot?" she asked.

"It looks like you spilled something on the burners and shorted out the igniters. They'll be fine as soon as they dry out. I could set up a fan to help them dry out faster if you'd like."

"Oh. Complete idiot, it is." She had poured water all over the cook top last night to clean up a tipped jar of honey. "I'm so sorry to drag you over here. You were probably doing something really important." She was used to looking like an idiot, but it stung so much more in front of Noel. Why couldn't she have run into him while winning something? Not that she'd won anything recently, but still, it would have been nice.

He flashed her an adorably quirky half smile and said, "No. I'd much rather be here." He looked over at the stove. Her French press was out and filled with coffee grounds, clearly waiting for hot water. "Were you trying to make some coffee?" he asked. If Ruby didn't know better, she would guess he was looking for an excuse to stay longer.

She nodded, feeling confused and hopeful.

"Let me see if I can do anything about it. Why don't you sit down and let the cats out or something." He opened up the cabinet below the kitchen sink and rooted around for a minute until he came up with a prize. "Found it. You have some canned air. This should do the trick." He sprayed the offending burner, reset the breaker, and turned the stove on. It lit no problem. "Voila. While I'm at it, I'll just finish this up." He put the kettle back on the burner.

"Thanks so much." A little bewildered, but grateful,

Ruby sat down. While she watched, Noel found the cream and sugar (without asking for direction), poured her a cup of very fine-looking French press into her favorite Café du Nord cup, and handed it to her as if he did this every day. Incidentally, he drank from the cup with a picture of her and a sorority sister screaming on the downside of a roller coaster at Funland. She hoped he had picked it out on purpose.

Just then, Todd, who Ruby had thought was at work, appeared from seemingly out of nowhere and poured himself the last of the coffee. He brought the coffee cup up to his face and said, "Smells gooood." Looking at Noel, he said, "Hey, dude, nice suit. Did you get that at the Big and Tall?"

"Uh, no." Noel looked to Ruby. He was clearly wondering who Todd was.

"Oh. Well you should check them out. I heard they have nice stuff." And with that, he stumbled back from whence he came, probably to get ready for work for which he was already about three hours late.

"So who was that guy?" he asked.

"Oh, sorry! I forgot to introduce you. That's Todd." She said this as if everyone had a half-naked dude living on their couch.

Noel nodded skeptically, but made no further mention of the mystery that was Todd. Instead, he said, "I'm glad you called. I wasn't thrilled to be stuck in a meeting all afternoon anyway."

"Oh, if you need to get back—"

Noel waved off her suggestion. "No worries. I've had it with the guy I'm supposed to meet with. He's putting together that new development over on Hyacinth Ave. It's mixed use, business and residential. Basically, it's a bunch of

McMansions and high-end stores, an Organic Food Hollow, a Crate and Barrel, four Starbucks, a Pottery Barn Kids, that sort of thing. I think he has an exclusive fitness place too."

"Ooh. That sounds…" She trailed off when she noticed her cat pawing at his legs. She grabbed Vera Wang just before she inserted her claws into his pant leg.

"Atrocious, I know."

Actually, Ruby had been thinking, *Amazing! When can I move?*

"I know just what you're thinking: what a soul-sucking, consumption-oriented, apathetic black hole. I can just see my college friends—the ones who I thought would change the world—moving into the development, buying a minivan, patting themselves on the back for shopping at Food Hollow, and letting mainstream news and a short commute lull them into a false sense of security while they ignore poverty and the declining literacy rate right outside their doors." He looked at Ruby for affirmation.

She smiled. *Literacy rate declining? Where did he hear that?* Instead she said, "Exactly what I was thinking. Food Hole is such a poser," (Food Hole being the local nickname for Organic Food Hollow). She actually lived to buy five-dollar-a-pound apples from Food Hollow and congratulate herself on saving the planet while reading *Luxury Spa Finder* in the checkout.

Then, she asked, "Did you say Hyacinth Ave? I bet you're talking about the same developer who is trying to buy my client's house." Estelle's place was on Hyacinth Ave. If the development was as big and fancy as Noel made it sound, Estelle could probably score a sweet deal, *if* she decided to sell. She'd have to check in with Estelle and make sure that

Destinee didn't swindle her out of her property.

Noel glanced at the clock and said, "I better get going. I'll be stuck at the office all night if I don't get out now. By the way, what are you doing at home? Shouldn't you be in a cubicle buried in files or something?"

"I'm working from home." Then, while she had her courage up she said, "Before you leave, I was wondering... I know this probably sounds ridiculous, but I don't really know what happened that night I woke up with you. Do you remember anything?"

"I... uhhh—" Noel started stammering like a bad actor trying to pull off a dramatic role. He began squinting and nodding too much, as if intensely consider her question.

A diehard fan of bad acting, Ruby watched Noel and tried to understand him. Seeing him stumble over his own words, Ruby forever extinguished the idea that he had taken advantage of her. He was adorable and sweet and Ruby loved it. What girl doesn't enjoy watching a boy stammer a little?

Finally, he wrangled his thoughts and said, "I actually, I can't remember. The whole night is really foggy."

Relieved and incredulous, Ruby said, "How could both of us—"

Todd yelled from the back room, "Uhhh, has anyone seen my socks?"

Ruby didn't answer, but the interruption caused a flash of connection between "Todd" and "amnesia."

Still struggling with the memory problem, Noel said, "I don't get it. It doesn't make any sense, but it's one big blank for me. I remember coming over to your place because of a call from the neighbor. I remember leaving with you, but that's about it."

From the way he said "about it" Ruby thought he was leaving something out. Giving him her best third-degree look, she asked, "What do you mean that's *about it*? What else happened?"

With an embarrassed laugh, he said, "It doesn't make any sense, but I think we might have gone to the Dollar Store."

Ruby sighed with relief. At least she hadn't shown up on his doorstep with a box of condoms like some sort of de-ranged Girl Scout. They had embarked on that hair-brained mission together. She smiled and said, "Well, I hope we had fun."

With a knowing grin that made her doubt his blackout equaled her own, Noel said, "I'm pretty sure we did."

Ruby felt herself blush at his tone, but she liked the way this conversation was heading.

Then he dropped the hammer. "I would have called you, but I'm actually seeing someone. That's part of why I was so shocked about waking up with you."

Her heart sank. *Rolly Bag. He is seeing Rolly Bag.*

On his way out the door, it didn't feel right simply say-ing, "See you later," not with the fresh acknowledgement of their lost night together, but Ruby didn't know what else to say. She wanted to hug him, but she didn't.

He had a girlfriend.

He must have felt the same because he reached out and pulled her into an awkward half hug. She had hugged teach-ers, parents, and friends this way countless times, but she'd imagined Noel's touch too many times for this to be casual. Closing her eyes, she inhaled. He smelled like her favorite brand of dryer sheets. She couldn't be sure, but it seemed like he kept his arm around her a fraction of a second too long. In a quiet voice she said, "Thanks for all the help today, Noel. You must think I'm an absolute mess."

When he pulled away, he let his hand trail down her arm in a way that made her skin tingle and the look on his face— it wasn't professional. Softly, he said, "I don't think you're a mess at all, Ruby." Then, giving her hand one last squeeze, he turned to walk away.

She whispered, "Bye, Noel," feeling more sure than ever that the man of her dreams was walking out of her life and into the arms of a woman who traveled with a rolling file cabinet. She could almost hear the sound of tiny plastic wheels rolling away her dreams, *roooooooll, thunk, roooooooll, thunk*.

Chapter Seven

ALL BOYFRIENDS LOOK THE SAME

Later that evening, Ruby changed into garb more fitting her mood: sweatpants, a robe from her grandmother complete with appliquéd kitty cat, and slippers. Then she curled into a semi-fetal position on the couch and put in *Bum Bum Rapido!* She sat transfixed as Leonardo energetically jumped from side to side doing a double diamond move, but she didn't manage to get off the couch to join him. For whatever reason, she felt like a completely run-down shell of her former self. Her auburn hair color had faded to pinkish brown and the last tub of ice cream had gone straight to her ass. Todd sat down next to her and offered her some Cheetos.

"Thanks," she said, reaching for a handful and stuffing too many into her mouth.

"Want me to turn up the heat?" he offered.

"No, I just wanted to cozy up a bit," she said with her

mouth full.

"Cool." Without questioning her choice of programming, he commented, "Man. That guy's fucking aaawwwesome. Whoa."

"How are things going at the lab?" Ruby asked. While she talked, she opened up a tub of cellulite cream she'd picked up on her way home that day. It was worth a try.

Bum Bum Rapido! ended and Todd started flipping through the channels as he talked. "Not sure, to tell you the truth. Ming has me boil stuff and take notes. Seems okay. She gave me a white coat that looks pretty awesome. That's about it." He nodded and shrugged, apparently satisfied with the state of things.

"Nice. 'Bout the same as my job, except for the part about boiling things. Where's Ming?"

"She's at work still. Boiling some shit, probably. She kicked me out. Said I was driving her nuts and getting in the way. Gonna be another half hour probably."

"So you came to her place?" Ruby looked at him with a look of shared mischief. "Good move."

"My place now, too, man," Todd clarified.

After *Entertainment Tonight* faded into a *Seinfeld* rerun and then *Law and Order*, Ming came home. She looked straight at Todd and said, "*What* are you doing here?" This was obviously bravado since she was well aware that Todd had been living on her couch for over a month.

Neither Ruby nor Todd was bothered by Ming's blustery mood. When Ming was on the warpath for real, they'd run for the storm cellar like someone had just yelled "Twister!" but she was just blowing off steam. Between the fledgling underwear empire and the lab work, she had too much on her plate. While Ming slammed cabinet doors and told Todd about his horrible results from the day, "That column you ran—it looks like you ran sheep manure through it. What was that?"

Todd shrugged.

"You definitely added something. Your percent yield can't be 125 percent. You're going to have to do it again."

In his best Igor voice, Todd said, "Yes, mastuh." Then, he swallowed his mouthful of Cheetos and said, "125 percent no good. Tomorrow, I give 200 percent."

Ming rolled her eyes, but before she could respond, the doorbell rang. True to form, she greeted the knocker without any pretense of welcome. With a saucy pose and a glare over the top of her cat-eye glasses, she said, "No soliciting. Didn't you see the sign?" She pointed to the NO SOLICITING sign to his left.

"Not here to sell anything. I'm picking up Ruby," Eric said in an unruffled tone. "I'm taking her on a date."

Ming simply said, "Be my guest," and pointed towards Ruby who was staring with horror at Eric. What was Too Sexy doing at her door?

"*Miss O'Deare.*" He swaggered over like John Wayne and gave her a once over. After taking in the robe, the hair, and the bag of Cheetos, he commented, "Did you forget our date?"

She stared at him with confusion. "What? What are you doing here?"

"We have a date. Seven o'clock. Dessert. Don't you remember?"

"We don't have a date. We never confirmed or picked a time. And, that was *so* long ago." Scrutinizing his expression, she said, "What are you doing?" Taking in his appearance, she thought maybe the better question was—did she care what he was doing? He looked like a sexy Norse god in jeans and a T-shirt, a tattoo of a ship's wheel on his upper arm and blond wind-whipped hair.

With a casual shrug, he said, "Doesn't look like you have any plans." Ruby stared back, wondering if she wanted to trade in her kitty cat robe for a something cute and go out with Eric. She paused, though. The man looked ready for a *Sexiest Man Alive* photo shoot and all he wanted was for her to postpone rubbing in cellulite cream so they could go on a date. It didn't add up. There had to be something wrong with him. How did he even know where she lived?

Eric ignored her hesitation and said, "How about we start with introductions?"

"Oh, sorry. Eric, this is Ming and Todd," she said, pointing to her housemates. "Ming and Todd, Eric. Ming is a chemist-slash-underwear designer and Todd is her assistant." Turning her gaze to Eric, Ruby added, "Eric was the arresting officer on one of my cases."

Even Eric, seasoned police officer that he was, raised his eyebrows at Todd and Ming. "Nice to meet you. What kind of underwear you people designing?" His tone implied that he assumed it was S&M.

Ming just rolled her eyes and went to the fridge to look for something to make for dinner. She clearly didn't give a damn if Eric or anyone else thought she was a whips and chains freak.

"Where you guys going?" Todd asked. Like a Labrador, he perked up at the mention of food.

Todd didn't really get the concept of dating, or privacy

at all for that matter, obviously. This was probably due to his upbringing. From what Ruby could piece together, he grew up on a kibbutz in Israel until his parents split, at which time he had moved to Grand Targhee where his dad worked as a ski instructor. From the sound of it, Todd had become a certified ski bum in Targhee. In Kansas, where the tallest ski hill was a 200-foot icy incline that ran straight into the interstate, Todd's description probably ended at bum. Only Ruby and Ming's couch saved him from violating local homeless statutes.

"I was going to take her out for pie at the fifties diner."

"Nice. If Ruby doesn't want to go, I will. I'm *starving*." He looked down at his stomach as if it were a separate being.

"Are you serious, man?" Eric asked with an incredulous look.

"Totally," said Todd.

Eric shrugged and said, "I guess, if Ruby would feel more comfortable, it's fine with me. It's not like I can't find another date. I mean, I could just set up a speed trap and get phone numbers that way."

With raised eyebrows, Ming said, "You dispense tickets and collect phone numbers. For real?"

"Basically," he said. "What's your problem, Fifty Shades? Do you really believe in the 'First comes appetizer sampler platter, then comes love' crap that Hollywood and corporate food giants feed us?" He shook his head. "Applebee's and Carmike Cinemas only foster the concept of 'dating' to keep stiffs in neighboring cubicles from getting married without spending a fortune on fried cheese sticks and tickets to the latest Jennifer Anniston movie." From his expression, he didn't appear to be a Jennifer Anniston fan.

Ming rolled her eyes. "Whatever. You sound stingy to me. Just make sure to have Todd back by midnight and try not to get him drunk."

Rolling with it, Eric responded, "That'll be hard to do because he already looks high as a kite to me. And, *that* is a professional opinion. Ruby, you coming?"

She was going to say no, but she imagined the noise of the rolling bag, tiny plastic wheels rolling over evenly spaced tiles, *roooooooll, thunk, roooooooll, thunk, roooooooll.* "Fine, I'll go." If Noel was going to date Rolly Bag, she might as well have some fun, even if there was something wrong with Eric.

"Okay, I'm coming too. Someone responsible needs to be present," Ming said.

So they all piled into Eric's ride, incidentally a three-quarter ton diesel pickup with lights on top and an American flag attached to the antenna. It came with everything but the giant dick, which was presumably attached to the owner of the pickup. Like a bunch of high-school kids, they filed into a booth at the diner and ordered mugs of coffee and pie. Against her objection, Eric paid for Ruby's slice of strawberry pie, opened doors for her, and casually slung his arm over her shoulders in the booth—not in a snuggly way or a poised-to-grope way, just in an "I'm a big man and I take up a lot of space" way, pretty much the same as his truck. He didn't ask before he encroached, he just did. If there was an armrest, he would have taken that, too.

Ming noticed. "Why do men always see the need to take up all the space in a booth?" She was looking at Eric.

"What? I'm just sitting."

"No, you're not. You're taking up most of the booth. Are

men all born with some sense of imperialistic entitlement to take up more space than women? It's ridiculous." She kicked Todd into the corner of their shared space for effect. "You might as well take that flag off your pickup and plant it on Ruby's side of the booth. Chinese men are never this impolite."

"Chill out, woman. We're just sitting here," said Todd.

Ming had lost Ruby a while ago. She was delighted to be tucked into Eric's arm. Who wouldn't be? It brought to mind a Kim Kardashian interview. "Ming, didn't you hear that interview where Kim Kardashian said, 'Having a big boyfriend makes me feel protected and small.'" It was true. Also, since Eric's hair was so straight, she almost felt like her hair was curly.

"Aren't the Kardashians from *Star Trek*?" Todd wondered aloud.

While Todd struggled to locate the Kardashians in the jumbled files in his mind, Eric casually asked Ruby, "You still in touch with Estelle?"

"What? Why?" She couldn't imagine why Eric would care.

"Just wondering. I was talking to Destinee. She asked about Estelle's house."

"What's it to you?" Her hackles stood up. Why would Eric care about Destinee's business or Estelle's?

"Nothing, baby. Dee just mentioned it to me yesterday."

Dee? Ruby mentally added another tick into Eric's "suspicious" column, right next to "insisted on buying me pie." Though it was tempting to believe, she didn't think Eric had spent a month working up the courage to invite her out. To Eric she said, "Estelle's a client. I can't violate attorney-client privilege."

Ming changed the topic. "So the chemistry department is having its annual fall party. I offered to throw it at our place so there would be decent food. It's going to be a costume party because it's Halloween." She looked around the table. "I'm going to need some help with the set-up and I'll provide free beer to anyone who helps. It's this weekend."

Eric and Todd nodded assent. "Sounds good to me," said Eric. "I don't know about a costume, but I'll come."

"It's a *costume* party," said Ming. "Hence, you need to wear a costume."

"Fine. I'll be a swimmer," answered Eric with a shrug.

"Ugh. Nudity doesn't count as a costume."

"You haven't seen my abs, yet." He started to pull the hem of his shirt up.

Ming didn't look impressed. "Come as a police officer if you have to. That's basically a costume anyway."

"When did you say the party is?" asked Ruby. "You know, I'm sort of busy at work."

"This Friday, two days from now. I'm having it catered. All you have to do is move your pile of magazines and fingernail polish and put on a costume. It's almost all men, many of them moderately attractive with good earning potential, so you might find a good prospect in there besides this yahoo." She gestured to Eric. "Todd and Eric, you're pretty much out of luck. I'm about the only chick in the department, but I'd like if you came over and moved the couch out of the way."

"Can I invite Noel?" Ruby asked, suddenly excited at the prospect of dressing in a slutty costume and flirting outrageously.

"No, Ruby. You absolutely cannot invite the landlord."

Ruby started to protest, but Ming shut her down. "What

are you even thinking with that guy? He's cute enough, but I don't get what you see in him. He's always standing around like he's waiting to play in a polo match or something. On second thought, maybe that's why you like him."

"That's *not fair*, Ming. He totally looks like Mister Right."

Eric cut in. "Who's Mister Right, that sissy zoning commissioner?"

Ignoring Eric, Ruby said, "My mom would say Noel's…" She stared at her plate for a few seconds. "Who is that guy, you know the one from the comic strip with Betty and Veronica?"

"You mean Reggie? Where are you coming up with this?"

"My Mom, I guess."

With an amused expression, Ming said. "I hate to break it to you, but not everyone fits neatly into a TV character trope."

"You're wrong." Ruby shook her head. "You're Veronica. I'm Betty. Noel is probably the cute boy one and you guys are…" Ruby bit her lip and tried to remember the other characters from *Archie*. "Whatever. I'm sure you all fit one of the characters, *exactly*. My mom could tell you which ones."

Ming started laughing. "I love how you can't even remember any of the male characters. It's a hell of a way to classify potential boyfriends."

"Whatever." Neither of the guys appeared to be listening. Todd was making a statue out of his silverware and Eric was eating everyone's leftover pie while she talked.

"You are basically operating in a Barbie framework, or

any other world that has only one male character. Ken or whoever, is only there as a prop. If you want to get married or go to a premiere, you need Ken." She looked at Ruby to make sure she was listening. "You see guys in terms of Ken or Not Ken."

"Shut up." She tried to think of a response, but nothing came to mind immediately, so she added. "That is the dumbest thing I've ever heard. Of course I have a more nuanced understanding of men than that."

"No, it explains all of your past relationships. Every guy who would look good in a tux is a 'Ken,' regardless of all other traits. After a few dates, you end up wondering why the guy, who usually has a side part, isn't bringing you flowers or driving you around in a convertible." Ming started laughing, "It's worse than I thought. Remember Ty?"

Ruby felt her cheeks burn. She and Tyrone, Estelle's prosecutor, had dated for about a month. During Constitutional Law they talked about *Brown v. Board of Education* and separate but equal. Casually, Ruby had asked him, "Why do you say us when you're talking about the black kids?" He'd given her a funny look and said, "Uh…'cause I'm black."

She hadn't known. Granted, he wasn't super dark-skinned, but after meeting his sister (who sported a fabulous afro) and a month of heavy petting in the library, she probably should have guessed. He'd dumped her not long after that (because she was an idiot) which had been a bummer because she really liked him. At least she thought she did. Even she had to wonder at her lack of perception. Ming was right, she was man-blind. Give her any man with the basic dimensions of Ken and she'd fill in the rest—likes, dislikes, sexual preference, even ethnicity.

Todd's tower of forks collapsed and broke her train of thought. He said, "I'm totally Ken, aren't I?"

Ming said, "No, Todd, you're someone else, but we can't remember because we didn't watch any shows with boy characters."

Swallowing a mouthful of pie, Eric said, "What about you, Ming, are you into Barbie or Ken?"

Ming redirected. "Oh, silly boy, I don't classify dates by cartoon characters. We're talking about Ruby."

"Ming doesn't even want to get married," Ruby said, hoping to keep the attention on someone else.

"Of course not. I don't want to give up my independence just because of my biological drive to reproduce."

Eric and Ming eyed each other from across the table, like a couple of circling tigers. Eric sized her up again and said, "I might have to come visit that underwear shop of yours when it opens."

Ming stared back with a look of boredom. "I'm done. Let's go home."

Ruby reflected on Ming's observation. Had she ever really known any of her boyfriends? Between work and free time, Ruby spent most of her time in the mall with Gap's version of the average male posted on every wall. At night she came home to *The Bachelor*. As for her formative years, her mother had directed their household like a madcap version of *Father Knows Best*. She wasn't sure if it was possible to be physically blinded by your expectations, but it might explain the last few guys she dated. It made her wonder if Noel West was as good as he looked. Maybe if she squinted, she'd be able to parse out the details.

Chapter Eight

Trudi Over-salts the Chicken

Ruby woke up the next morning feeling a bit woozy. She stared out the window for a while, not even able to drink her coffee. *What is the matter with me?* She didn't feel nauseous, but she did feel like the floor was moving without her. The room was swaying, just a little. If she'd been more of a control freak, she definitely would have felt really sick, but being Ruby, she figured she'd just add coffee. Going straight to work sounded awful, so she decided to drop by Estelle's first. If Eric was wondering about the real estate deal, it was probably time to check in. She picked up the phone and dialed.

Estelle answered on about the fortieth ring. "This is Estelle," she said in a wavering voice.

"Estelle, it's Ruby. I was wondering if you had time to talk this morning?"

"Isn't that a coincidence? I finished leaving you a

message about one second ago."

Ruby exclaimed, "We're psychic!" and then added, "Well, I guess we can just skip the messages." This was convenient because Ruby never checked her messages anyway. Who needed to talk with Bank of the West Collection? "I was calling to see if you wanted to go out for a coffee this morning. We can catch up and go over the offer from that developer."

"Oh, you don't have to take me out, sugar. Trudi is over and she'd probably love to have a girl around to visit with."

"If you want to stay home, we can do it another time, but it is important to talk about your legal issues without anyone else around." *Especially Trudi*, thought Ruby. "All the same, I'd like to take you out. Where'd you like to go?"

"Oh, I don't know. Wherever you normally go," Estelle replied.

• • •

Estelle may have played it cool on the phone, but the woman was dressed for an occasion with a floral church frock, a hat, and matching rhinestone jewelry. The outfit screamed shopping followed by a late lunch of finger sandwiches, not coffee date with your lawyer.

"Well, I was going to take you to Starbucks, but maybe we should aim a little higher," said Ruby. Estelle would probably hate the menu of lattes and macchiatos as much as anyone else's grandmother anyway.

"Can you wait a minute, honey? I still need to put my face on."

"Of course, I'll just sit down."

"Trudi's in the kitchen if you want to chat for a minute. She was just telling me about Jermaine. He's doing so well."

"In jail?" asked Ruby. Her voice sounded as confused as she felt.

"Of course, Trudi tells me that he quit smoking and he's working out. It's just wonderful. I've been trying to get him to quit for ages."

That's one way to put a positive spin on a prison sentence. She was willing to bet that Trudi hadn't described Jermaine's experience in exactly those terms.

Ruby steeled herself for a verbal whipping and walked into the kitchen where Trudi was supposedly preparing a Crockpot meal for Estelle's dinner, something that struck Ruby as wildly out of character.

"Hi, Trudi. Good to see you," said Ruby politely.

"Where *the fuck* is the salt?" Trudi spat out as she rummaged through Estelle's cabinets. She stomped around the kitchen, looking through every drawer and cabinet, slamming doors, and muttering obscenities like Ruby wasn't there. It looked more like she was ransacking the house than making dinner.

"What are you making, Trudi?" Ruby asked, standing back a few paces.

"Some food. What do you care?"

We're making progress! She didn't call me a bitch.

Trudi finally found a shaker of table salt and said, "Who *the fuck* keeps salt with the spices?"

Ruby thought this made perfect sense, but kept her mouth shut.

"No wonder I couldn't find it."

After all of that, Trudi dumped the salt out of the shaker

and refilled it. Ruby couldn't imagine why. Then, with a liberal hand, Trudi shook it into the Crockpot and into Estelle's large jar of unsalted peanuts before setting the shaker back on the counter. Estelle snacked on peanuts obsessively because of a tip she'd heard on Dr. Oz, something about omega fatty acid and memory.

Before Ruby could help herself, the words shot out of her mouth, "Estelle has high blood pressure. I'd take it easy on the salt."

With that piece of unwelcome advice, Trudi got all up in her face. "Mind your own business. Estelle likes it salty. Plus, this is special low-sodium salt. Pastor Rick recommended it."

Ruby held up her hands in surrender. "If Pastor Rick likes it, I'm in." Estelle had mentioned that Jermaine had taken a shine to Pastor Rick. Rick, apparently, preached the Gospel at jail, which tickled Estelle to no end.

Estelle saved Ruby from further conversational shrapnel by coming back into the kitchen. She had stepped into some canary-yellow shoes and too much blush, but managed to look sweet in a batty old lady sort of way. "You look beautiful, Estelle."

"Aren't you just a honey! So, I was wondering if you'd like to go to Auntie Em's? I used to go there when I was girl. Jermaine says they still make homemade pie and soup."

• • •

Ruby helped Estelle into the restaurant, a coffee shop-diner offering local foods and filled with high-school art projects. There were a variety of gluten-free selections. A pierced barista wearing a look of affected boredom loitered behind the counter and stared purposefully at the ceiling tiles. Estelle fussed over hanging up coats and hats before settling into a booth. After noticing the pierced baristas, she commented, "Must be new owners."

"Yeah, I think so. They still make great soup, though." Ruby glanced at her watch and realized she had definitely not set aside enough time for a lunch date with an eighty-year old who hadn't been out in… "Estelle, when was the last time you were out to lunch?"

"Well, this makes the second time this month, actually." She paused to make sure Ruby was listening and added, "You'll never believe where I went."

"Where?"

"Clementine's," Estelle exclaimed.

Clementine's happened to be the new happening spot in town with a Parisian chef and a waiting list for reservations, not the kind of place where people who can't afford a new coat of house paint normally hung out.

"Wow! You get around. Who was your date?"

"Never you mind," Estelle shook her head cryptically. "Just an old friend who needed a little favor." In a sassy voice she said, "Turns out he's gonna do a little favor for me."

Unsure what to make of all that sass, which was so unlike Estelle, Ruby probed, "What do you mean? What kind of favor?"

Estelle smiled the self-satisfied smile of a woman holding all the cards and said, "Never you mind." Then, she casually mentioned, "As for Clementine's, that restaurant acted like it was the first place to put nuts in brownies." Estelle gave a little chuckle.

"And I thought you never went out," Ruby teased.

"Oh, I don't normally. What does an old lady like me need to get out for anyway? I have *The Pastor Rick Hour* on TV, cooking, and a to-do list a mile long. Not to mention, it's easier to stay put. I have a pretty tight schedule." She looked at the clock. "I'm probably missing *Dr. Oz* right now and *The Doctors* if we stay past eleven, but he was only going to talk about snoring today so no matter. No one to complain if I snore! Now, when I was with Clarence I would have paid good money to figure that one out." She stopped, conscious that she'd been talking about herself for longer than she thought polite.

Ruby smiled. "We better talk about your house, though. Is anyone from Ozcorp still sniffing around, trying to buy your place?"

"Well, I was going to need your help with that, but turns out I took care of that issue all by myself. Thanks to that little lunch date, I'm gonna keep the house *and* get Jermaine out of jail. How's that for an old lady!"

"What do you mean? What'd you do?" Estelle's claims made no sense.

"I'll tell you next week after all the details are hammered out." Then she looked at her menu. "I wonder if they make a good pumpkin pie?"

"Well, if you change your mind, call me."

The route home from Em's took them straight up Biomall Promenade. Approaching the shopping center always reminded Ruby of driving up to the Denver International Airport. Both structures grew out of the plains, strange, beautiful, and filled to capacity with Starbucks. Estelle's neighborhood was no farther from the mall than a rental car agency from DIA, making it a perfect place for Elysian Fields. As the only poor neighborhood left in the vicinity of the mall, it was ripe for development. To Ruby, it looked like the Biomall was about ready to swallow up Estelle's house, even if Estelle thought it was the other way around.

That thought was for another day, though. Today, Ruby needed to meet her daily quota at work and then rush home to entertain a bunch of drunk chemists. Tonight was Ming's departmental Halloween party. With a wistful sigh, Ruby thought of Noel. If he didn't have a girlfriend, she would have invited him regardless of Ming's protest. He didn't look like a landlord. He probably wouldn't act like one either. She wondered what sort of Halloween costume he would have worn. She imagined him as Prince Charming. But then again, he already looked just like Prince Charming in his zoning commissioner costume.

Chapter Nine

Halloween

As she walked up to her front door that afternoon, the wind sent a pile of leaves skittering in front of her feet. The sun shone brightly, but in a post-apocalyptic, over-exposed way. Instead of warming things up, the world looked colder, flatter, and meaner—at least until the holiday decorations went up. Ruby pulled her sweater around her shoulders a little tighter and hurried into the house. In the kitchen, she opened the fridge door and stared for several moments before deciding that none of its contents could revive her. Nothing even tempted her.

Resigned to her fate of spending her evening co-hosting the chemistry department's drunken festivities, she shimmied into her white satin costume. She sucked in hard, but the zipper wouldn't budge, so she plopped despondently onto the bed in the half-zipped costume. If the sexy nurse costume failed her, she had nothing to wear. She searched the depths of her imagination for ideas... Sexy cat. No. She didn't have any black leggings. Bond girl. Maybe. She had a lot of big rhinestones.

Partially squeezed into a decidedly unsexy nurse costume, Ruby slumped down at the kitchen table with a carton of leftover Chinese and a Diet Coke. Out of ideas, she picked up her cell and dialed Ming's lab. No answer. Channeling all the desperation she felt into one plaintive plea for help, she said, "Miiinnng, where are you? I had a rancid day and my costume doesn't fit. Everyone is going to be here and I'm getting fat. *Help!*" Ruby tossed her phone across the table in frustration and grabbed her egg roll.

The nurse costume malfunction stretched Ruby's optimism past its breaking point. An afternoon of reading about people with terminal illness in her office had laid her bare. Without an optimistic glow to soften reality or expose possibility she saw herself in the harshest light possible: a failed attorney—worse yet, a failed *asbestos* attorney with more than two-hundred-grand in debt, unloved and unsuccessful, still trying to wriggle into a costume from her sorority days to impress...she wasn't sure who. Ruby felt more than sad. She felt hollow.

Ming found Ruby in just this pose, listlessly holding her uneaten egg roll and staring vacantly. "My God, Ruby. *Seriously*. The nurse costume isn't even that good."

Ruby looked at Ming and gave her a weak smile. "I know. Have any other ideas?"

"How 'bout a sexy doctor? I brought home a lab coat and some chemistry goggles. If you wear a push-up bra with the lab coat, it might look sexy."

Ruby normally would have balked at the suggestion of wearing a lab coat stained with toxic residues and a pair of oversized goggles, something she wouldn't even wear during chemistry class, but she couldn't bring herself to care about such trifles when other people had real lives with more important concerns like children, careers, mesothelioma. The only responsibility she had in life was making her hair appointments with Chaz, lest he feel stood up. "Thanks, Ming. I'm going to go carve a pumpkin now."

Somehow, hollowing out a gourd and carving a fake smile into its flesh fit Ruby's mood perfectly. She took a serrated blade and jabbed it into a huge pumpkin. She sawed deliberately, eradicating thoughts of her stupid nurse costume and the fact that she sucked at her job and didn't have a life. Ruby scooped out the seeds with disregard for the mess she was making.

Ming stopped fixing appetizers to watch Ruby's reckless knife handling. "Um, Ruby. You doing okay? Want me to help out with that pumpkin?"

"I'm fine," she snapped. "I'm carving eyelashes into my pumpkin."

Ruby was indeed trying to carve eyelashes into her pumpkin, but not doing a good job. She had never learned to properly handle a knife. Her mother would say this was because Ruby's father never came home from work to teach her such things. Ruby gripped the knife awkwardly and pushed into the orange flesh really hard, trying to make the angle of the eyelash a perfect 45 degrees from the large eyeball she had already finished. She slipped. The knife deflected off the pumpkin's cheek, veered left, and jabbed into her left hand. She stared for a split second and then hurried to the sink.

With wide eyes, she held out her hand and asked Ming, "Will you look at this?" Ming called Todd over. He had been on ski patrol once and was therefore the biggest medical expert on the scene. Ruby shut her eyes and extended her hand limply. Unperturbed by the gushing blood, Todd peeled open the wound to see how deep it went while Ming looked over his shoulder.

"Wicked! You hit bone!" He paused and looked thoughtful for a second before saying, "I did the same thing with a shovel once." Before Todd could explain how he had managed to slice through one of his own appendages with such a crude implement, Ruby grabbed a kitchen towel and sat down on the couch.

Meanwhile, a knock sounded at the door. A moment later, Noel let himself in and called out, "Ruby? You here? Is it a bad time?" He poked his head around the corner, but then stopped short when he saw Ruby's hand. Her blood had started to soak through the towel she had wrapped it in. With a concerned look, he asked, "What happened? You're bleeding."

"I cut myself, but I'm fine." As she told him she was "fine," she did start to feel a little faint.

"Ruby, I think you need to sit back. That looks like a nasty cut." After propping another pillow on the couch, he lifted her hand gently and looked at the finger. "I think you might need stitches."

"It's fine. Todd looked at it." Ruby cocked her head in Todd's direction. She wished her finger wasn't throbbing so she could enjoy Noel holding her hand. At any rate, he was fulfilling all of her gorgeous doctor fantasies. Last time, he'd saved her from a malfunctioning igniter, this time a bad finger cut—it was as if he'd written the Mr. Right playbook.

Apparently not as distracted as she was by the hand holding, he looked skeptically at Todd. "Is he a medical expert?"

"He used to be on ski patrol."

"Ski patrol?" Noel looked in the direction she indicated, only to see a man slopping a Jell-O shot onto his hockey mask.

"Fuuuuck! Forgot I was wearing that," Todd said. He took off the mask to wipe it off and shook his head. "What a waste." He began to lick the red splatter off the plastic mask. When Todd noticed Noel staring at him, he asked, "You want to do a shot, man? They're red." He raised another shot and threw it back. "But that cut doesn't look too bad. If you go to the ER, they'll probably just prescribe her an antibiotic that she doesn't need and stitch her." After another moment of reflection he added, "I wouldn't worry. It's just a finger. Maybe if it was a thumb or something. I mean you can't do jack without a thumb."

Noel looked at Ruby and said, "That settles it. You're going to the ER and I'm driving." Taking stock of her lab coat, Noel said, "I'm glad to see you have something warm on. Can you walk?"

"It's just my finger, Noel. I'm not even sure I need to see a doctor."

"Of course you do. I won't be able to sleep tonight unless you have someone look at this." He looked very concerned.

"You're joking, right?"

"No, I'm not. I'm perfectly serious. What if it turns out to be broken or infected?" he asked, looking like a responsible adult, which she found amusing.

Sure, she wanted to spend time with Noel, but not because he thought it was his duty. Also, she'd prefer to be wearing something other than a lab coat. She was desperate to go put on something sexier. "Noel, it's so sweet of you to offer, but I don't want you to spend your night chauffeuring me to the ER."

Looking her straight in the eyes, apparently not distracted by the cleavage-bearing lab coat, he said, "I came over to see you. I don't care if we're at the ER or a wine bar, but I was hoping to see you."

Ruby suddenly felt weightless and giddy, but before she got too excited, she asked, "What about your girlfriend?"

"I broke up with Moira."

She managed to say, "Oh!" even though she wanted to squeal in delight like a teenage girl. "In that case, let's have a glass of wine. I'm sure my finger will be fine." As she said this, the blood soaked through the towel she had pressed to her hand. "You can order since that's your area of expertise."

With a laugh, he said, "I don't know where you got that idea."

"Well, duh!" she said. "I thought you knew everything about grapes." Marvel had told her all about the winery.

With a look of even greater concern, he said, "I think you might have lost more blood than you think. Liquor might not be the best idea right now." He raised his eyebrows and added, "You already woke up at my house after a blackout once."

Todd pulled out a flask and filled it with some sort of liquor from the booze table. He handed it to Noel. "Here. You can have a drink and go to the ER. Best of both worlds, dude."

Chapter Ten

SHOULD HAVE CAST JODI FOSTER

The emergency-room crowd looked about how you would expect it to on Halloween. There were a couple of kids in superhero costumes with Spiderman masks flipped back to reveal blotchy, tear-streaked faces, a few college kids in various states of intoxication, as well as the usual crowd of high fevers and broken bones. Judging by the college kids, Ruby and Noel were probably not the only ones in the waiting room with a flask full of Jägermeister. Ruby took a sip and grimaced. "Maybe you'll like this. Jäger isn't really my thing."

"Might as well," he said with a glance at his surroundings. He took a long swig and continued scrolling through headlines on his phone. Once or twice he mentioned corn subsidies and the Farm Bill.

Ruby smiled and nodded. Was the Farm Bill his go-to conversational gap filler or was he was really that boring?

Then, she remembered, it was probably relevant to the winery. A winery, she marveled. He was *so* sophisticated! Ruby desperately wanted to talk about his single status, which he had so casually mentioned, but her finger hurt, so she decided to bring it up after some pain meds. In the meantime, she skimmed a magazine article titled, "Is Your Shampoo Making You Fat?" She chuckled in a superior, little laugh. She pointed it out to Noel, saying, "Look, Noel, isn't this dumb?"

Before he could answer, the nurse called her name.

Noel got up to follow her, but when Ruby saw the scale, she said, "Noel, why don't you wait out here. I'm sure this won't take long." There was no need for Noel to know everything before they even went on their first real date.

"Okay, I'll just be out here then." He smiled and sat down next to a kid in a Spiderman costume.

The preliminary weighing went poorly. The nurse costume did not lie—she weighed a solid fifteen pounds more than expected. *Fifteen pounds*, basically the equivalent of a Thanksgiving turkey. Clearly, the extra spandex in her pants had been lulling her into the false belief that she didn't really need to work out. She was mentally working out a diet and exercise plan (a French diet maybe?) and perhaps a shampoo switch (just to be safe) when the doctor knocked and walked in. Staring blandly at the chart, he said, "Miss O'Deare, I see you have a finger injury." He sat down across from her and asked her to hold out her hand. He looked it over and said. "Hmm. Looks like you have a pretty deep cut. I think you're going to need some stitches and maybe a round of antibiotics. Are you up to date on tetanus?"

Ruby nodded, still thinking about a French diet plan and trying to reconcile bread, wine, and cheese with her desired weight loss. The French were all skinny, so it had to work, she reasoned.

"Do you have any known allergies?"

"No."

"Are you pregnant?"

"No." As she said no, Ruby tried to remember when her last period was.

The doctor sensed her uncertainty. "Are you sure that you're not pregnant?"

"Pretty sure." She thought of the sexy nurse costume. Maybe there was a reason it didn't fit.

Catching her hesitation, the doctor asked, "When was your last period?"

"You know, I'm just here for my finger. I'm not pregnant." Even saying the word out loud sounded preposterous. "Sure, I put on a little weight recently...but I'm totally not here about that." She paused, "Why does it matter if I'm pregnant anyway?"

"Well, I don't mean to pester you. It's just that the medication I normally prescribe would not be my first choice if I also had to consider how it might affect a fetus. The pregnancy question is routine. I only inquired further because you hesitated."

Ruby's blood pressure lowered a tad. "Sorry. I was just surprised you asked." She thought for a minute. The last time she could remember having her period was on her weekend trip to visit Ming's family in Malibu. That had been a great vacation. "I guess my last period was sometime around Labor Day. I think."

When she said it out loud, she realized it had been almost two months ago. She'd never missed a period before.

He paused long enough to calculate the elapsed time. "Well, Miss O'Deare, that's been about two months. Have you had unprotected sex since then?"

Ruby said, "No," then amended, "I don't think so," as she tried to remember the details of the infamous night with Noel. She'd woken up purple with a receipt for condoms. That much she knew. But had they used them? Even if they did, a little voice in the back of her mind yelled, *Glow-in-the-dark condoms. From the Dollar Store… Probably expired!* Still, she'd never thought of herself as the fertile type, whatever that might be. To her, unplanned pregnancies were like tornadoes—they only struck trailer parks.

"If you don't mind, I'd like to rule out pregnancy before I prescribe any medication for you."

"Fine. But…" Her high school guidance counselor's mantra "*It only takes once*" cut her off her would-be protest.

After peeing into a cup, Ruby sat and waited. She tried to read, but couldn't focus. She scanned the multitude of posters hanging in the room encouraging diabetic foot care and vaccinations. The obligatory poster of the female reproductive system glared down at her, somehow making her feel like an animal, a verging-on-chubby specimen of the female variety. Make that an irresponsible specimen, never mind $150 haircut and law job, not to mention Ming's lab coat. In truth, she felt more like an unwed teenage mother than a responsible lawyer.

When he finally came in, he sat down calmly. "Miss O'Deare, I know that you might not have been expecting this news." He waited a moment to let her steel her nerves. Instead of steeling her defenses, she felt them crumble around her. When he said, "You are pregnant," she felt the tears well up involuntarily.

She blinked and said, "You said I'm pregnant?"

"Yes."

Looking at her knees, she exhaled a few times and propped her head in her hands. She had planned on doing so many things before she had kids—traveling, learning French, paying off *all* of her credit cards, reading some of those books she had pretended to read in college. Even higher up the list of things she should have done before this moment was marriage with a honeymoon (in Hawaii) to a man she had spent more than one night with. Instead, the father was in the lobby, oblivious to this possibility, reading about corn subsidies. It was too much to bear.

And the whole baby aspect of the pregnancy… She had never even held a baby. Just the thought of a baby stole all of her resolve. Boneless, she sank farther into the chair. Her life was turning into a serious movie, something Oscar-worthy, a movie that required a strong lead, probably Jodi Foster or maybe Natalie Portman. Maybe Kristin Wiig. No one would *ever* cast Ruby O'Deare for this role. It would be like casting Tori Spelling. She closed her eyes and took a deep breath. Then, because there was nothing to be done, she put on her courtroom face, wiped away the tears that were threatening to spill, and asked, "Are you sure I'm pregnant?" Tori Spelling had like four kids, right?

"Yes." He pulled out a little calendar and counted back. "It looks to me like you are ten, no wait, six weeks pregnant, based on the date of your last period." He paused for a second and put on his diplomatic face. "So, Miss O'Deare, have you given any thought to whether you want to keep the baby?"

"Seriously?" She had never imagined a doctor would ask her that question. This was the question she expected someone else from her high-school class to hear, probably that girl who took yearbook and low math. She squinted a little, but couldn't stop her eyes from welling up again. Ruby couldn't believe she was having this conversation. She wasn't opposed to abortion for religious reasons. She hadn't attended church since her confirmation class ended when she was thirteen. Still, she knew she didn't want one. It just seemed wrong since she was twenty-eight. She had life insurance. At least she assumed she did. And she had a job and a nice-enough car. Well, a temp job and a convertible, but still, she was an adult. Her birth certificate said so. With conviction she said, "I'm keeping the baby."

"Excellent. In that case, congratulations are in order."

"Well, I don't know if I'd go that far." Ruby had trouble focusing on the doctor as he told a few basics about prenatal health. She needed to schedule an appointment with a family practice doc or OB/GYN, stop eating tuna, and eat more legumes. This statement gave pause to her runaway thoughts. *What are legumes?* Then, she thought of that Jäger and everything else she'd drunk in the last two months. *Yikes!* "I haven't been watching my alcohol intake or anything. Will the baby be okay?"

"I wouldn't worry. That's how half the people I see end up pregnant in the first place." He chuckled and added, "Just be careful from now on."

She was ready to leave when the doctor said, "Now for the finger. How did you manage to do this?"

"Oh." Ruby tried to smile. "I forgot about the finger. I was carving eyelashes into a jack-o-lantern." Next Halloween, she would have a baby to stuff into a little costume, a cute little thing with a pink cheeks and a toothless smile. She imagined she'd have a cute one. Maybe she could make enough to live comfortably, just her and the baby. Or maybe…she didn't dare think about Noel or the (three!) of them yet, but she couldn't help herself. In her rebellious imagination, they were living in a sun-dappled villa on a winery somewhere between Emerald and Topeka. Marvel had said the villa was a ways out of town.

He put a couple of stitches in her finger, but she was so distracted by the other news that it barely even registered. After he finished the stitches he told her the nurse would come by with a splint in a minute. The doctor's words snapped her out of her reverie and she looked up. The poster about diabetic foot rot stared back at her and she nodded as the doctor recommended that she change the bandages on her finger regularly. But, she was still thinking about Noel, who she would have to face in approximately one minute. Her stomach heaved.

"Are you okay, Miss O'Deare? Do you have anyone here with you?"

"I'm fine. Just a little nauseous." The thought of Noel made the vomit rise up in her throat.

"Well don't worry about it. That'll happen from time to time. But it should get better in a week or two. If you haven't had much morning sickness thus far, you're probably in the clear."

She bid the doctor a quick good-bye and greeted a nurse who came in to bring her a fancy blue finger splint. She was the motherly type of nurse who probably gave all the kids suckers and extra stickers.

"How you holding up, sweetheart? Do you want me to get that handsome young man who came with you?"

Ruby smiled. "I'm just fine. Definitely don't get him. I'll be fine."

"I'm sure you will. Such a nice, young couple. I can tell you will be great parents. He looks so caring *and handsome*."

Ruby's feelings began to overflow again and she felt the tears run down her cheeks. A baby was one thing, thinking of herself as a mother was something entirely different. And, Noel, she wondered how he would take going from landlord to father before they even managed one date.

Ruby walked into the waiting room with a freshly bandaged hand, a splotchy red face and a complementary bottle of prenatal vitamins that she quickly shoved into her lab coat pocket. She gave Noel a weak smile and said nothing because, really, what do you say in that situation?

"Is everything okay? You look like you could use some more Jäger," he teased, handing her the flask. When she didn't laugh, he joked, "Do they have to amputate?"

She smiled a little. "I'm just a little worn out. *Long* day." She looked so beleaguered that he put his arm around her and gave her a squeeze on the way out of the door. The doctor, who was standing at the patient counter discussing something with the staff noticed and assumed this was a "congratulations honey!" hug and called out, "Congratulations! Good luck with everything, Mr. and Mrs. O'Deare."

Noel looked from her to the doctor with a confused expression. Ruby eked out a shallow laugh and started walking to the door and avoided eye contact with Noel. They needed to get out before anyone said anything else.

"Wonder what that was about?"

Ruby shook her head and shrugged.

"Are you sure you're okay?" He took her arm, unsure of how else to help her. "Let's sit you down." He ushered her to the car, opened the door, and insisted on ensuring that she sat down without further injury.

Ruby rode home, almost completely silent except for a little sniffling as she tried to keep from crying. She tried to say something so that she didn't look like such a nut, but when she opened her mouth, she couldn't think of anything to say. By the time he got her home, he insisted that she go straight to bed and kicked the last chemistry revelers out of the house. He gave Ming instructions to "keep an eye on her" and drove home.

After an hour or so, Ming who'd been watching *America's Most Wanted* re-runs, peeked in to make sure Ruby was still breathing. She was sitting up in bed staring at her wall. Even Vera Wang looked concerned, mewling a little in the corner. "What's the matter? I thought it was just a finger thing… Do you need something? I bet Todd has something."

"No. The finger is fine. It's something else." Looking at her hands, she said, "The doctor made me take a pregnancy test and I found out that I'm… I'm pregnant."

"What?"

"I'm pregnant." The fact sounded so much worse out loud than it did in her head.

"Are you serious? With Noel?" She answered her own question, since she knew Ruby hadn't been with anyone else. "*What* were you thinking? Aren't you on birth control?"

"Well, yeah, but I must have skipped one or two days… or maybe last month. I wasn't exactly worried, you know." She didn't mention the expired condoms. Ming would get too much material from that.

"Okay, in the morning we'll take care of it. I'll drive you to the clinic and then we'll go out for coffee or something." Ming was not the motherly type. She was militantly against children, actually. She was *the* woman, probably the only one that Michelle Bachman warned about, ruthlessly picking an abortion clinic conveniently located next to a Starbucks and a nail salon so that she'd have something do while Ruby took care of business.

"No. No. I think I'm going to keep it."

"What? You can barely remember to feed the cats. You had to get an automatic feeder, Ruby. By the way, I think you forgot to fill it this week. I think the neighbor might be taking care of them." Ming scowled. "You need to stop buying animals like they're handbags."

Ruby rolled her eyes, her conviction strengthening against Ming's arguments. "I feel like it's the right decision. Do you know that I've been craving crème brûleé and caramel rolls for the last six weeks? I think the baby likes caramel. She also must be a morning person because I've been waking up *really* early every day. She already feels like a person to me."

"Ruby, I'm sure you feel that way, but you should think it over. It's just a cluster of pluripotent cells. It has the potential for humanity, but nothing more. I think you should get some sleep and think about it tomorrow, after a good breakfast and coffee, my treat. Also, you should sleep in. It's late."

Chapter Eleven

MURDER

In the morning Ruby felt drained before she even opened her eyes or could recall the source of her lingering despair. For a minute she just lay there feeling as disoriented as a sci-fi traveler waking from cryo-sleep. Instead of finding herself in the Andromeda Galaxy with an alien race to fight, she remembered. She was pregnant, her finger was sort of broken, and she couldn't take anything stronger than Tylenol. Pretty much as bad as the alien race scenario. She pulled the covers over her head and shut her eyes until she managed to fall asleep again.

Next time she woke up, Ming was pulling the covers off her face. "Ruby, wake up. I'm starving and I need to start cheering you up over breakfast *now*." She handed Ruby a cup of coffee.

"I'm just not up to it, Ming. Let me sleep in today."

"It's already ten o'clock. Time to buck up." Ming only had about a half-hour's worth of sympathy and one bedside coffee delivery in her and Ruby had just used up both.

"Are you serious, Ming? I just found out that I'm about to be an unwed single mother. It's sort of a shock to go from debutante to Jerry Springer in one night. Give me a minute." This was no exaggeration. Not only was Ruby a former county fair princess, she was literally a graduate of a social etiquette club with a full-fledged debutante ball. Probably not the best life training in hindsight.

"Oh, come off it. You've been dancing around Jerry Springer ever since freshman year when you lived in the AOII house. Do you know what everyone else called that place?" She paused before the answer. "The 'ate her pie' house. Debutante went out the door a while ago. And so what? You made a bad decision. Just start making some good ones now. We're leaving for breakfast in fifteen minutes. No excuses."

"Oh my God. Who are you? Jillian Michaels?" Ruby complained as she swung her legs over the side of the bed dramatically.

Showered, but bare of jewelry and mascara, Ruby climbed into Ming's black hybrid SUV, a vehicle as unfathomable and contradictory as Ming herself. Ming drove to Auntie Em's, belying the fact that she felt no sympathy. She was about to break her macrobiotic diet with sugar-coated beignets, Em's Saturday morning specialty.

Ruby looked at Ming gratefully, "Thanks, Ming."

Toward the end of the beignet binge, during which there was no discussion of Noel or the baby, Ruby's phone rang. She pulled it out and looked at the caller ID. "It's Eric."

"Answer it. You might need a baby daddy," Ming said, as if Eric would ever voluntarily take on responsibility.

Ruby followed Ming's command and picked up the phone. "Hi, Ruby," Eric said in an unusually professional tone of voice.

"Hey, Eric. Why so serious?"

"It's Estelle."

"Is she okay? What happened?"

"She's dead, Ruby."

"*What*?" She must have misheard. She felt like she had that morning when she couldn't quite distinguish her reality from her dream. Estelle couldn't be dead. Yesterday, she'd eaten pie at Auntie Em's wearing a canary yellow outfit with too much blush.

"We found her this morning."

Ruby set down the beignet she had been about to eat and wiped the sugar off her fingers robotically. She couldn't eat. Ruby had never experienced a loved one's death before. Being notified about a death unexpectedly over doughnuts, it was wrong in so many ways. There was no reason he would make it up, but she couldn't process it. She knew what she was supposed to say and think—"she was fine yesterday" or "how did it happen"—so she uttered her lines, not even bothering to listen to the answers.

"I'm meeting the medical examiner over at her place in fifteen minutes. I wanted to let you know, but I also wanted to come by and ask you some questions later. I know you saw her yesterday."

Numbly she asked, "Do you want me to do anything?"

"No, I'll be over later. Just thought I'd give you a heads-up."

"Okay. Bye."

Ruby set down the phone and stared at her last two beignets and the latte she'd ordered. *Estelle is dead*. Ruby tried telling herself again. *Estelle is dead*. It just didn't ring true. She'd seen Estelle yesterday. Her stomach still hadn't recovered from Estelle's tar-slick black coffee. She had been looking forward to finding out how Estelle had saved her house.

Ming looked at her, "What's the matter? You look like your fairy godmother just died."

Ming's unintentionally apt description made her tear up. Estelle was her fairy godmother. "It's Estelle, the pro bono client I've been helping recently. She died this morning." Announcing this felt strange, especially when she hadn't absorbed the shock herself. It felt wrong to even say it out loud. Ruby's announcement hung in the air for a moment unacknowledged.

With a look of annoyance on her face, Ming said, "Is one crisis at a time too much to ask? Could you please hold the drama for five minutes and let me finish breakfast?" Ming finished a few beignets and drank her coffee before asking, "How did she die?"

"I don't know. Eric didn't say. Would you mind driving me by her place on the way home? I want to see for myself." If nothing else, Ruby felt like she had to confront the reality of Estelle's absence before she could believe it. And maybe she could help. She felt like she had to do something, anything. Though everyone always expected her to be useless in a crisis, one of those overly dramatic girls who needed to be consoled when someone else was bleeding, Ruby wasn't that girl. This morning, she wanted to do something useful.

"What for? Did you really know her that well? I know you liked her, but you just started helping her a few months ago. She's a client. They die sometimes."

"I'm not a surgeon, Ming. It's not like I lose people on the table 15 percent of the time. Not to mention, she's my *only* client. And, I just feel like I should go. Eric needs to ask me some questions anyway. He can drive me home."

"Fine by me."

Ming pulled up in front of 835 Hyacinth Blvd. It looked the same, big old tatty house with a beat-up sofa on the front porch and a Christmas wreath that was probably attractive fifteen years ago, before the pine bows melded to the shape of its storage box and the glitter wore off the Styrofoam cardinals. Poor Estelle. Ruby wished she could drop by with a brand new wreath for her friend tomorrow, one with more glitter. She started to tear up because she hadn't thought of that sooner.

Eric was in front of the house strutting about like a seasoned investigator, taking note of this and that. He said something to Trudi, who had her butt parked on the front stairs. Trudi looked sullen and definitely less mean than usual, more like the outcast high-schooler Ruby remembered than the bitch throwing a fit in Estelle's kitchen. Oblivious to the pitiful wreath, Eric walked right through the front door and headed for the other officials, probably guys with names like "Detective Lynch" and "Detective Ryan." They looked important. They made some official noises and looked around them in an engaged and alert sort of way, very *CSI*.

"Will you wait just one minute?" Ruby asked Ming.

"Sure. Just wave if you're going to leave with Eric."

"Thanks." Ruby stepped out of the car and walked

hesitantly up to the house. She stopped in front of Trudi. "I'm sorry about Estelle."

"Don't be. She wasn't anything to me." Trudi's tears belied the awful statement. Between her tears, blotchy red face, and shaking hands, she looked like a complete wreck.

"Sorry anyways." She brushed past Trudi, who refused to budge, on the way up the stairs. At the door she gently touched the boughs of the sad wreath. She looked in the door and saw Eric in a group with some other cops. "Eric!" she called. "I came by to—" She lost the words in her throat when she caught sight of a black body bag. She still stood upright, but inside she crumpled. Tears pricked at the back of her eyes. Her vibrant, sparkly friend should not be in that horrible bag. Though swamped with sadness, a flash of anger caught her unaware like a stitch in her side. As she stared at the bag, she didn't think she would lose that stitch anytime soon.

"Ruby, what are you doing here?" Eric wrapped an arm around her and steered her back down the stairs onto the lawn. "You should go straight home. I just called to let you know, as a courtesy. You shouldn't be here."

"I'm sorry. I don't know why I came."

"It doesn't matter." He saw Ming and ushered Ruby back to the car.

"I'll come by in a bit. You go home and relax. Drink some tea or something."

Ruby nodded meekly. Ming said, "See you later, Viking."

As they drove off, Ruby looked out the side window and noticed the development sign planted firmly on the front corner of an industrial looking lot, *"Future home of Elysian Fields Green Luxury Development. Live green and live well!"* The sign looked like it had been there for a while. The upside-down orange couch rested in front of it and, strangely enough, part of a refrigerator was surfacing a little to the left of the sign. Apparently Elysian Fields was taking a while to get off the ground.

Ming asked, "Isn't that the old dump?" as they drove past the sign.

"How would I know? Do you know anything about Elysian Fields?"

"Yeah. I read a piece in the paper on it a few weeks ago. It's supposed to be some über-sexy, green-living development—all sorts of Feng Shui-ed neighborhoods and upscale shops for the 'urban elite.' They didn't mention the development was being built on the dump." She chuckled.

"Sounds good to me. Cute houses and shopping. What's not to like?"

"I have to admit, I like the no commute thing, the shopping, but I'd prefer not to bunk with anyone who calls themselves the urban elite, especially when it is built on top of a bunch of old toasters and microwaves. I'm 99 percent sure that is the old appliance dump. Oz operated it before the Biomall took off." Ming paused to reflect for a moment. "And why live in a country club if it doesn't have a pool or tennis courts? It's all snob factor without the benefits, except proximity to the shopping, which we already have."

"Isn't it supposed to have some sort of lower-income house built in? I know Destinee was trying to sell Estelle a place."

"Supposedly, *but really*, do food stamps work at Banana Republic and Starbucks? If they'd been trying to help the poor they could have put in someplace where their food stamps would go a little farther than Food Hollow. Maybe a worker's center. It's just a ploy to fast-track it through the zoning board. They're all about mixed use/mixed income levels. Living next to janitors is very *en vogue* these days."

"You're such a snot, Ming. If Noel is working on it, it has to be nice."

"*Ohhh.* I see how it is."

Ruby's mind began to drift. As they drove past The Great Wall, she smelled delicious Chinese food. She started thinking about egg rolls and her mouth watered. When she realized that she was thinking about egg rolls while Estelle was dead, she couldn't believe how callous she was. She was much too selfish to be a good mother. She started to cry. Then she started to cry harder because she was crying for herself, not Estelle.

"Ruby, really, can't we get through ten minutes without crying? Your hormones must be whacked. What is it this time?"

"I'm fine," Ruby said, still crying. "I really want an egg roll, though. I feel like such a jerk for wanting an egg roll. Estelle is never going to have an egg roll again."

Ming said, "Let's get an egg roll."

· · ·

A few hours later, at her place, Eric gave her the official report. "The neighbors called and reported a fight, which is why the cops investigated in the first place. When the cops arrived they found Estelle dead in the kitchen and Trudi on the porch crying. Trudi admits that they had a fight. About you, actually."

Ruby cut in. "About the Giddyup deal?"

"I don't know. She didn't say anything about that. From what I gathered, she and Jermaine just didn't want Estelle to 'lawyer up.' Trudi claims that she left in a hurry. When she went back a few minutes later to retrieve her purse, she found Estelle dead in the kitchen." He paused to let that soak in, then explained, "It looks like she had a heart attack. We wouldn't have investigated at all except for the 911 call." Eric said this with more finality than the statement probably deserved, meaning, *Don't abuse our friendship by making me look into this old lady's death.*

"Oh." Ruby sat silently for a moment. "That just doesn't make sense to me. Estelle was healthy." Ruby could picture Estelle going up and down the ladder retrieving Isotoners from the attic. The woman started every morning with a "Get fit while you sit" workout that she'd ordered from an infomercial. "That just doesn't make sense to me, Eric. I don't think she had a heart attack."

Eric patted her on the shoulder sympathetically, too polite to say, "Old people have heart attacks all the time." After he left, Ruby changed into sweatpants and didn't get out of them for the next thirty-six hours, about eighteen of which she spent sleeping.

Chapter Twelve

ASBESTOS PURGATORY

At work, she sat down in cubicle wearing a T-shirt that smelled vaguely of Chinese take-out from a few days ago and stared at the "Follow your dreams! Way Up High!" poster hanging squarely in front of her workspace, cheering her on like a backstabbing cheerleader, the kind who says nice things, but really hopes you fall off the top of the pyramid. This morning, its commandment pissed her off more than usual. She hated cheerleaders (she had been on the color guard), so she stood up, took it off the wall, and let it fall behind her desk, where it landed with a satisfying thud.

She smiled at the clean rectangle outlined in dust where the poster had been. It was almost as good as beating the fax machine with a baseball bat.

With that out of the way, she slumped into her chair and pulled her phone out of her purse. She scrolled through her contacts until she came to Noel, but she couldn't bring herself to press "send." Notifying Noel that she was pregnant was just too much for a Monday morning. She set the phone on the desk. A little too forcefully, she slid it across the surface. It slammed against the wall and dropped behind her desk. That decided it. She'd call Noel later. At this point, she'd have to move the desk if she wanted to talk him, which tipped the scales from epically daunting to impossible.

Moving on to the next order of business, she needed to call Eric. With her office phone, of course. She could have used that to call Noel, too, she supposed, but pregnancy defied logic. It only felt right to talk about pregnancy on her personal phone. She might also need to wrap herself in a fuzzy warm blanket and hold a teddy bear.

Eric might not want to get involved in Estelle's case, but it didn't hurt to ask. If there was foul play she wanted to make sure someone investigated properly. Jermaine and Trudi certainly weren't going to do anything.

"Eric, hi. It's Ruby."

"Hey, Ruby. How are you feeling?"

"Okay," she lied. "I was just wondering if you got Estelle's autopsy report back."

"Yeah."

He paused for a minute, making it was clear that he didn't want to tell her the results.

"So tell me already. What did it say?"

"It's inconclusive. The medical examiner sent out toxicology, but the results won't be back for a week. I don't expect anything that disputes the presumption of natural causes."

"So you'll be looking into her death, treating it as a

homicide until then?" Ruby asked hopefully.

"I wouldn't go that far. I don't think there's anything to find, Ruby."

"If there's anything you can do, I'd appreciate it. Estelle was my friend."

"All right. I'll give you a call when I find anything out." He paused and shifted his tones, a little less policeman and a little more Barry White. "I had something else to ask you, too. I've been meaning to call and see if you want to go out for a date, maybe one *without* your roommate. She's cool and all, but I would sort of like to make it to second base without her, that is, unless we all want to go there together?"

"Eric, are you serious? I just called about Estelle's autopsy results. Is that how you roll? I realize that you didn't know Estelle, but it's not really the time. You aren't getting off home plate today."

"Okay. Guess I'm just used to it. Plus, I thought a date might cheer you up. In my experience, a trip to second base, or even a full home-run, is the best way to help the bereaved. Much more effective than a casserole."

As nasty as he was, she couldn't help but laugh. "I'll keep that in mind."

Gratuitous flirting or not, she still felt pregnant and depressed when she hung up the phone. She wanted Eric to get on the horse and investigate. The woman might have been eighty-something, but she didn't have a bad heart.

She pushed thoughts of Estelle aside as her computer inconsiderately reminded her of the "59,666 documents left to review," asbestos purgatory still waiting for her to clock in. On Friday, she would have forged on with glazed eyes, thoughts of her mid-morning coffee break dancing in her head, but after experiencing death and impending mother-hood, something started to snap. Her shiny veneer of cheerful indifference began to crack. It turns out Ruby didn't have much time for document review.

But her boss certainly did.

Her email *pinged* and a message from Destinee briefly flashed across the screen and faded like an unwelcome desert mirage. Destinee wrote:

Ruby, Please put together a three-page memorandum describing the highlights of the Medina evidence so far. In addition, I want a list of all the employees who smoke and those who live in dwellings built before 1950. If your memo is good enough, I might be able to include it in the summary judgment motion.

Destinee clearly thought she was tossing Ruby a juicy leftover from the pile of real lawyer work. Granted, if Destinee had sent the email to her more eager co-workers, like Olivia or Ted, she'd immediately receive a response asking for the opportunity to draft the whole document and give a ten-minute presentation on potential litigation strategies. Just like Olivia would have, Ruby dutifully started the requested memorandum. She typed:

To: Destinee Childs
From: Ruby O'Deare
Date: November 5
Re: Medina Asbestos Evidence Summary

Then, she clicked onto the document viewer to look through her reviewed documents. She stared at the number again: 11,005 out of 59,666. Reflexively, she opened another window and typed in petfinder.com where she scrolled through all of the medium-sized dogs within one hundred miles of Emerald. When she clicked on a matched set of cocker spaniels named Debbie and Charmaine the excitement swamped her depression faster than a triple grande pumpkin-spice latte laced with Prozac delivered intravenously. Without even stopping to think, she typed a quick note: *Are Debbie and Charmaine still available?* She could see it now: Cocker spaniels sleeping in front of her fireplace on monogrammed dog beds. Walking cocker spaniels in the manner of a Louis Icart model, 20s-style chiffon dress clinging to her willowy frame while spaniels pulled her toward vanilla latte with eager glee.

Almost instantaneously, a woman responded. She explained that Debbie and Charmaine weren't just run-of-the-mill cockers. They were OzDogs, genetically modified to be cuter than every other dog; i.e., act fast because they wouldn't last! Moreover, she wrote that Debbie and Charmaine were still looking for their "forever home" and advised Ruby to fill out the attached application. More often than not, Ruby equated available with destined-to-be. For example, size eight Jimmy Choos in stock (or a largish seven or seven and a half or smallish size eight and a half or nine). Not buying them would be akin to composting a tortilla with Jesus's face burned into it.

Now she knew it—God wanted her to have cockers. She glanced furtively at the memo, her cursor blinking anxiously at the top of the page. She minimized it and pulled up the application. If there was a God, he wanted her to ignore Destinee, fill out the application, and rescue those dogs as soon as possible.

1. Do you have a fenced back yard?

2. Have you ever owned a dog before?

3. Do you have other animals? If so, do they get along well with dogs?

4. Do you have time to walk the dog every day?

Ruby quickly answered "Yes!" to all of the questions and shot the application back to the cockers' foster mom, Debbie. She figured it didn't really matter that her back yard only had a decorative fence, her cats had never met a dog, and she had only owned a near-comatose Bernese Mountain Dog that had died while she was still wearing Care Bear underwear. Another bonus of having dogs was that she would have more in common with Noel. He had a dog. She felt like it was named Lupo…or maybe that was someone else? At any rate, she envisioned getting lattes on Saturday mornings and walking to the park, just her, Noel, and a bunch of dogs. And the baby, of course. Front packs these days were so fashionable.

Her call to dog ownership answered, she looked back at the asbestos documents and began to read an old miner's health insurance plan. She didn't get past, "The insured agrees," which she read approximately thirteen times, when Olivia walked in.

"Ruby, how are you doing? Marvel told me you broke it or something."

Ruby held up the finger. She had nearly forgotten about it. "It's just a bad cut." Ruby looked at the finger and thought about her "other news." She was planning on keeping that to herself for a good long while so as to avoid becoming office gossip and questions she wasn't prepared to answer. Perhaps if she wore the right clothes, she would never have to tell.

"Okay, Marvel has finally pressured me into joining her Smiddy's Biggest Loser club. We're all supposed to go on walks, eat salads, and generally encourage each other to be healthier and lose weight. Whoever loses the most weight by Thanksgiving has to buy a round of drinks for the rest. Marvel promised there won't be a weigh-in in the lobby, at least until the end. Are you in?"

Ruby looked at Olivia. She thought carefully before going on. "I know I've been bugging you to exercise with me, but this might not be the best timing." She tried to think of why without spilling the beans. "You know…with all the work we've got coming up, I'm not going to have time to make salads and pack little snacks of almonds and cranberries. Maybe we should wait."

Olivia looked stunned. "Seriously?"

Ruby decided not to bother arguing. Liv would win, so she might as well give in. "Oh, whatever, why not?"

"Nice. I knew you'd join. None of the attorneys in this firm manage to eat well or exercise. We have to take a stand and make it a priority."

Ruby looked out at the other attorneys. She could see several from her desk, most staring at their computer screens. Ted was typing feverishly to meet a deadline, Meg was shielding her screen so no one could see that she was on Gmail, and Zach was facing the wall with an iPad propped in his lap, probably napping. They were all putting in their time like lifers. Their days in a cube and any free hours now designated for supervised exercise.

She managed to review twenty more documents before lunch, still not enough to write an updated review of evidence highlights, but she didn't give a damn. She was so far behind, what did it matter anyway? She picked up her purse and walked with Olivia to the appointed meeting spot of the

Biggest Loser crowd, which now included partners and su-
pervisors, probably to show they cared about the little people.

Marvel explained that the point of the group was to set
fitness goals and spend the lunch hour exercising. Though
Ruby tried her best to look busy talking with Olivia, Destinee cornered her.

"Ruby, I'm so glad you're here! I bet you didn't think I
would be!" Destinee laughed a little, as if it was preposterous
that she needed to lose weight. "I was hoping I would run
into you. We can talk business while we're feeling the burn."

Ruby nodded and smiled like a bobble-head doll. Behind
her empty smile she wondered what Destinee was up to.

"First of all, how does the evidence look?"

Ruby fixated on Destinee's nose, which looked perfect.
She wondered if Destinee's plastic-surgeon father had
anything to do with that, but she answered, "It looks pretty
good. I think plenty of the workers smoked."

"Excellent. I want a detailed list of all the smokers and
please include any other negative health information available from the medical records, autopsy reports, or depositions. And I mean *anything* at this stage. We'll prioritize
later. If they had pernicious toenail fungus, I want to know
about it. I need you to give me all the ammo you can to
throw a wrench into their causation argument. Asbestos isn't
the only thing that causes lung damage."

Keep telling yourself that! She nodded and politely said,
"Sounds like a good plan."

"This is the way it's going to work: I will be the lead on
the Medina case with Dworkin, only checking in from time
to time. I envision you and Olivia as my field officers. You
will get your hands dirty with document review. As needed,

I will have you draft documents to the court and help with depositions."

Translation: You do all the work, I'll take the credit.

"Sounds great!" Ruby smiled brightly. It was actually good news. Dworkin had given her the impression that she was in charge, so it was a relief to be demoted. Destinee sounded as if she would just love to assign Ruby to urinal cake replacement and toilet cleaning, the little skuzzy bits around the hinges, not just general scrubbing.

"I have another major case I'm heading up as well, which will go to trial in the spring, I think. You and Olivia will need to be first in command at that point."

"Okay, sounds like a wonderful opportunity," said Ruby. She was starting to think delivering a baby sounded like a great alternative to being a field officer on the Medina Asbestos defense team. She wondered if Noel liked babies.

Just when Ruby thought she was done, Destinee imparted one more piece of advice, but without the veneer of civility this time. "I would like you to cease any investigation of the Estelle Harris case. I need all of your energy going into the asbestos litigation." She said this as if she knew that Ruby had already been poking around, which made zero sense because she had done nothing but talk to Eric. Destinee explained further, "The family has requested that I help manage the dispensation of the estate."

Ruby knew one thing. Jermaine did not request any "dispensation."

• • •

After her fitness walk with Destinee, Ruby wrote the memo.

She didn't pretty it up. She had only reviewed the first 400 documents out of 60,000, definitely a flirtation with substandard work, at least compared to the other associates. She identified two smokers and one guy who lived in an old house that probably had some asbestos tiles in it. She didn't mention that he probably didn't shred and inhale his tiles, making it unlikely that they caused his mesothelioma.

Before she left the office, her phone rang from under the desk. Ruby's heart sputtered at the thought Noel might be calling. It'd be so much easier if he called her. She dropped to all fours and grabbed the phone just before the call went to voicemail. It turned out to be the cocker spaniel lady. "Hello, Ruby. Your application has been approved."

When Ruby heard this, she pressed send on the memo without bothering to proofread. She had puppies on the brain. Destinee would be delighted for the opportunity to inform her of any misspellings anyway. She reached for her purse and turned off her computer. "That's great! When can I pick them up? Would tonight be okay?"

"Actually, I won't be around to meet you tonight. You can pick them up as early as tomorrow, but it'll have to be before two o'clock because I have an appointment after that."

Ruby did a little mental math. Estelle's funeral was at three o'clock tomorrow. She had planned on working until two and then heading over… *But*, if she worked during the morning, she could pick up the dogs and still make it to the funeral in plenty of time. She *needed* those dogs. Estelle would have loved those dogs. Debbie and Charmaine were going to get her through the next few months of her life. Besides, kids loved dogs. Her kid was going to be so lucky!

She went home mostly content. While the valet retrieved

her car, she stared out the window and rested her mind. Her day at work at least helped distract her from pregnancy and Estelle, sort of like getting a punch in the gut to take your mind off your headache.

At home, she threw her briefcase in the corner and slumped onto the couch next to Todd.

"Whatchya watchin'?" she asked.

"MTV. Some show about pregnant chicks. I can't find the remote."

It was *Sixteen and Pregnant*.

"Think I'll pass, Todd. Little too close to home." Of course, Todd had no clue why *Sixteen and Pregnant* "hit too close to home" because Ruby hadn't told anyone besides Ming, but he nodded in understanding and flipped the channel. She could have used the same line for *Star Trek* or *Total Recall* and he would have blindly accepted. Last person on Earth capable of overthrowing the robot overlords, yep, too close to home for Ruby.

He flipped the channel to the six o'clock news. Ruby sat bolt upright as she saw a reporter standing right in front of the Elysian Fields sign. The camera panned the area giving her a glimpse of the sign, the orange couch, the fridge, and Estelle's place with a single streamer of crime-scene tape trailing from the porch. Then the camera cut back to the local newscaster.

The newscaster began, "Tonight, I would like to introduce you to the future home of Elysian Fields." She pointed at the vacant lot behind her. "Elysian Fields will be the Biomall's first official shopping community. Also, it's going to be green. As part of a land reclamation project, Ozcorp is building it right on top of an old appliance landfill. There will be extensive land rehabilitation, as well as LEED-certified housing."

The reporter tossed her hair and continued. "So what does this mean? I have it for you in one word: *Discounts!* All residents of Elysian Fields will receive a Biomall credit card with an extra-high limit and low interest rate. Not to mention, Oz is connecting Elysian Fields to the Biomall via a monorail luxury caboose!" She fanned her face and said, "You can count me in. I've already pre-purchased a condo and intend to exercise my shiny new credit card ASAP." She held up her credit card for the camera like she had just won a ticket to Willy Wonka's. The credit card was gold with no writing except her name: "Janine," as if she and the credit card company were on a first-name basis.

Last week Ruby would have run to pre-order a condo. Tonight, she just stared. She flashed back to her conversation with Noel. He'd called the place a "soul-sucking, apathetic black hole." Maybe he was right.

Before she fell asleep that night, her phone beeped. It was a text. From *Noel.* Her heart began to race as she read it. He'd written, *Hope you're feeling better today. Wanted to call but didn't have chance. Dinner Friday?*

Once again, she picked up the phone to call him. It was as good a time as any, but she wasn't ready to say it out loud to him. It's not like they were a nesting pair and he would be like, "Great, an egg!" They were just two birds who got drunk and he probably didn't even want an egg or her, especially if she came with an egg. For a second, she thought about responding with news of their chick. Unable to find the right words, she decided to do the sensible thing and continue with the charade. She texted: *Yes! Can't wait for Friday.*

Chapter Thirteen

DEBBIE AND CHARMAINE GO TO A FUNERAL

Ruby looked at the map and noticed that Hackamore, Kansas, where she needed to pick up the dogs, was farther away from Emerald than she had imagined, so she punched the gas and set the cruise control to eighty mph. She felt like she was making a prison break from her angsty, depressed life. Three consecutive days of depression marked a new record for Ruby, if you didn't include her identity crisis before law school. She had been seriously depressed, not just a touch of ennui, but an American-sized "let's eat a double cheeseburger and rot because there aren't any dolphins in Kansas" type depression. She hated to admit it, but her dad had been right about marine biology. No one had ever heard of a bachelor of *arts* in marine bio, especially in Kansas. Now, five years and another degree later, she still didn't feel as if she'd made much headway.

Cocker spaniels, she was sure, would make it all better. And when her kid was born, she was gonna tell it to her straight, or better yet, have Ming do it. Instead of the la-di-da, "you can be president if you put your mind to it or save the whales after you major in freaking dolphin appreciation" shtick she believed growing up, she would raise her kid on reality, straight up. She would let her know, "Better get used to gas station cappuccinos. Either that, or be an engineer."

She rolled down the window, felt the wind whip her hair, and cranked up the radio to a Beyoncé song that soon faded into Neil Diamond and then a Pastor Rick sermon about cheating on Jesus by devoting too much energy to work. Ruby found it convincing. By the time she began her approach into Hackamore, the caffeine high had completely faded and the rural radio had brought her down to an emotional state where she wondered what the hell she was doing playing hooky from work to buy dogs.

Where Ruby had expected to pick up the dogs at a shelter actually turned out to be a farmhouse way out in the boonies, a structure ripe for an episode of *Hoarders*, surrounded by ramshackle outbuildings and thigh-high grass. Debbie, a woman in a stained gray sweatshirt answered the door. A quick glance over Debbie's shoulder gave Ruby the impression of a computer graveyard. Old radios, telephones, computer monitors, and pretty much anything else that you could plug in lined the walls. Debbie didn't invite Ruby in, but led the way to the back yard.

"So, you're a lawyer?"

"Uh, yep. I work at Smith, Dworkin, and LeBlue in Emerald."

"I used to work down at the Attorney General's office,"

Debbie mentioned. "White collar crimes division."

"Wow." Ruby did a blatant double take. Debbie was about five years older than she was, but she looked like she'd been rode hard and put up wet. She'd had highlights once, but they'd grown out about six inches back and she appeared to be wearing maternity pants. Ruby eyed the elastic waist jeans with apprehension. To her, donning a pair of elastic pants was like waving the white flag of surrender.

"I got out of the job when I got pregnant the first time. I started fostering dogs and Facebooking for money and some other stuff. No office politics with dogs, at least none that concern me. I'm not a people person." The way she said that, Ruby believed her. In fact, it probably went without saying.

Ruby fought competing urges: 1. To drive back to Smiddy as fast as possible and buy a dog at a pet store like a normal person, or 2. To ask Debbie for mentoring advice; i.e., how she had achieved true bliss: Facebooking for money.

Debbie had a third-world menagerie in the back: goats, chickens, a couple of Chihuahuas, and the cocker spaniels. The cockers, luckily, were everything Ruby had dreamed, adorable dogs with the look of animated stuffed animals, sad eyes, droopy ears, and wagging tails. "I'm glad you are able to take both. They're sisters. I found them out on County Road 55 when they were just a couple of months old. Oz, or whoever is running his puppy mill, dumps the dogs that don't meet the standards out there every now and then.

"*You* named them?" Ruby was suddenly wondering why Debbie had named one of the puppies after herself.

"Funny, huh? About the time I rescued the mother I read about this butterfly release idea, where you symbolically release butterflies into the world. They are supposed

to represent you flying toward your dreams. I thought butterflies, cocker spaniels, what's the dif?"

Legs, fur, walking, piddling on the floor, Ruby began to
list in her head.

"Anyway, so I named the puppies after myself and
intended to send them off into the world, but I ended up
keeping them."

Still trying to put two and two together, Ruby asked,
"They're both named after you?"

"Yeah, Charmaine's named after me too, the woman I
want to be. That's my stage name."

"Oh… That's pretty. Are you an actress?" Ruby took in
the elastic pants again.

"You could say that. My husband said it would be more
symbolic if we just offed Debbie and kept Charmaine, but I
decided to go the Petfinder route."

Ruby waited for Debbie to laugh at the absurdity of
that statement, but Debbie just stared at the horizon for a
moment with a steely-eyed Clint Eastwood gaze. Then, she
let the dogs out of their run.

"I can't believe someone dumped these dogs. They're so
cute." Ruby had heard about the OzDogs. Oz had created a
non-shed spaniel without using poodles. Without the poodle
gene, the dogs had silky, non-shed fur—the holy grail of the
dog world.

"They end up with a few Danny DeVitos in every litter,
sort of like in *Twins*, that movie with Arnold Schwarzenegger.
These two certainly got the looks. They might be missing
their brains, though."

Who needs a brain? Todd barely had one and she loved
him. She couldn't understand why Debbie would get rid of

such cutie pies. "Why part with them now?"

"Just wait until you have a couple of kids. The chickens take care of themselves, but the dogs are too much work with a new baby in the house. They're only about a year old, still puppies themselves, really. Plus, I gave up on the symbolism thing after the second kid was born. Debbie and Charmaine are both dead. 'Mom' is the only one left."

"Oh." Ruby smiled, the same panicked smile she'd give personal finance expert, Suze Orman, if she ever met her in person. She dampened her panic, reasoning that Debbie was probably a run-of-the-mill nutso backwoods gal and not the ghost of Christmas future.

Debbie started to give her the run-down. "You need to walk them twice a day. I've been feeding them a half-cup of dry food in the morning and at night. No treats because Debbie is on a diet."

Ruby scratched Debbie behind the ears and baby-talked her, "Ooh, Debbie. You look too pretty to be on a diet. Coochie coochie coo."

"Well, thanks, honey. If my husband sweet-talked that dog, I might have kept her around. Might have been good for our marriage. Also, you might want to clean them up before you kiss them." Debbie pointed toward the pen as she said this. "There's only so much cleaning I can do with a new baby."

Ruby looked back. Indeed, the run where they had been staying was filled with dog turds. "Good tip." With nothing left to do but put the dogs in her car, she asked, "Do you have leashes for them?"

"None that I can spare."

"Boy, do I feel silly. I was so excited I didn't think of

that." Ruby ran back to her car and shuffled through the trunk until she found something just as good as dog leashes: two Hermes scarves that she'd been meaning to return. Too expensive, even from overstock.com, but now that she needed dog leashes ASAP, she figured what's another couple hundred on top of two-hundred-grand in student loans? She ran back to the dogs and tied a scarf around each one's neck.

"That should do the trick." Ruby felt more resourceful than ever. The dogs looked so cute with their golden fur and the scarves slung around their necks like accessories for a *Vogue* photo shoot. She knew she had done the right thing adopting them.

"Is that really how you're going to walk them?" Debbie asked, her brows drawn together skeptically.

Ruby nodded.

Debbie glanced meaningfully at Ruby's "leashes" and said, "Let me tell you about the trackers. Both dogs have GPS microchips installed. You might need them."

"Oh. Okay."

"You'll need to download a tracker app for your phone." She fished around in her pockets for the numbers and handed them to Ruby. "Once you program in the numbers, you'll be able to track them on GPS. I'm actually getting some for my kids."

Ruby pulled out her phone and started fiddling with it to download the app.

"It's a fancy service, sort of like BlondeStar, but for finding lost dogs. If you dial customer service, someone will walk you through finding your dog.

"Now I just have to keep from losing my phone!" Ruby laughed crazily because it was true.

With the dogs loaded in the backseat, Ruby looked at Debbie. She was *American Gothic* personified, except with one hundred or so years of deferred maintenance (if you included Debbie and the house). Leaving Debbie like this while her dogs left in couture was unfair. Ruby untied one of the scarves for Debbie and gave it to her, hoping desperately that she wouldn't pair it with the sweat suit.

"You take it, Debbie. They can share one scarf. I'm sure I have another floating around somewhere. And really, they don't look too sweet to run away."

Debbie put the scarf on with her sweatshirt, looked at Ruby as if she were a giant freak, and said, "Uh, thanks."

With the dogs loaded into the back seat, wiggling around, sniffing everything, and leaving suspicious brown dog prints all over the upholstery, Ruby drove back to the highway. She watched them in her rearview mirror with satisfaction. The farther she got from Debbie's, the better she felt about her decision. She could handle a new baby and new dogs. Debbie was clearly dysfunctional. Feeling generous and grateful all at once, she decided to share the wealth and opened up the windows for the dogs. Debbie and Charmaine eagerly stuck their heads out to let the wind whip their droopy cocker ears like wind socks in a gale-force wind.

Tooling down the road, Ruby glanced at the clock: 2:45. She was still half an hour from Emerald.

Shit!

She was going to be late to the funeral as it was and would be even later if she dropped the dogs off at home first. Skipping the funeral wasn't an option. Ruby really wanted to say good-bye to Estelle. She settled on leaving the dogs in the car, reasoning that people do that all the time.

Only fifteen minutes late, she pulled up to the church and unrolled the windows a little. Debbie and Charmaine tried to squeeze out the door with her, but she held them back with her knee and a few false kicks. She couldn't imagine anything worse than chasing an unleashed dog down the street at someone's funeral.

"You two be good. I'll be back in a little bit." She said this as if they understood.

Ruby smoothed her dress, tried to brush a little dog hair off (luckily she had worn an animal print), and reapplied her lipstick using her reflection in the window while the dogs panted, their noses pressed up against the glass. She blew them a little kiss through the window and tried to compose herself for Estelle's funeral. She had never been to Emerald Baptist Church before, a white building with peeling paint sandwiched between homes in Estelle's neighborhood. The church was probably well on its way to being purchased and redone as a trendy home with glass tile bathrooms and recycled quartz countertops, but for now, it was a church. The congregation was largely minority and less affluent than the shopping district. Those who had hung onto their houses worked at the Biomall, but they didn't shop there.

She tried to sneak into the back of the church and slide discretely into the last pew, but the *click-clacking* of her heels sounded her arrival clearly in the cavernous space of the church. Her leopard-print dress and four-inch heels didn't help. She had intended to go home and change into something more funeral-like until she ran out of time. Why she thought it was a good idea to pick up dogs in rural Kansas wearing heels and leopard print was another matter. Several women shook their heads as if to say, "Help her,

God, because that woman cannot help herself." Ruby gave a demure half smile and sat down.

Two prayers and one "Amazing Grace" later, Estelle's funeral was over. The preacher directed all the mourners to follow the hearse to the cemetery where Estelle was to be buried.

Ruby joined the procession right behind a rusting Oldsmobile Cutlass, a car that went down even before Detroit and immediately in front of a low-slung pimpmobile with flashy rims and neon lights on the undercarriage. She drove along sedately in her red convertible, letting the cockers (still wearing Hermes) catch a breeze out the back window. She felt a little out of place, but not nearly as much as she should have.

The mix of people at Estelle's funeral was odd: Trudi stuffed into a black spandex number weeping a few crocodile tears, Jermaine in a zip-up track suit, along with the Wednesday-night Bingo crowd. Ruby started to revise her opinion on whether or not Estelle truly had her head in the sand. From the looks of sadness and respect Estelle was getting from this crowd, Ruby half wondered if she was the kingpin of whatever drama was afoot.

Ruby admired Trudi's funeral attire. "I love that necklace, Trudi!" For the occasion, Trudi had layered five or so cross necklaces. Ruby particularly liked a pink lacquer cross covered in black lace. It dangled from a goth glam rosary. "Betsy Johnson does God better than anyone. That's Betsy, right?"

Trudi shrugged. "Estelle bought it for me."

This made both of them tear up.

"I'm gonna miss Estelle so hard," said Trudi as she

fingered one of the crosses.

Ruby gave her a hug and revised her previous opinion. Maybe Trudi wasn't so bad.

Lingering near the back of the crowd and not speaking to anyone, Ruby recognized Estelle's handsome mailman. He wore what was probably his best suit and had been for the better part of forty years. He carried a bouquet of daisies. Estelle would have loved them. If Ruby knew Estelle, she probably refused to date the poor man because of her busy schedule cooking for her grandson's Giddyup crew.

After the prayers and burial, she ran into Jermaine, who she had never met before. He was her age and pretty hot, if you went for prison tats. He certainly didn't look like the boy scout Estelle described and Ruby wondered why he was at the funeral instead of in jail. Because it was Estelle's funeral, she tried to cultivate all of her sympathy. With real feeling she said, "I'm so sorry, Jermaine. Your grandma was a saint on earth."

Jermaine didn't respond. He didn't even look at her. Not used to being ignored, Ruby answered for him as if she was reading two parts in a play. "You must be so sad. You're going to miss everything about her. How could you not?"

"Uh huh, that's right," he said, giving her leopard-print wrap dress and yellow rhinestone earrings a once over.

"By the way, how did you get out for the day? I thought that was against the rules, even for family deaths."

He gave her an affronted look. "What, do you think that's where all the black men belong?"

"No! Of course not. I'm just surprised. I mean you were in jail. Now you're not." Ruby looked around for someone else to talk to. She didn't know what to say. He stared at her intensely, seemingly demanding an answer. Vaguely, she commented, "Structural racism. It's a bitch. I know." She flipped her hair.

A tall, slim, golden mustachioed man appeared from seemingly out of nowhere to rescue Ruby from herself. Co-incidentally, he had also rescued Jermaine from jail that day. With great pomp, he announced, "I bailed the boy out. No sense having him sit in jail when he has a strong back for work and the spirit of the lord filling his soul." Ruby's jaw slackened as she stared up at the stranger. She felt as if she had just met…Brad Pitt.

"I'm Pastor Rick," said Brad Pitt in a throaty, masculine voice.

"I'm Ruby. I'm so glad to meet you." She was so going to church on Sunday. As with most celebrity encounters, she said too much. "I've only seen you on the cover of *Kansas Monthly* up until now. I thought I was behind you in line at IKEA once, but I wasn't sure. The guy I thought was you bought purple throw pillows and a spatula."

Pastor Rick tilted his head slightly and looked at her as if this was the most interesting thing he had ever heard, as if he deeply wished they had once been in line at IKEA together. "Wonderful to meet you, my lamb."

Ruby nodded and smiled. "Why did you bail out Jermaine again?" It seemed preposterous.

"I take care of my flock, especially gems like Trudi and Jermaine."

Jermaine, who'd probably never heard himself described as a "gem," grinned from behind his gold grill.

"When did you find religion, Jermaine?" Ruby was guessing yesterday.

Rick confirmed her suspicion. "I introduce many a lost soul to Jesus while they are in jail."

Ruby smiled and nodded, because what do you say to that? While smiling, she noticed a flash of movement out of the corner of her eye. Her car was parked twenty yards away in a line with the rest of the vehicles. One of the dogs was doing her best to squeeze out the window. She had one leg and her head hanging out the eight-inch gap Ruby had left in the window. Eight inches? The dog wouldn't be able to squeeze out. There was no way.

As she stood by Estelle's grave she watched as the dog wriggled all the way out and dropped to the ground. Ruby gasped, worried the dog might have broken a leg.

Rick asked, "Are you okay?"

She smiled like nothing had happened. "Of course. I think I better be off, though. Nice to meet you, Pastor Rick." She wished Trudi and Jermaine a final condolence, while letting her eyes linger on Trudi's cross. The fabulous cross wasn't just a fashion statement. Jermaine and Trudi had found God, or at the very least, a purveyor of fabulous accessories.

She hurried to the car as fast as she could in her heels and watched her dog. Nose to the ground, it was weaving between headstones and running like crazy. Instead of chasing the animal around right in front of the crowd of mourners like a lunatic, she picked up her phone and pulled up the tracker app. It worked great. She picked up the dog on the way home. Easy peasy. That was the last time she was bringing dogs to a funeral, though.

· · ·

When she pulled up to the house, Ming met her at the door.

"Ruby, whose dogs are these?" asked Ming.

"Mine. I'm sure our lease said dogs are okay." If it didn't, she was sleeping with the landlord. She could always pull that card. "You know I've always talked about getting a dog."

Ming shook her head. "I hate dogs. These things aren't even non-shed. And what are they doing? Are they always like this?"

Ruby certainly hoped not. They were running through the house sniffing every surface frantically and panting like a pair of brainless hairballs. "Oh, they're going to be really good. And they are non-shed. They're OzDogs. Debbie said they're very well behaved."

"Who the fuck is Debbie?"

Ruby just stared.

"Whatever. You're in charge of these things. If they get in my way I'm skinning them and making a shrug to go with my new fawn-colored sheath."

"You're gonna love 'em. By the way, you're coming to dinner with me at my parents tomorrow, right?"

"Of course not. I don't even hang out with my own parents."

"I still don't get that. Your mom seems so nice."

"Nice to *you*. Plus, hanging out with my mother is about as fun as staring at my reflection in a fun-house mirror. No, I take it back. It's worse. I don't want to know what my thighs are going to look like in thirty years."

Ruby rolled her eyes. "So, you're coming, right?"

"I guess it depends on how bored I am."

"Yes! It'll be so much better with you there."

Chapter Fourteen

RUBY'S FAMILY DINNER

The morning after the funeral, Ruby could barely squeeze into any of her regular clothes. Luckily, she'd bought a pair of black leather pants a size too big. *Score!* she thought, zipping herself into her first pair of "maternity" pants. As long as she stood up straight, they practically felt loose. So she grabbed a piece of toast and left the house with unusually good posture. Her first stop of the morning was the police department. When she walked in, she found Eric casually draped across the reception desk. If you traded out the desk for a car, he would look ready for a photo shoot for *Hot Rod Magazine*. Ruby shook her head. "Do you *ever* work?"

He winked. "I was just charging up before heading out for some police business."

In a it's-time-to-get-to-work-mister tone of voice, she said, "Well, I'm here to see you. About Estelle."

With obvious regret he pried himself up from his hot-rod pose. "Walk with me and I'll tell ya what I know." As they started walking back toward the front door, he said, "You're not gonna like it, though."

"Just tell me."

"The medical examiner confirmed that Estelle had a heart attack."

Ruby exhaled loudly and drew her brows together. "That doesn't make sense. There was something strange going on with her property. I just have a feeling. I wish you would just look into it anyway."

He nodded noncommittally. "I can mention something, but I don't think your hunch is going to inspire the department to reopen the case." Either in an attempt to change the conversation or because he was truly distracted, he nodded appreciatively and said, "Nice pants." Because he had to take everything to the next level, he placed his hand on her right butt cheek and gave it a nice squeeze. With his hand thus occupied, he gave her a sideways look and raised an eyebrow.

She rolled her eyes and leaned in. With a quiet authority she didn't exercise all that often, she said, "Eric, kindly remove your hand from my ass."

Holding up his hand in mock surrender, he said, "I get it. We're at work."

"Yeah, and there's a photographer. I'd prefer not to have this documented." Not that anyone would care.

By the time she got to her car, she'd already forgotten Eric's ass grabbing, but she was still confused about Estelle's case. She supposed she should be glad that Estelle was killed by her one true love: butter, but it just didn't sit right and

she'd watched enough *CSI: Miami* to expect more from in-
vestigators. If only David Caruso would come in and explain
in that husky, arrogant tone: "It only looks like a heart attack. It was actually blankety, blank, blank." She couldn't
think of anyone to call or even how to phrase her suspicions
intelligently.

With no sensible ideas about Estelle's death, but distracted to no end, she reviewed an embarrassingly small
number of documents, Facebooked half-heartedly, and
called doggie daycare to check in on Charmaine and Debbie, who were fine. (They had just been out for exercise time
and were enjoying chewies.) Finally, she made a desperate
call to Debbie.

"Debbie, this is Ruby. I'm just wondering how you got
a job Facebooking? It sounds like a dream job, so I just had
to ask."

"Um. I have a degree in programming. I actually write
script for them, plus some others. Ozcorp, Delta Airlines,
lots of places. I don't even have a Facebook account."

"Oh." And that's when her bottom dropped out. Even
Debbie/Charmaine with a muffin-top and a yard full of
goats had more sense than her.

"How're the dogs?" Debbie asked.

"They're doing great. I left them at doggie daycare
today." Ruby had almost wanted to stay herself. It looked
like the kind of place she wanted to get her hair cut, but
couldn't afford.

Debbie laughed. "You're shittin' me? What's that costin'
ya?"

"I know it's expensive, but the dogs just love it. It's
like a dog spa or something." Ruby just figured this is what

people with dogs did. *What else would your dogs do during the day?* She had never taken an active role in caring for her childhood Bernese Mountain Dog, Barker.

"Uh huh. Well, you have fun with that. Good luck with the job search and the doggie daycare."

• • •

By the end of the day, Ruby was feeling the exhaustion of the pregnant and the despair of the disenfranchised. Hell, she didn't even vote for *American Idol* anymore. She dropped onto the couch dramatically and reached half-heartedly for the remote, but Todd had fallen asleep on top of it. When she reached for it, he shifted and turned up the volume. To top it all off, her pants were too tight. She popped the top button and slumped into the couch. "Ugh, Ming. I hate my life."

Ming ignored her and asked, "When are we going to dinner? That's tonight, right? I'm out of food. By the way, where are Shizzle and Nizzle?"

Ruby shot out of her chair. "Oh my God! Oh my God! Oh my God!"

"What is it?" asked Ming.

"I forgot them at doggie daycare! Can we run down there on the way to my parents?"

Ming shot green tea through her nose at this statement. "I'm not going to say anything. It's just too easy." After wiping off her face, she said, "But seriously, I'll still drive you to the abortion clinic if you want."

"Just get in the car fast. Let's pick them up on the way to my parents' house."

Ruby drove to daycare in a state of complete panic, a

full two hours past her scheduled pick-up time on Debbie and Charmaine's first day. She rushed in and said, "So sorry I got stuck in a meeting with clients." She thought it sounded better than, "I forgot I had dogs." Sure, she forgot about the cats pretty often, but cats took care of themselves. She couldn't even remember the last time she bought cat food and they looked fine. Hopefully Noel was more responsible than she was. Of course, he didn't even know about the baby. It would be a bit premature to start relying on him to do daycare pick-ups and midnight feedings.

Luckily, half the other dog owners must have been late, too. Ruby recognized a sleek Doberman in a hot-pink collar as Destinee's prized show dog, Karma. Once, Karma had snarled at Ruby, a nasty, tooth-baring snarl. Destinee had smiled and said, "Watch out. Karma bites," as if Ruby would be responsible for any injuries sustained while provoking Karma.

The doggie daycare lady said, "No problem. These two are sweeties. We're all excited to have them here." Her tone almost sounded reverent.

"Why?" Sure, Ruby thought they were cute, but why the tone?

"They're the first Enzo puppies we've had here."

Ming snickered.

"How do you know that?" asked Ruby.

"Enzo puppies are the only ones that come out with naturally platinum fur like this." In a hushed tone she said, "Some people actually have us dye their dog's fur." She shuddered. "You wouldn't believe the upkeep!"

Ming started laughing and choked on her spit, but Ruby smiled with pride at being the lucky owner of naturally blond dogs. "Well, I'm so sorry I'm late. It won't happen again."

"Don't worry. You aren't that late. However, if you can't get here before seven, we board them overnight and you have to pick them up the next day."

Under her breath Ming asked, "I wonder if they'll do that with your kid, too? That'd be convenient."

Debbie and Charmaine wiggled their behinds in excitement when they saw Ruby, who felt completely undeserving and humbled at their display of love and trust. She reunited with them as would a mother whose kid had been lost in a mineshaft for three days, crying and blubbering, and carrying on about how much she "lubbed dem." She told herself that she would never be so self-absorbed as to forget her dogs again.

Or her kid.

. . .

The O'Deares had earned just enough money to appear richer than they actually were. When they came into money, they'd moved out of their trailer into a two-story manufactured home delivered on a truck from Denver. They'd ordered the model with two and a half baths and decorative columns (foam core) like your average strip-mall bank. The next owners could just trade out the columns for an open concept patio if they wanted. Inside, the home was encrusted with crystal chandeliers, gilding, and outrageously formal portraits of the family—portraits that made them look like trailer trash pretending to be rich. In that way, they were accurate.

Of course, the O'Deares' white column wealth wasn't

much stronger than their home's Styrofoam facade. Sure, they had a decent income, but their lifestyle was financed almost 100 percent by Visa, Mastercard, and Maurine's Bed, Bath, & Beyond card. They were American enough to believe that next month would always be better than the last.

When Ruby, Ming, and the dogs walked in, her mother greeted them with mock annoyance, glaring out from under a dramatic sweep of freshly dyed hair. "Ruby Bird O'Deare! You are an hour late for dinner. We are all starving waiting on you, Miss. And where did these dogs come from?" Maurine was Spanxed into an hourglass figure and wearing a white shirt with the collar flipped up. From a distance, she could be mistaken for Sharon Osbourne.

Ming started snickering, as she did every time she heard Ruby's mother call her Ruby Bird. "Maurine, I've always wanted to ask you where you came up with that middle name."

Maurine forgot the dogs when asked to recount her story. "Oh no. It was my pet name for Rubes while I was pregnant. I called her 'my Lil' Bird' so much, it felt like her name. I thought I might as well put it on the certificate."

"That's sort of sweet," said Ming, whose family wasn't the type to acknowledge sentiment. Ming's family was of the "no Santa Claus, no Easter Bunny, and no free lunch" school of thought.

Still fixated on the name conversation, Maurine said, "I started calling her Lil' Bird because there were some mama birds nesting right across the street when I was pregnant. They were so sweet and I felt a sort of kinship with them, us all being mamas."

"You mean where the Biomall is?"

"Yep, it used to be a marsh over there and the birds loved it. They were some kind of sweet little bluebird. In the 1800s, settlers shot most of them and made them into hats." Like many of Maurine's statements, no one knew exactly the right response, so after a moment, she embellished the story. "I don't just mean the feathers. I saw pictures of the hats at the museum once. They must have had taxidermists mount the whole bird. The poor little things died for fashion."

"Sounds like an honorable death to me," said Ming.

Maurine ignored Ming's statement. "Believe it or not, I was president of the bird-watching club in those days." Ruby took her mom's tears for what they were. If given the choice between a really great hat and the continued existence of birds, her mom would choose the hat any day of the week and twice on Sunday. Not that Ruby wouldn't.

Shaking off the remembered bird drama, Maurine breathed in and squared her shoulders. "Ruby, someone special is dropping by a little later." Her voice dripped with suggestion.

Ruby let loose a multi-pitched squeel of protest. "Ugh, *Mom*. Are you serious?"

"Oh. You're not going to complain when you seem him. He's just dropping by for a minute. I have his briefcase. He left it at a meeting I was at today." Maurine tittered in a self-satisfied way and fluffed her Sharon Osbourne 'do.

Ruby's dad, Ray, laughed. Without looking away from the TV, he said, "More like she ran away with it while he wasn't looking. I'd say she stole his briefcase." Ruby noticed that her dad's hair was also freshly dyed. Between the jet-black hair and sideburns, he looked like a man dressed up for a part in a play. Ruby wasn't sure which play, but her mother was the costume designer.

"I did no such thing, Ray."

"Most people don't take their briefcases to the rest room during a meeting," he said under his breath.

Maurine raised her penciled-in eyebrows at Ray and shook her head. "Well, at any rate, he's coming by to pick it up. Ruby, you might want to go freshen up a bit." She stared for a fraction of a second too long at Ruby's bloated tummy and unbuttoned leather pants.

Thinking, *Oh my Gaawd!* (teenage inflection brought out by mother/daughter dynamics), Ruby looked at Ming and said, "Do you want something to drink?"

"Yes, please," Ming said. She already looked like she was second-guessing her decision to tag along for the family dinner. As Ruby started walking to the kitchen to pour Ming a glass of wine or maybe just disappear for half an hour, the doorbell rang.

Like Mrs. Bennet on 'roids, Maurine snapped, "Ruby, I'll answer the door. Go button your pants."

Ruby, who was standing around the corner on the way to the kitchen, rolled her eyes and made a show of gagging and choking herself for Ming's benefit. When the door opened, she heard a male voice say, "Hello. You called about my briefcase."

Noel.

Holy bejeezus!

She flattened herself against the wall and tried to button her pants. She could barely suck in anymore.

Her mother blabbered, "I'm so glad I found it before some hooligan ran off with it!" as if the Zoning Commission was a hangout for gangsters. "Come in while I fetch your

briefcase. Why don't you sit down? My daughter is here, too."
Ruby didn't see the wink, but she was sure it had happened.
"Ruby, come meet Noel."

She just managed to button her pants and smooth her
hair before Noel caught sight of her. "Ruby! What are you
doing here?"

She took a deep breath and confessed. "This is my parents' house."

Maurine practically squealed with delight, "Oh! You two
already know each other. How nice! Why don't you come in
for dessert and a nightcap?"

Even though he looked a little confused, Noel gave
Ruby his adorable half smile, the one that made her feel like
the only girl in the world. To her mom he said, "Thanks so
much, but I really can't."

Ming whispered, "You realize your mother is going
to claim the baby was all her doing now regardless of the
timing."

Maurine feigned deafness and began pouring Noel the
drink he'd just declined.

Louder, he said, "Thanks, but I really can't stay."

Maurine redoubled her efforts. Still pretending not to
have heard Noel, she said (too loudly), "Ruby, do you remember when you won that beauty pageant?"

Ruby looked at Noel and mouthed, "I'm sorry."

"Isn't she a doll? None of the men she dates are good
enough for her. For instance, that boy who is living with you
girls." Maurine just shook her head.

Ruby seethed through her grin. Her mother always did
this, made up fake boyfriends, sort of like a realtor dropping
hints that multiple buyers were interested. It made her feel

like a desperate floozy. She smiled harder and took the drink from her mother. "Noel can't stay, Mom."

"Really? Well, why don't you walk him to the door?" Maurine's tone was unmistakable. She wanted Ruby to walk him to the door and close the deal now that she had pitched her as a high-end property with multiple bidders.

Ruby, who simply wanted to extract Noel from her mother's company as soon as possible, said, "Feel free to start dinner. I'll be right back."

She opened the door and ushered Noel outside, mainly so her mother couldn't eavesdrop. Standing on her parents' front step with Noel, she had a flashback to high school, something that had been happening way too often recently. She started to apologize, "I'm really sorry my mom—"

"Don't worry about it. It was good to see you." He pushed a few wisps of hair out of her face. Then, with a voice that was as much inquisitive as joking, he asked, "So seriously, you're not seeing anyone else?"

"No, I'm not." She paused for emphasis and said, "I'm really excited for our date." She didn't bother to explain her mother's blathering about men. Her best strategy, she figured, was to pretend like it didn't happen.

"What about that other guy your mom mentioned?"

Ruby waved dismissively. "No worries."

"Well, how about seven o'clock on Friday? We can go out to the Biobar and then catch a concert." The Biobar was the Biomall's fanciest bar. It only served things like barrel-aged martinis and handcrafted liquors. Because it was on the main floor of the mall and only enclosed with James Bond-style aquarium walls, Biomall shoppers treated the bar like a zoo exhibit. It rarely disappointed.

"That sounds perfect." Ruby smiled brightly, but she was thinking, *I can't put it off much longer. I'm going to have to tell him I'm pregnant.* She pushed that thought aside to enjoy the moment. Standing before her was her dream man. He was asking her, Ruby O'Deare, out for a romantic evening—even *after* meeting her mother. She was standing on a step and he on the ground, which left them staring into each other's eyes. Well, she couldn't see his eyes too well. A car dealer had parked a bunch of luxury cars right across the street in the Biomall parking lot and lit them up with a dozen high-powered spotlights. A wayward light was shining into her eyes at an angle that left her squinting into Noel's face, obscuring his features and outlining him in a halo of light. Even though she couldn't see his face, she filled in the details with her mind's eye: heavy lidded blue eyes and lips slightly parted to whisper her name… Perfect.

The moment was tingly, exciting, and filled with promise. She moved a little closer to him. Then he to her, their attraction pulling them toward each other like magnets, the pull growing as the distance closed. Not able to stand it any longer, Ruby leaned all the way in. After she made the first move, Noel didn't hesitate. He placed his hands gently on her upper arms and kissed her gently, but the kiss quickly turned breathless. She wrapped her arms around his neck and pressed herself into him. After a moment he picked her up and lifted her down to his level and she ran her hands up his arms feeling deliriously giddy. Not wanting the moment to end, she stood up on her tip-toes for one more kiss.

In a husky voice tinged with amusement, he said, "I'm going to have to merge into the fast lane to keep up with you and all your boyfriends, aren't I, Miss O'Deare?"

The way he said "Miss O'Deare" made her insides tingle. She was going to laugh and tell him her mother made up all those stories about other men, but as she reflected on her history with Noel, she realized it might take a while to undo his assumptions and her mother's insinuations. After all, the first time they'd hung out she blacked out and got pregnant. She'd have to tell him that soon, but for tonight she whispered into his collar, "I can't wait for Friday."

With a smile, he said, "Me, either."

This time, when she looked up at his face, they had traded positions. The lights from the Biomall weren't in her face anymore. With his features clear, she realized his eyes weren't blue. They were brown. Ming's comment hit her like a fly ball from left field. *Am I seeing in Ken-Vision? If so, what else do I have wrong?*

With a final good-bye kiss, he left her standing on her parents' stoop, thoroughly kissed, tasting of pumpkitini, and hoping that she wasn't blinded by her infatuation.

Chapter Fifteen

Follow the Yellow Brick Road

The next morning Ruby decided to take care of business. Since this didn't happen often, she rode the wave of taskmaster energy until she'd exhausted her list. Not only did she schedule a baby appointment and an ultrasound, she called a contractor to install a fence in the back yard. Next, she found a neighbor kid to walk Debbie and Charmaine after school for seven dollars a pop. Debbie had been right to laugh at her. At sixty dollars a day, Doggie Daycare should provide Debbie and Charmaine with steak in a crystal dish and velvet beds. Instead, they got dry biscuits and cramped quarters, which they shared with Karma. As she ate dry cereal and anticipated seeing Destinee at work, Ruby decided it would be unethical to inflict her own life on her dogs. She wanted better for them.

At work she kept it together, even for a meeting with

Destinee. By two o'clock, Ruby needed a break, but from legal work, rather than the mind-numbing exhaustion of obliquely confronting the void of existence through meaningless social media interactions. "Hey, Liv. I'm going to stretch my legs. I'll be back in half an hour."

"See you then," Olivia said.

As Ruby wandered out of the office toward the shops, she caught herself wondering if Noel would call or email while she was out. She could hope.

She hit the Biomall's Yellow Brick Road, or as locals called it, the YBR. Emerald didn't pander to *Wizard* fans much, at least intentionally. The munchkin statues decorating every street corner had been nothing but a happy accident. Usually, the town tried to avoid the whole cliché, but in this one instance, Oz had caved, partially because the gold-tone tiles he'd picked out for the mall walkway happened to look yellow anyway. Instead of fighting it, he let it happen.

The "Yellow Brick Road" meandered through the entire mall, looping past every store, and basically winding in a circle with no discernible beginning or end, just one big parade of high-end stores, expensive snack food, and the occasional water feature. Without really advanced spatial skills, the looping feature wasn't immediately apparent. Ruby had a blind date once who suggested they meet at the end of the Yellow Brick Road. Ruby thought it ended at the Limited and her date thought Sports Authority. Only old folks realized it was basically a perfect 10K loop with no beginning or end, making it the Mount Everest of old-timer mall walking.

Ruby never really thought about it, even after the blind-date mishap. She just put one foot in front the other and hoped not to bump into other shoppers while she gawked at the latest bags and shoes. Taking a "walk" on the YBR translated to strolling by the new Prada bags and Betsey Johnson baubles.

Today she headed straight for Enzo's, which was like Kansas's version of Barneys. She closed her eyes for a moment and absorbed the aromas, letting the smell of perfume, the cheerful chatter, the obscenely early Christmas music, and the click-clack of heels on tile floors chase away her demons. She began her routine, spritzing on perfume, flipping through some sweaters, and scoping out the formal wear.

Then she saw them. If this were a movie, the director would cue backlighting and choral music. Brown leather, western tassels, cowgirl style. She had never liked cowboy boots, until now. Ruby felt like a cowgirl—alone, but capable. She also liked horses. The boots reminded her of her quarter horse, Pansy, a beautiful chestnut mare with a mild manner and a flowing mane. Ruby missed Pansy. Her parents had sold the horse to the neighbors when Ruby graduated from college and her mom had converted the stable to storage for extra clothes and all that Mary Kay she never sold. Ruby preferred Pansy.

Ruby flagged down a cute red-haired clerk. "Excuse me, Miss, could I see these boots in a size eight?"

"Aren't they cute? We just got them in," the clerk gushed.

Ruby didn't think they were cute at all. They represented the next phase of her life as an urban cowgirl, a cowgirl who could manage to have a real conversation with Noel and tell him they'd already skipped past the dating phase. If she had some cute boots, that'd be easier.

She put the boots on. They kind of pinched her pinky toe a little, but Ruby didn't care, assuming she could break them in. "I'll take them."

"They look *great* on you! Totally badass."

"Thanks. I think I'll just wear them out," she said, throwing caution to the office dress-code policy. Dworkin certainly wasn't paying attention, and Destinee, well, if Destinee had a problem, they could just have it out once and for all over a pair of cowboy boots. When Ruby had told her mom how Destinee was such a bitch, her mom had offered some insight. "That's got to be about my 1990 nose job. I asked for the Jane Pauley and her dad gave me the Deborah Norville. Our families never spoke again after that." Ruby figured this theory offered more insight into her parents' debt problems than her boss's vendetta against her.

As she was about to stand up, Ruby saw a pair of outrageous red, high-heeled, plastic ankle booties. She flipped open the tag, which said, "High fashion PVC shoes only worn by supermodel. Very popular in Asia, Middle East, Europe, and so on."

Ruby was sold. "Wow! Those things are *unbelievable*. Are they jellies?"

Mistaking Ruby's tone for sarcasm, which it definitely wasn't—Ruby would have worn those things to Burger King without blinking—the salesgirl said, "I know. They are so over-the-top, especially for Kansas. So far only one Judy Garland impersonator tried them on."

Not surprisingly, Emerald had the highest per capita number of Judy Garland impersonators. "The Judies" and Ruby always shopped at the same stores. Ruby had fought over a pair of shoes with more than one Judy.

Ruby would have bought them on the spot, but one glance at the price tag and she said, "Whoa. Two thousand is a lot for jellies. Maybe if they go on sale."

On her way out, Ruby walked past the baby section. She paused for a moment. She had never seen anything sweeter than the baby snowsuits and plush blankies decorated with furry little duckies and bears. The fabrics blew her mind. She watched a fashionable mom stroll a chubby little baby through the racks of onesies. She stepped into the baby area and started flipping through some sweaters.

On impulse, she purchased a pair of tiny footie pajamas. They were soft as a teddy bear and the color of a daffodil. While she purchased the item, she wondered about Noel and what he would think of the tiny outfit. She needed to stop being a chicken and just tell him. When she got back to her office, she slipped it under her desk. She'd tell the people at work when she felt good and ready. For the moment, the little pair of pajamas made her happy, a tangible reminder that she had something to look forward to in life besides finishing her document review project.

Before getting back to work, she decided to indulge in her usual stroll through Facebook. Facebook, though, had nothing. She picked up *The Emerald Rag* from Olivia's desk. To her shock, her picture was on the cover. With Eric. She was walking out of the police station and he had his hand on her ass.

The headline of the article was, "Emerald's Bad Boy Cop." The caption under the photo said, "Eric Peterson and Ruby O'Deare leaving the police station hand in, ahem, (that's not her hand)." The article discussed Eric's use of the DMV and other official government databases as his own private dating websites. Ruby vaguely remembered seeing a photographer outside the station. She had assumed there was a press conference. But no, he'd been snapping a picture of her getting groped in a pair of leather pants.

It made her look like a total floozy. Pretty cute, but a floozy. Why did it have to come out right after Noel finally asked her on a date?

• • •

Ruby spent the rest of the day hiding out in her office. She waited until most everyone had cleared out to make her exit. She plodded down the hall more slowly than usual, the burden of public ridicule slowing her down, along with the too-expensive cowboy boots. They pinched her toes.

"Ruby!" Destinee's voice came from the depths of the office somewhere.

Ruby looked left and right. She wanted to drop to the floor and belly crawl out of the office before Destinee could give her another assignment.

"Ruby, I need you to fill out a conflict form."

"No problem." Ruby breathed a sigh of relief. She could do that. No big deal. At least it wasn't an assignment.

While Destinee fished through a drawer for the form, Ruby took inventory of the office.

Glamour shot: Check.

Glamour shot with Karma: Check.

Posed photo with Pastor Rick: Check.

The photo with Rick surprised her. They appeared to be at a dog show. Destinee was holding Karma's leash. Rick also held a leash but his dog was cut out of the frame. This confirmed her suspicion about dog shows, largely based on *Best in Show*—they attracted the biggest freaks.

Destinee surfaced with the form. "Here you go."

Ruby scanned it. "Ozcorp? Ozcorp hired us?"

"Yep. I'm going to be the lead attorney, but I might need you to do some research."

"Oh."

"I assume you don't have any conflicts?"

Ruby shrugged. "I guess not. I'll fill this out and drop it in your box." She picked up her purse again to leave. "Is that all?"

"One more thing. I need your full attention on the firm's business."

"I'm sorry about that photo. I know it looks bad, but I'm not dating that police officer." She tried to remember if she had any active cases Eric was working. She could get in trouble for that.

Destinee cut her off before she could go on. "I could give a damn about Eric. I need you to leave the Harris case." With an accusatory look, she said, "I hear you were at the funeral."

"Is that a problem?"

"No, I just want to make sure you understand where your loyalties lie. Ozcorp and Ms. Harris had some business dealings." She angled her chin down and leveled Ruby with a heavy gaze. "Adversarial business dealings."

Ruby nodded as if it made sense. After she filled out the conflict form, she drove straight to Estelle's.

Chapter Sixteen

Ruby Red (Orthopedic) Slippers

When she arrived at Estelle's, the Elysian Fields sign was in the front yard. Ruby paused to contemplate that oddity. She couldn't imagine that Estelle left her house to Ozcorp, which meant that Jermaine or whoever she left the property to must have already sold it, but it seemed too fast. Before walking in, she hesitated. The house looked abandoned, no car in the driveway and no lights in the windows. When she tried the knob, it turned, so she walked in. If someone caught her, she'd just say she forgot... She couldn't think of anything she was missing except her favorite tube of lipstick. She laughed to herself. Hopefully no one asked.

She pushed the door open. The air smelled stale and the house looked untouched, except for an accumulation of pizza boxes and Gatorade bottles in the vicinity of the couch.

Ruby started her search for her Crimson Vixen lipstick in the attic. A fit of giggles hit her as she climbed the ladder. Or maybe it was just nerves. At any rate, if someone found her laughing in Estelle's attic, they'd probably be too confused to call the police. They might even believe she was looking for lipstick. As she looked around the piles of infomercial paraphernalia, Ruby tried to imagine what she might even be looking for. It looked as if Isotoners were not Estelle's only quirky obsession. Social Security might as well have made out her checks directly to QVC.

After the attic, she headed to the kitchen. Like the rest of the house, Estelle had crammed the kitchen full of all manner of knickknacks. Every postcard she'd ever received hung on a bulletin board and yellowed pictures signed "Jermaine" in childish handwriting still decorated the fridge. A picture of two stick figures, a big one and a little one holding hands, must have represented Estelle and Jermaine. Next to that relic of Jermaine's childhood, Estelle had posted a reminder for his arraignment hearing.

A long row of dusty cookbooks rested in a kitchen hutch. As she stared, she noticed that they were unused. None of the cookbooks had cracked spines. Then, she saw a shoebox next to the family recipe box. It appeared to be filled with every document Estelle had ever felt reluctant to throw away, an RCA television manual, a garage door opener, insurance policies, a schedule of classes at the community center, some orange Tic Tacs, and her will.

Estelle definitely wouldn't have made it as a secretary, but Ruby wasn't going to complain. Grabbing one of Estelle's bags of unsalted nuts, Ruby sat down to read the will. Though sort of uncouth to eat a dead lady's food, Ruby figured Estelle would have offered them. She sprinkled some salt in the bag and poured herself a glass of water.

The will looked pretty standard. Estelle left her collection of jewelry, fur coats, Ginsu, and all other "special collections" to her niece, Monette. *Lucky Monette!* As expected, she'd left the bulk of the estate to Pastor Rick at the Glass Chapel, which still struck Ruby as weird. She'd heard other people describe Glass Chapel donations as "beaming money straight to heaven!" as if everyone in heaven watched their bank accounts and played the stock market. Estelle seemed more the type to take her religion with a large helping of Jell-O salad and a couple of lightning bolts. The Glass Chapel's pastel-colored version of the world, not to mention Pastor Rick's skinny jeans, were the polar opposite.

Still pondering why Estelle would donate to the Chapel, Ruby began to see a pattern: the Ginsu knives, the George Foreman countertop grills (two of them), the jumbo juicer (only available through QVC), the Thigh Masters—Estelle might not care about the Glass Chapel's message, but it was on TV. Estelle loved TV. Leaving the estate to Pastor Rick was probably more about leaving money to her favorite actor or television program and less about ideology.

Ruby tried to imagine if Jermaine would kill his grandma out of revenge. Sure, it was plausible, but it didn't fit. For one, he would lose access to the house and her money. Jermaine didn't strike Ruby as the type of parasite that would kill its host. Really, he seemed more like a standard jerk than a killer.

As Ruby thumbed through Estelle's collection of books and papers one more time, she picked out a clean sheet of card stock shoved between books. It was the menu from

Clementine's, the fancy restaurant Estelle had eaten at a week before she died. On the top, Estelle had scrawled "lunch with Oz," as if to document the occasion for her scrapbook. She had circled the butternut squash ravioli and leg of lamb, probably what they ordered for lunch.

Lunch with Oz.

That didn't make any sense. Ruby tried to recall the conversation she'd had with Estelle about the lunch. She thought she remembered her saying something about an old friend agreeing to do her a favor. Did Estelle mean Oz? Ruby shoved the menu into her bag.

Before she left, she saw Estelle's favorite pair of red sequined house slippers. They were so Estelle, with their practical old lady rubber soles and sparkly red sequins. On impulse, she grabbed them and headed for the door.

As she walked down Estelle's front steps, Destinee pulled her sleek black car in across the street. As she swung her legs out and reached for her purse, Ruby pivoted. If Destinee caught her, she'd probably lose her job. She ducked behind one of the chairs on Estelle's porch. Thinking of the price tag on her cowgirl boots, she dropped her head to her hands and prayed Destinee would just walk on by. Instead, she heard the *clickety-clack* of high heels on pavement coming her way. Destinee walked right up the stairs.

While fishing in her purse, Destinee looked right at her, as if she'd known Ruby was there all along.

Ruby made like she had been looking for something and said, "I dropped my lipstick. Guess it's a goner." With Destinee still watching she got up from her awkward crouch and sat down in the chair like that was what she'd been planning on all day.

In a quiet, I-don't-need-to-get-worked-up-about-the-little-people tone, Destinee said, "You're fired." Then, like Ruby wasn't even there, she pulled out a hand mirror and applied a coat of lipstick. It was the same shade of red as the tube Ruby had lost.

"Is that Crimson Vixen?"

Destinee rubbed her lips together and touched up a smear in the mirror, "Yep."

"Where'd you get it? I thought they discontinued that color." Would Destinee have stolen used lipstick? Ruby wasn't sure.

"It pays to work for Ozcorp. I ordered a case." With no judgment in her voice, Destinee said, "It could have been you, you know. All you had to do was follow the rules, stay on the path."

"Follow the Yellow Brick Road" ran through Ruby's head. She didn't understand everything that was going on, but she was glad she'd veered off course into Munchkin-land. If she ever found that tube of lipstick, she was going to throw it away. She was moving on. To another shade of red, something with more sparkle. She didn't even care that Destinee had just fired her. She said, "I'll swing by and pick up my things later."

Destinee shook her head. "No. I'll have someone deliver them. That way we won't have to involve security."

Ruby stood up tall and proud from Estelle's soggy front porch chair. In her most gracious voice, she said, "Even better. Thank you for the opportunity, Destinee."

If Destinee wanted to fire her for doing right by Estelle, Ruby didn't need her anyway or the stupid job. She tucked Estelle's red slippers firmly under her arm and walked to her car. She probably should have felt depressed, but she was happy to be done with Smiddy. No more pantyhose, document review, asbestos defense. No more Destinee. All she felt was relief, the hallmark of a relationship that had ended long before the death knell sounded.

• • •

On her way home, Ruby took stock. Her job with Smiddy was over. This was good and bad: good for her happiness, and bad for her bank account. In unequivocally good news, she had a date with Noel on Friday. After that picture with Eric in the Emerald Rag he probably wouldn't think the baby was his. Hopefully he wouldn't think she was a big slut trying to bag a zoning commissioner by lying about paternity. Enough was enough. Whatever the issues, she would put all the cards on the table and they could deal with the pregnancy like the two responsible adults they were.

Before she could chicken out, she drove to the Zoning Commission. She pulled up and marched in without letting herself second-guess her goal. She would ask him if he wanted to go out for a coffee and tell it to him straight.

Noel saw her walk into the office. He came out to the reception area to greet her, a big smile on his face. "Ruby, what a surprise! It's great to see you."

She smiled back. He was such a nice guy. No matter what they decided, they'd be able to get through this just fine. He was exactly the kind of solid, caring person a girl could count on.

"I was just going to call you. I have to cancel our date for Friday."

"Oh," she tried to hide her disappointment. "Any reason?"

"Yes. I have huge news. I'm leaving the country for a while. I finally got into this program for sustainability management. I've been trying to get into it for years and a spot finally opened up."

"Wha?" Ruby heard the words "sustainability" and "management" come out of his mouth and she saw his excitement. It didn't make sense. He was talking nonsense. "You're leaving?"

"Yes. Just for two months."

Two months. She would be three months along when he got back from whatever it was he was doing. That was still early in the pregnancy.

While she tried to make sense of it, he kept talking. Apparently, he'd been awarded a grant from the State of Kansas to study sustainability management. The Biomall, he said, was using too many resources: water, power, consumable goods. She couldn't put it together. The Biomall, apparently, was in trouble unless it started to economize. It sounded nerdy, but he was talking a million miles an hour and he looked so excited, like he had just downed three Red Bulls and an espresso. He used the word sustainability over and over, getting more jacked up each time. "My dad pulled some strings to put the trip together so quickly."

"Oh."

"He's just come back into my life. I think he's trying make up for lost time with this."

It looked like the strategy was working.

"It's going to be a really long trip, but I'll be back by Christmas."

Ruby's hopes sank.

"I'm going home to pack and leaving tonight. I'm catching a red-eye out of Kansas City. I didn't think the grant was going to come through. That's why I didn't mention anything. I've got to go now or never. I have to get the trip in before the holidays. I'm visiting the ten largest malls in the world based on gross leasable space, not revenue. Then, I'm going to Africa."

Ruby's head spun. He stopped talking long enough to squeeze her hand and say, "You'll wait for me, right? I'm still planning on that date, hopefully more than one."

She nodded. "I guess." She felt like a war bride, one of those women who saw their men off to war and greeted them with surprise babies and pregnancies. "Can I call you?" she asked, dazed.

"Of course, but I'm going to be hard to reach. Eight of the ten malls are in Asia. Then I'm off to Africa to learn about water saving techniques in the Sub-Saharan region. I'll be in remote locations half the time."

She followed him limply to the front of the building. "In two months, I'll be back." Like a man going off to war, he tipped her back and kissed her senseless. He stared into her eyes intently. With a hint of mischief, he said, "Stay away from Eric. I'll be back before you know it."

A few minutes later, she sat in the driver's seat of her car, all the things she meant to tell him still on her tongue.

When she got home, Ming asked, "Did you finally tell him?"

"I tried. I went to his office, but he was on his way out of the country. For two months."

Ming scoffed. "For what?"

Ruby shook her head in a perplexed way. "I think he's

going on a tour of the world's malls, something about the Biomall. It's the first I've heard of it, but I guess it's not sustainable as is and Emerald has to manage it better. As a city official, he's trying to help. I don't know. It felt like he was going off to war to save our way of life, at least the shopping part."

Ming laughed. "He's totally going to tour a bunch of malls in Asia with a clipboard."

Ruby sat down at the table and dropped her head to her hands. "I don't know what to do. I mean I'm only a month along. I think I'll just wait and tell him when he gets back." At the moment it seemed like a better idea than texting him on his vacation.

Chapter Seventeen

MEET THE BUMP (TWO MONTHS LATER)

In the weeks following Noel's departure and her "job loss" (the unemployment officer's patronizing term), Ruby spent the bulk of her time molding the couch cushion to her ever-expanding ass. As for Estelle's death, she gave up asking questions. If the medical examiner said it was a heart attack, so be it. At the moment, Ruby had more pressing concerns, like finding a job.

The Great Recession had squarely stepped on the legal business. She read about it in *US News & World Report*, as if she needed someone to tell her. Luckily there was a lot on TV and there was always Facebook, but she couldn't really get into it. Why update your status when you have nothing to report? She watched the world move on without her in a constant stream of status updates—Angela trying a new restaurant, Lainey having a baby, Tyrone going to Hawaii,

Noel posting photos of shopping centers in Malaysia. Her investigation into Estelle's death suffered from her mental state. Sure, she texted Eric a bunch, but that was about it.

Then, a week before Christmas, Ruby woke up with a bump. Actually, a "bump" was being generous. She looked bloated, not bloated like a Hollywood starlet after a Chinese dinner, but really thick through the middle. Like a porpoise. She clearly needed to put aside her shiny nylon mini-dress or really any fabrics that reflected light. Her boobs were relatively enormous, in a painful sort of way, but they at least helped to distract attention from her mid-section.

Ruby didn't know how Marvel could accuse her of being too skinny, even with a bun in the oven. The woman clearly needed new glasses. When Ruby turned sideways in front of the bathroom mirror and sucked in nothing happened. What would Noel think?

Today was the day of Noel's return. After two months of shopping in malls around the world, he had learned everything he could about "making our modern lifestyle sustainable"—his words. Ruby still didn't get it, but Noel seemed convinced the Biomall needed a makeover. It was a shame, though. Ruby would have loved to "research" at the mall. The state of Kansas should have paid her to go on a two-month shopping trip.

After two months of waiting, tonight was the night. She was going to march down to Noel's and tell him the news. In a moment of bravery, she donned a skintight mini dress and a pair of tights. That way, when the time came she could just point to her belly and say something like, "See what you did!" In her bedroom, surrounded by her favorite books and magazines, framed pictures of her family, and the cats, this seemed like a perfect idea. Vera meowed and rubbed herself against her leg.

She put on her new boots and fur-lined hoodie and set out for Noel's, deciding to walk because it would give her a little time to think over how to break the news. Plus, Debbie and Charmaine needed to get out. She stared vacantly as the dogs pulled her past the beautiful homes. Even after months, she wasn't sure how to break the news.

Noel, you remember that night we slept together?

Noel, remember when we had sex?

Noel, we had sex. You were there. Remember?

By the time she got to Noel's doorstep she had nothing better than: *I'm pregnant* followed by a quick line reminding him that they had, in fact, had sex. After three months of elapsed time and a trip around the world, he'd probably forgotten.

Unbeknownst to Ruby, Noel was not engaged in a dignified solitary activity, as a proper object of romantic fancy should be. He was not brooding over unrequited love for Ruby in a leather-backed armchair, managing his rambling estate, contemplating buying a new horse, or even playing a video game like the star of a Judd Apatow movie. Instead, he was entertaining his family.

Grand Theft Auto would have been better.

It just slipped her mind that he had a family. Romance without family is perhaps one of the great fallacies. Really, it could explain the insanely high divorce rate. Instead of the obligatory premarital counseling sessions where a pastor verifies that the couple might or might not be from the same faith and might or might not want to have children, engaged couples should be required to spend a solid month with their future in-laws. At the very least, those who survived the experience could not complain that they did not see "it" coming—"it" being the propensity to let dishes pile up, passive-aggressive name-calling, obsessive list-making, genetic predisposition to toenail fungus, familial hypochondria. "It" is impossible to predict.

If Ruby had any inkling about Noel's weekend plans, she would have waited to tell him. She certainly wouldn't have shown up on his doorstep with a couple of dogs in a spandex hooker dress. When a middle-aged woman answered the door, Ruby stammered, "Uh, uh, hello. I think I have the wrong house." She stepped back to take a look at the house number. "Is this Noel's?"

"Yes. I'm his mother." Upon inspection, Ruby noted the similarities. Noel's mom was tall and statuesque with strong features and the build of a linebacker, but dressed head to toe in Ralph Lauren, sort of like a female impersonator decked out for charity golf event. Ruby's mother would probably nod gravely and say, just a little too loudly, "Poor thing."

Noel's mom waited for a second and asked pointedly, "And, who might you be?" In a louder voice meant for Noel, she said, "I didn't realize Noel invited *another friend* to dinner."

"Uh. I'm Ruby. I…" She stopped, uncertain how to classify her relationship with Noel. Workmate didn't really capture the pregnancy part, ex-girlfriend didn't work since they never dated. Finally she went with Mrs. West's description: "I'm a *friend* of Noel's." Then she added, "We're both lawyers," as if that explained why she was knocking on Noel's door in hooker garb.

"Come on in. I always love to meet Noel's *friends*."

"Where are you from, Mrs. West?"

"Please call me Victoria. Noel's stepfather and I are both from Emerald, of course." She said this as if Ruby should know, which she didn't. Nothing is more boring than history and geography than *local* history and geography, so Ruby certainly knew nothing about the Wests, despite numerous field trips to the local history center in grade school. She certainly didn't read the plaques in front of each display explaining the local West empire who started out in wheat and cattle, then moved into banking and credit. She had even attended West Middle School and had two accounts at Bank of the West, though, in her defense locals referred to these institutions as "the middle school" and "the bank." Victoria said, "We were just about to sit down for dessert. Why don't join us."

"Okay. That would be nice."

After settling the dogs in the garage, she walked into the living room. Noel, who must not have heard her knock, stood up. "Ruby!" he exclaimed. "I didn't hear you come in. It's so good to see you!" After almost two months, it was a surprise to see him. It was like meeting Prince Charming all over again, except this time he was a little tanner than she remembered. Apparently, he hadn't spent his entire trip in the mall. She saw his eyes graze her belly and move back to her face. He probably just thought she'd put on weight. "I see you've met my mom. Have you met my stepdad?"

"No."

John, the stepdad, looked up from his paper briefly and mumbled, "Hello. Always nice to meet a friend of Noel's." Then, he looked right back at the paper, clearly not nearly as interested in his son's dating life as his wife.

"How was your trip?" she asked Noel.

"Great," he said. "I learned so much. Glad to be back, though."

Ruby's heart sank as another woman walked out of Noel's kitchen. In her kitschy apron and pearls, she looked like a young Jacqueline Kennedy posing for a *Good Housekeeping* photo shoot. It was Rolly Bag in the flesh. Even without a file cabinet she looked fully alphabetized. Rolly Bag stopped and tilted her head. Through a tight-lipped smile, she asked, "And who might this be?"

Victoria said, "Ruby, I'm sure you know Moira, Noel's *fiancée*." She might as well have dragged out the word fiancée and tagged it as "Exhibit A" in list of reasons Ruby should go home.

"No we haven't met," Moira said, looking Ruby up and down. To Noel's mom she said, "You know we're not engaged anymore." Her smile said, *But we will be again soon.*

Victoria smiled conspiratorially and said, "Of course, darling. How about we sit down? The table is set and I am dying to try Moira's pear *tatin*," pronouncing *tatin* in a perfect French accent. "Did you say you were serving it with a brandy-infused cream?"

"Yes. It's my grandmother's recipe," answered Moira. "She was French."

"How lovely!" answered Victoria. "I've always admired the French. We're 100 percent Welsh. If the Windsors hadn't married in and turned the whole family into a bunch of Hanoverians, we would still be royals." She laughed as if it was funny rather than simply pretentious.

"Really?" Moira asked with a little too much interest, as

if investigating the pedigree of her future children.

Ruby smiled in secret amusement, delighted that she was the one incubating the royal bloodline.

"What does your family do, Ruby?" Victoria asked.

"They're parking lot contractors. They put in all of the Biomall lots." Paving Emerald was a big job being that the Biomall had more parking spaces than any other structure in the country. You had to ride a tram to get to the mall from some of the farther spaces. Her dad liked to brag that his lots could cover the state of Rhode Island twice over. Some "alarmist liberals," according to her Dad, even claimed that the Biomall and its parking facilities were creating their own weather patterns.

"Your mother is in the parking business too?" Victoria asked in a superior tone.

"She designs the lots and does the books."

"Did she go to school for that?" Victoria laughed.

Noel's stepdad, still sitting the corner, and speaking to no one in particular said, "Too bad Oz isn't renewing their contract."

"Really?" Ruby hadn't heard that one, but maybe it explained why her parents hadn't repainted the house or gone on their yearly gambling trip to Vegas.

"Yep. Oz is starting to cut costs. He's banking on that new development, Elysian Fields, saving his skin. Wonder what those places are going for?"

Noel said, "I have some more ideas after the trip. There are so many ways to make the Biomall more sustainable and save money. The place is essentially a greenhouse. We should be using it to grow food for shoppers. Solar power is a no-brainer. So many things."

Victoria looked at John with pure hatred. Her mouth formed the words, "John, you're keeping everyone from the table. It's time for dessert," but everyone clearly understood, "I hate you. Get to the table before I divorce you."

In a bland tone, John answered, "Thanks, sweetheart." To no one in particular he said, "Can you believe your mother and I have been married for thirty-five years?" Then, he flashed his wife a smile that said, "Eat it."

Ruby sat down next to Noel. She was on one side, Moira on the other. She felt as if she were in a bad reality TV show, maybe an episode where Jerry Springer drops in on the royal family. As each moment passed Ruby became more aware of her incongruous presence. Her skirt felt too short, her hair too done-up, her nails too pink, her belly too protuberant. She sat in silence as Victoria fussed about Moira's *tatin* recipe and inquired about her French relatives who turned out to be from Champagne, which she pronounced shompon-ya. "Shom-pon-ya! How delightful! Noel's father and I happened to stop there for lunch a few years ago and have wanted to go back for a proper visit. Maybe you could do us the honor of being our guide sometime."

Noel remained mysteriously silent until his mother brought up the governor's race. The way she talked about it made it sound like Noel was running.

"Governor's race?" asked Ruby.

Noel clarified, "Joel Smelch is running for governor. He asked me to join him on the ticket as lieutenant governor. I haven't decided."

"Oh." Lieutenant governor. That sounded like Miss Congeniality to Ruby. It was probably all photo ops or something.

John raised his eyebrows and said. "I suppose he picked you because you'll fit in with his 'Average Joel' campaign. I hope he didn't pick you only because of the name, Noel."

Noel's mother shooed that topic under the rug. "Flashy campaigns win elections, John."

Ruby wondered if this remained true even if the campaign was a little on the dumb side, but she didn't comment. She wanted to leave. "I think I'm going to walk home before the snow piles up. I wore the wrong shoes."

Noel stood up, "I'll give you a ride."

"Definitely." When she stood her belly ended up at the family's eye level, the electric blue fabric stretched taut and the tiny tinsel threads reflected the light, emphasizing her rounded belly. Moira noticed and smiled, her first eye-wrinkling smile of the evening, clearly delighted that her competition was a bloated prostitute.

Ruby wasn't sure she wanted to talk to Noel anymore, but she desperately wanted to get out. Noel went to get her coat, a thigh-grazing hoodie lined with faux fur.

"I'll be back shortly. Moira, if you need to leave, I'll see you at work next week."

Noel walked Ruby to the door and pointed towards his antique Ford pickup. He loaded the dogs, who looked eager for car ride, into the back. To Ruby, his pickup looked more like a hobby than transportation and completely lacked a back seat. She wouldn't have guessed that Noel, the *Economist* subscriber/political candidate, would drive an old truck. This truck also provided a quick reminder of Noel's lack of plans for a baby. Discussing her electric blue baby bump would have felt more appropriate if he already drove a minivan or maybe a Volvo. Of course, if he drove a Volvo, they wouldn't be in this situation. Volvo owners probably didn't have unexpected pregnancies, at least no more often than statistical failure rate on birth control pills. She pushed the thoughts aside. She hated Volvos anyway.

In the intimate atmosphere of a pick-up cab, Ruby felt almost like his girlfriend, especially after meeting his family. The whole experience shone with the surreal varnish that generally coats a life-altering experience. It transported Ruby back to the night she had met her prom date's parents, senior year of high school. That night she had been concerned about third base and keeping her strapless bra up, events which had felt just as daunting at the time.

Noel started the truck and eased out of the driveway without saying a word. Ruby couldn't think of a thing to say but, *I'm having a baby*. As the moments passed, it became clear that this drive was to be more awkward than prom, even considering that her date's dad had chauffeured them around town while making awkward jokes about "leaving enough room for the holy ghost."

Noel looked at her and said, "Whadya say, do you want to out for a drink while we're at it? Are you still dating that police officer?"

"I never was dating him. The picture just made it look like it." She stopped to catch her breath. "What about you? Your mom introduced Moira as your fiancée."

"I told her to stop that. Moira is not my fiancée. We broke up months ago, but my mom is attached and Moira is lingering. I'm sorry you had to end up in the middle of that. I need to have a serious talk with my mom."

"Oh." Well that was at least a start, him not being engaged to someone else. It wasn't as if she had unrealistically high expectations about their future. Well she did, but she had hoped that they wouldn't crumble this early. "I need to talk to you about something else, too. Something…important." Ruby was thankful that he was staring at the road rather than at her. He pulled up to a stoplight. She looked directly at him and said, "You know our one night?"

He nodded.

She waited a moment, giving him time to draw his own conclusions. As a fairly smart individual, Noel connected the dots. His placid expression changed to panic in the span of a few seconds. He looked at her for confirmation.

Ruby confirmed. "I'm pregnant."

Noel didn't react dramatically. He expelled his breath and sagged into the driver's seat. She would have thought that he hadn't heard her, except he accidentally sat through nearly an entire green light.

"The light's green."

He put his foot on the gas. "Are you sure? Have you already been to the doctor?"

"Yes." She pointed at her belly. "I know I haven't been eating *that* much."

"Are you sure it's mine?"

Shocked, she said, "Yes. I haven't been with anyone else."

He didn't say anything, but she could see the question written in his eyes. He didn't believe her. He confirmed this by asking again, "I don't mean to be rude, but are you sure it's mine, 100 percent sure?"

The question made her want to die. She was the kind of girl who made fun of Jerry Springer, not the kind of girl who would be *on* Jerry Springer. Why didn't Noel know this?

Emphatically, she answered, "The baby is yours."

Noel continued staring at the steering wheel like a frozen computer in need of a reboot.

Because she couldn't stand the silence she tried to think of something to say. "Well, your family seemed...nice," she lied.

He laughed. "They did not."

"Well, your dad did."

"Stepdad," Noel clarified. "Everyone I'm related to is an ass, except maybe my real dad. I'm finally getting to know him."

"Who's your dad?"

"You really don't know?"

Ruby shook her head.

"Oz."

Ruby felt like was she living in a child's Viewmaster toy. Every time the kid pressed the button the slide changed and her world turned upside down. *Click*, Estelle's dead. *Click*, you're pregnant. *Click*, Oz is your baby's grandpa. "Oswald Rancka," she confirmed. "As in *Ozcorp*?"

"That's the one."

She looked at Noel more closely. He had Oz's dark hair and his charismatic personality.

"Do you talk to your dad?"

He gave her a funny look. "Only just recently. He helped me with that trip."

She took a troubled breath and rubbed her belly. Her baby's father was the heir to Ozcorp, the same company that cost Ruby her job and planted a sign in Estelle's yard the day after she died. This did not sit well.

Her life was getting way too complicated. Tonight alone

was like five episodes of *Gossip Girl* rolled into three hours. She wasn't sure how she felt about this new information. Now that'd faced her fears, she got nothing but a lukewarm response and bad news. If she played out her fantasy and married Noel, she'd have her number one murder suspect for a father-in-law. Sure, they'd get whatever venue and caterer they wanted with his pull, but still, yuck. All she wanted to do was go to bed.

"Want me to come in?" he asked.

A minute ago she would have said yes, but not now. "I think I need a little space tonight."

Inside, she made herself a cup of coffee and sat down at the kitchen table with a fresh yellow legal pad and a brand new Bic pen. She started on a list. Besides figuring out Estelle's murder, she also needed a paycheck and probably health insurance. Her options included:

A. **Start own firm.** Pros: knew how to "be a lawyer," opportunity to be own boss. Cons: required an office, clients, management skills, fax machine, people skills, secretary (Todd maybe?). Also not too keen on "being a lawyer."

B. **Marry Noel.** Pros: immediate insurance, husband with income, marriage to biological father of baby, possible move to a vineyard, also a fairly trendy choice, as it followed the plot line of *Knocked Up*, a popular Katherine Heigl movie. Cons: basing her career on the plot of a Katherine Heigl's movie might not be as good of an idea as it seemed on the outside.

C. **Job at Starbucks.** Pros: free coffee and employer-provided insurance. Cons: Might have to fib on resume about barista experience (list Ming as reference?).

D. **COBRA.** Pros: Olivia recommended. Cons: What is COBRA? Also, sounded expensive. Definitely would have to fill out form.

Looking at her hastily scrawled list, she thought, *"C" is always the best answer.* Ignoring the fact that she had created the list and assigned the letters, she decided, *Starbucks it is!*

Chapter Eighteen

Roses are Red, Violets are Blue

Ming walked into the kitchen and switched off the Christmas music.

"Hey, I was listening to that," said Ruby.

"When you start paying your half of the rent again, you can pick the station."

"You're such a scrooge. Christmas is in like two days." Ruby poured her fourth cup of coffee and sighed dramatically. "Ming, I don't know what to do. Everything is so confusing...my job, Noel, and I keep thinking about Estelle. I feel like I gave up on her." Despite her nonexistent budget, she'd picked up a glittery Christmas wreath the other day. It reminded her of Estelle. She'd intended to hang it up. Instead, it sat in a box next to the front door. That also reminded her of Estelle.

Ming looked up from her chemistry journal. "Just update

your LinkedIn profile and finish your coffee."

The thought of LinkedIn floated over her world just long enough to make her shudder. "Maybe it isn't that bad that Noel is Oz's son?"

"Who cares? Look at your parents."

"What about them?" said Ruby with a questioning look.

"Not to mention your parents used the Biomall as free childcare while you were growing up. Oz might be Noel's father, but he was basically your babysitter. You're both equally screwed up probably. More importantly, did he say anything about the baby?"

Ruby shook her head. "Not really."

Before Ming could let loose with an anti-Noel diatribe, Ruby's phone beeped with a text. From Noel: *Is your dryer hose still plugged?*

Ruby stared at the misbegotten text for a fraction of a second, baffled that he had just texted her about the dryer. Hadn't she just twelve hours earlier announced that he was going to be a father? She averted her eyes and showed it to Ming.

Ming looked at the text as if it was a dog turd on a Persian rug. "Tell me that isn't a euphemism. Whatever it is, you should cut him loose right now." She picked up Ruby's phone for her and asked, "You mind if I respond?"

"Go ahead."

Ming texted: *Shut up about the laundry. Just told you I'm pregnant.*

On the other end, Ming received: *RARVAB!* @->->--

She showed it to Ruby with a look of incipient disgust and asked, "Does this mean anything to you?"

Ruby squinted at the message for a second. "No."

With her disgust fully realized, Ming texted back: *WTF?*

"Ruby, this is beyond appalling. He just texted a frowny face." Ming held the phone out like a bad report card for Ruby to see. "A grown man should NEVER text a frowny face."

Ming typed in: *Be a man.*

· · ·

Ruby sank into her chair wondering what Noel's problem was. There was clearly something off. She felt too mentally exhausted to read or cook breakfast, so she tuned into NPR. She had begun to listen lately, hoping to absorb whatever it was she had missed during law school. A professor-type announced in an ominous voice: "Today, Earth's population reached seven billion people," darkly implying that the Earth was reeling toward a sustainability crisis, clearly steering listeners to think of tragic countries with way too many mouths to feed. The figure awed Ruby: "*One of seven billion!*" and in a flash of nihilism (her first), Ruby realized seven billion other people were striving to fill the void, eating Greek yogurt, trying to find *the* ultimate handbag, etc., and she began to cry a little.

For some reason, the population crisis and the bad texts made her think of a pivotal moment in *Clueless*: Alicia Silverstone walking down the street in her moment of despair wearing a ruffled shirt and platform shoes. She stops in front of the Bellagio. As the fountains erupt, her light bulb turns on she realizes that she *loves* Paul Rudd—the one who had always been there, not flashy and dramatic, but dependable. *Who is my Paul Rudd?* There had to be a Paul Rudd for her in the sea of seven billion.

She didn't need to be special and she didn't need to be the best lawyer around, but she wanted a Paul Rudd. Until the dryer hose text and RARVAB @->--->--, she was 99 percent sure Noel was the Paul Rudd to her Alicia Silverstone, even though he was technically way cuter than Paul Rudd, not her stepbrother, etc. etc.

Just then the phone rang and her heart fluttered. She glanced at the caller ID expecting to see Noel's name, maybe to explain the weird texts.

It was Eric.

"Hey, I've been thinking about you."

"Really?" She had a hard time believing that.

"I was wondering if you wanted to go out—"

"It's been like two months, Eric. That's a *long* time." They hadn't talked since their "scandal."

"Does love have an expiration date?"

"Plus, I hear you have plenty of other girlfriends." The article had reported that Eric used Kansas DMV and municipal databases as his little black book. Why the police department hadn't fired him, she couldn't imagine.

"I'm free now," he answered, plenty of swagger in his voice.

She laughed and started to shoot out with a sarcastic response, but she stopped. Partially because she was annoyed with Noel and partially because she was lonely, she thought, *Who cares? Why not go out with Eric?* "Fine, let's go. Pick me up whenever you get off and we can make an afternoon of it. I need to get out."

Eric said, "Let's see a movie. I checked and there's a new *Saw* playing at the mall or we can see *Citizen Kane* at the

Emerald. It's old, but supposedly the best movie of all time."

"That's easy. Let's see the best one."

He swung by and picked her up after work. She put on a cute black dress, rhinestone earrings, and red platform pumps, actually the same pair as Taylor Swift. Or was it Faith Hill? In any case, she looked hot and completely ready to embark on romance that would fill her life with meaning and passion with whoever showed up to take her out.

After they waited around for a while, the theater canceled the showing for *Citizen Kane* because no one showed up except Ruby and Eric, so they had to go to *Saw*, along with a hoard of high-school students. Looking around, Ruby realized who was scoring all the hot deals on size twos at Forever 21. They were all at *Saw* and most of them had braces. She wasn't sure if her ears were playing tricks on her, but Ruby thought she heard someone yell RARVAB.

"Do you know what RARVAB means?" Ruby asked.

"Not a clue."

"Me, either."

He shrugged his shoulders and they sat down for two hours of horror that felt more like five. Eric loved it, but Ruby left for the refreshment stand or bathroom eight times during the movie. It was the first time she'd embraced the way pregnancy made her have to pee every fifteen minutes. At least she didn't have to see the movie. When it was over, it didn't feel like the normal ending of a movie, it felt like she had just survived an event. Eric said, "Sorry, that probably wasn't your thing. We'll do a chick flick next time."

"No problem. It wasn't your fault. Who knew *Saw VI* was going to be such a bad movie?" she remarked without even a touch of sarcasm. She hadn't seen any of the previous

Saws. "I always thought Edward Norton was in them."

"Well, he wasn't in that one. How about a drink at my place?" he asked.

"That sounds really nice," she answered. She hadn't given up on having one of those "You complete me!" moments. Having a glass of wine by his fireplace or something would be much better than a movie. He looked like the type that would have lots of leather furniture and some hunting dogs, probably some pizza boxes. She smiled at the thought of Eric ordering pizzas by himself. *Poor guy!*

"Wow, you really live way out, don't you?" she commented as they drove deeper into the country, the canopy of trees nearly blocking out the sky. As far as the country went, Ruby preferred groomed pastoral landscapes or vineyards. She might have been only one generation into credit card debt, but she already believed trees should be carved into the shapes of cones and spaced far enough apart for a game of croquet. Eric...not so much.

He finally pulled into a driveway, actually an unmarked opening in the trees. Driving into the unlit woods felt more like the opening scene for the next *Saw* than the second act in their date. The tree branches scraped along the sides of the car like ghostly fingers until they emerged into a cramped and musty clearing which housed a strange building with no windows and a curved roof made of corrugated metal. A solitary light provided a feeble glow in the big, dark woods. Ruby didn't know she was looking at a Quonset hut, but she did know that buildings shouldn't rust. She hesitated, staring agog at the dismal building. Eric came around. "Need some help? Should have told you to wear tennis shoes, I guess." She stepped out onto the matted grass and marshy ground that made up his driveway. Her red heels sank deeply into the muck. Ruby's heart sank, too, knowing she would never be able to clean them up.

"It's just down here," he motioned. The boat was moored pretty close to the bank, but there was no dock.

"Oh…you live on a boat?" That sounded much preferable to the rusty, windowless hut. "Where's the dock?"

"There isn't one. This is an informal marina, if you catch my drift."

She didn't.

"I can't bring myself to pay marina fees for upkeep of a tennis court, pool, and bathroom I'm not going to use."

"How am I going to get on the boat?" She watched him jump from a rock onto the deck.

"Uh. Not sure."

She stared for a moment. She looked around her for options other than the boat, but the mosquitoes on the mucky shoreline were buzzing relentlessly. She took off her shoes, jumped to the rock, and stepped onto the boat with surprisingly little trouble. "Wow, I guess you don't want to come home drunk."

"That's for sure."

Once inside Ruby relaxed a little. She looked around. Eric had a mini-fridge like dorm kids, a stack of pizza boxes, and a couch that appeared to have been stolen from the set of *Roseanne*. "So do you entertain much?" she joked.

"You're the first person I've had out here in a while. Your boss came out a while back, but she refused to set foot in the place."

"Destinee? Really?"

"Yeah, but like I said, she didn't even get out of the car."

Ruby laughed at the thought of Destinee with her custom nose and one of her bridal-white business suits wandering around in the woods with Eric.

"She said it wasn't about not having a dock or a bathroom, it was about my freegan lifestyle with no responsibility or commitment. If you ask me, she's the one with commitment issues." He laughed a little. "I thought she was joking, but she demanded I take her home."

"Well, I can kind of see her point. This is not exactly glamorous." Everything on the boat was something he'd found for free. She didn't ask about the bathroom. She didn't want to know. "I didn't know you and Destinee dated," Ruby said, hoping for an explanation.

"We didn't." He didn't bother explaining the non-romantic reason that he'd invited her over. "You should see this place at sunrise. It's gorgeous. The sunlight on the water. Every day feels like a gift for me. It's 100 percent, unqualified, high-octane freedom." He waxed on, "What's more glamorous than pulling up anchor and hitting the open water in the morning? Nothing to tie you down. No mortgage. No rent."

Maybe on a yacht, not on a floating barge. Being Huck Finn held no appeal for her.

He paused a moment and walked over to his mini-fridge. Inside Ruby could see a take-out container sitting in a pool of its own juices, a package of beef jerky, and a couple of PBRs. "Want something to drink?"

"No thanks." She was actually dying of thirst, but the pickings looked slim, both for beverages and romance. Ruby decided to ask about Estelle, "Did you officially close Estelle's case?"

"Yep. She never even really had a case since there was no real suspicion of foul play. You quit looking into it as well, I hope?"

Mid-sentence she heard running water and she looked around to see Eric with his pants loose around his waist, presumably peeing. Into the river. He confirmed her suspicions when he leaned back and arced the stream a little higher.

As he sauntered back into the room, he noticed her look of shock—not repulsion, just pure shock. "Don't worry, there's an outhouse behind the Quonset over on the bank. I have a bathroom in here, but I don't use it. Plumbing's more trouble than it's worth in an old boat."

Ruby started to think she needed to go home. She was 100 percent sure that her salvation would not lie in the hands of a man who peed overboard. Eric was not her Paul Rudd. Eric must have reached the conclusion that she was not his Alicia because he was more than ready to drive her home when she mentioned she was getting tired.

In an unsurprising conclusion to the least romantic date ever, Eric asked if he could use her bathroom when they pulled into her driveway (for number two she assumed). She'd already seen him pee. It made sense given that the man didn't have a toilet. She said yes.

• • •

She found Noel in the laundry room with the dryer pulled out into the center of the room. He was fidgeting with the hose attachments and appeared to be replacing something. "Noel, what are you doing here? It's eleven o'clock." She hadn't seen his pickup out front. She never would have let

Eric in if she had.

"Didn't you get my text?"

"RARVAB?" she asked.

He shook his head. "No, the other one about the laundry."

"I got both of them."

"Ruby, I'm really sorry I texted you about the laundry this morning. It was horrible timing. I was just tired and not thinking." He looked tortured and filled with shame. Definitely pardonable.

"Hey, what's this stuff?" Eric called from the kitchen.

Ruby's gaze flashed to Noel at the sound of Eric's voice. Ruby wanted to sink into the floor and let it swallow her like quicksand. Noel looked less than pleased.

A second later Eric strode into the laundry room holding a take-out box and a pair of chopsticks. He shoved a giant pot sticker into his mouth and said, "Whatever it is, it's fucking delicious." Halfway through that sentence, he looked up and noticed Noel.

Noel scowled.

Eric looked smug. "Hey, man. You Rube's landlord or something?"

Noel gave Ruby a look that would blow the top off a pressure cooker. To Eric, he said, "Yep. I'm the landlord. How would you define your relationship with *Rube*?"

With the look of a man about to stir up trouble, he said, "I'll let Ruby do the defining. Her body, her rules, man." He shoved another pot sticker in his mouth.

Noel put all the force he could muster into loosening a bolt.

Eric picked up a wrench. "This one would work better."

Noel took it without a word.

Ruby would give anything to rewind five minutes or maybe twelve hours. Noel looked so handsome in his jeans and T-shirt, like that guy who always plays blue-collar hotties in rom-coms. With a tool box at his side and his shirtsleeves rolled up to reveal some very handsome forearms, Noel looked like Mr. Right. She wished he weren't scowling and beating on a pipe with a wrench.

He sucked in air and gave her a cold look. "You were right. There was something plugging the dryer hose."

"I'm sorry." She poured a lot of feeling into that apology, way more than a dryer hose plug deserved. "Thanks for fixing it."

With a violent jerk, Noel yanked a wad of fabric from the dryer hose and tossed it on the floor between them." A pair of pale pink, glittery underwear that said CHEEKY across the ass. "Nice underwear. You need to put a filter on this thing or your hose is going to get clogged all the time."

She looked at her belly. *Actually, he's the one who needs to put a filter on his hose.*

Eric laughed and said, "Like I said, man. Her body, her rules."

When Noel and Eric finally left, after Todd joined the party and offered them a beer (as if she needed to add a third man to the evening), she couldn't wash away the feeling of nearly missed happiness. Although she wanted to indulge in a fit of self-pity and an early bedtime, Debbie and Charmaine were wiggling and pawing at her legs. They had to pee, so she hooked them up, put on her Uggs, and walked them around the block in the crisp cool air, taking in the Christmas lights and the stillness. No one else in the neighborhood braved the unseasonably cool night, so Ruby had the whole world to herself, at least that's how it felt. Just her and the dogs. In the stillness, she untangled her thoughts and her feelings crystallized. Noel had reached out to her and she had botched it. She *needed* to make it up to him with some sort of meaningful gesture. After the dogs did their business, she yelled, "Bedtime" and they ran into the house and straight for the bed.

Before she turned in for the night, she Googled RARV-AB, which basically translated to "I'm sorry. I owe you flowers." It was a little weird that Noel knew this. It seemed a little teeny-bopperish, but it was sweet, and she had sent back a bitchy response. She read on a little more. Apparently, the appropriate response to a RARVAB text, was a sext, a take-off on some scene from the latest Judd Apatow movie. *Maybe that's what he'd been hoping for?*

Lying in bed, she couldn't shake the feeling that she should respond and let him know she cared. With Christmas two days away, she felt particularly lonely. She wanted Noel. *Maybe this is what it takes to be in a real relationship?* Yes, it was juvenile and stupid, something that would happen on *Keeping up with the Kardashians*. But, she knew that she had to risk failure, to risk looking like a fool, so that's what she was gonna do.

She upped the stakes and sexted him a picture of her boobs. Not her face. She'd already taken her make-up off. Or her bulging belly, which had obliterated her waist and given her the figure of a white porpoise. She managed to fill the whole frame with just her boobs. With grainy picture quality, they looked a little blurry and you had to stare for a minute to figure out what they were, but it's the thought that counts. Right?

Chapter Nineteen

Sextmas

Christmas Eve Ruby woke to an ice storm. The trees looked like glass and the streets looked like a nightmare. Charmaine and Debbie slid around the driveway like Bugs Bunny on an ice rink. For the millionth time she glanced at her phone. Noel hadn't responded to the sext. Apparently future lieutenant governors don't sext, only politicians farther up the food chain, like senators.

RARVAB was the extent of his flirtation. She imagined her boob shot floating in cyberspace unwanted and unclaimed. Single and pregnant is almost cool in July when it seems like everyone is doing it, all the celebrities strutting on the Malibu beach in bikinis comparing their baby bumps in *US Magazine*. Single and pregnant in December is another matter. She wished she could go to Estelle's and eat some caramel rolls in a nonjudgmental environment. That was true everyday actually, but especially today.

Todd said, "What's your problem, babe?"

While staring into her coffee cup, she admitted the facts. "I sexted Noel and he didn't respond."

"Ooh. Slammed!" Then, to make her feel better he added, "Don't worry. He was probably too busy jerking off to text back."

"God, I hope so," Ruby answered with a dramatic sigh. "As long as he doesn't hate me." After a brief pause, she asked, "What are you doing for Christmas?" She suddenly felt grateful and happy for Todd. She wanted to spend the rest of the day with him.

He stared into the fridge for a moment before answering. "I don't know. Gonna watch *Bond*. I think there's a marathon on."

"Oh, do you want to come to my parents'? You could be my date." A buffer suddenly sounded like a brilliant idea.

"Uh, what are they making?"

"Probably a goose and a ham and a bunch of other stuff. There's always too much."

"I'm in."

"Awesome!"

Later that day, Ruby dressed for Christmas Eve dinner in a red party dress, black peep toes, and a fur stole. She piled her hair on top of her head in a luscious, shiny mass of curls, *Seventeen's* "up-do" of the month. If nothing else, pregnancy had given her goddess hair. While she looked for her purse, she yelled, "Todd, you ready?"

"Totally." He shimmied out of the kitchen making jazz hands. It must have been the first time he tried it because he couldn't stop staring at them. He wore a pair of dirt-smeared, torn jeans and a sweatshirt with an elk head on it. He reeked of pot, but at least he was dressed.

"I forgot to tell you my family does a formal Christmas Eve." The O'Deares approached Christmas as if it was an event at the White House even though they lived in a modular home with detachable columns. Looking at the clock, Ruby said, "Oh well."

Todd didn't care, so why should she?

• • •

In her parents' driveway, she couldn't walk at all, her footwear being completely wrong for ice. Todd saw her distress and said, "No problem, babe. These boots have got crampons." He demonstrated by performing a few awkward lunges. The metal spikes of the crampons caught the ice and he stuck them like a pro. Because he could, he swept Ruby off her feet and carried her to the door like she was his woman. He knocked loudly.

Her parents answered the door and stared at the homeless-looking individual delivering their sparkling daughter. Todd greeted them, "Happy Chanukah." He set her down in the entryway and patted her on the ass for good measure. "What kind of cable package you folks got?"

Ruby swatted Todd's hand away from her ass and said, "Mom, Dad, this is Todd."

In a voice laced with fear and disapproval, her mom said, "The one who is living with you?" (Translation: *Oh my God. That is your boyfriend?*)

"Yep. He's the one." Then, to get it out of the way, she made her announcement. "Also, I'm pregnant." Ruby was sick to death of carrying around the baby like a secret.

Her mom reacted as if in slow motion. First, her face went slack. Next, the wine glass slowly slipped from her hand until it landed on the stoop and shattered into a hundred pieces. Todd and her dad were already headed for the living room. Neither even turned to see what happened.

She heard Todd ask her dad, "You wanna turn on the tube while the womenfolk cook? *Live and Let Die*'s on." He was practically deaf.

Ray nodded. "Sounds good. I'll grab some beers."

With trepidation, Ruby looked at her mom, who was still dramatically frozen in place and had yet to utter a word. It was as if Ruby had paused a movie at the absolute worst spot, right after the verbal instigation and a fraction of a second before shots rang out. All she wanted was to fast forward to the next scene. When her mom finally breathed in and exhaled dramatically, Ruby was relieved. They might as well get the scary part over with. Still not speaking, Maurine moved toward the broom closet while still performing perfect Lamaze breathing. Ruby started to say, "Let me. I'll sweep—"

"In. A. Minute. Ruby."

Recognizing the signs of a parental tantrum, Ruby decided this would be a good point in the show for her to make popcorn. "Okay, I'll go check the food." She took shelter in the kitchen and half-heartedly stirred something bubbling on the stove.

The tantrum started in the closet. First came crashing. Three guttural "fucks" rang out like shots. Then, Ruby watched a black work boot shoot across the room. "*Ray*. What are your fucking boots doing in here?"

Ray looked over his shoulder and cringed. Ruby heard him tell Todd in a knowing voice, "Christmas. She *always* loses it."

After tearing the closet apart, her mom emerged with a broom and stalked toward the front door, making zero eye contact with anyone. She swung the door open as if she was preparing to beat someone to death with her broom. For a minute, Ruby thought it might be over, but no. Just when she'd almost swept up all the glass, Maurine flung the dustpan into the yard and started hitting the glass shards with the broom. Then she hit the door.

Ray looked toward the front door. "Jesus Christ. Why can't someone else host the damn holiday for once?" Then, he turned up the TV to movie theater volume.

After the tantrum died off, Ruby's mom walked back in looking almost calm, the only sign of distress was her strained Stepford smile. Looking at Ruby, she said, "Ruby, turn off the stove. You're burning the cranberries." With an exasperated look she took the spoon from Ruby and said, "Just put together a tray of cheese and crackers. And Ray, turn down the TV."

While Ruby pulled out a box of crackers, she said, "Mom, it's not that bad. You've always wanted a grandbaby. Plus, I have a job and everything. I'm an adult. You should be excited." She would tell them about getting fired later. That would be too much for one day.

Maurine filled a new wine glass to the top and said, "Of course I want a grandbaby, but…I didn't even know you two were dating."

Ruby cringed. "Eww. Todd's not the dad. No." She held up her hand as if to shield her face from the very idea of sex with Todd.

Maurine crossed herself. "Thank you, Jesus. Who is it?"

At this point, Todd stood up and walked into the kitchen like he was looking for something. "Uh, ladies, could someone tell me where the bathroom is? I gotta piss like a racehorse. I totally forgot to pee today."

Ruby waved him down the hall, "Over there." She looked back at her mom and said, "Don't worry. The dad is really nice."

Maurine stared with her mouth open as Todd sauntered down the hall. "He forgot to pee?"

"He's transcended his physical self," answered Ruby.

A moment after the bathroom door clicked shut, a phone beeped. Ruby said, "Mom, will you check that? Uncle George said he'd text with his flight info and an ETA."

Maurine picked it up, opened the message, and looked at the phone. Then, she looked closer. She turned the phone around as if trying to figure what exactly she was looking at. When she did, her eyes shot open and her jaw dropped.

"What happened? Is his flight delayed?"

Maurine just kept staring at the phone and filled up her cup with punch, so Ruby let it drop. Her mom was sensitive about Uncle George skipping holidays. Last year's tantrum—because there was *always* a tantrum—had been triggered by one of George's lame excuses to skip the holiday.

"I'm going to finish dinner," Maurine took a deep breath. Then, she started to slam plates around the kitchen and shuffle silverware too loudly.

Ruby backed out. "I'll just go check on the men." She collapsed onto the couch next to Todd and rested her head on his shoulder. With a sigh, she said, "That didn't go well."

Todd yelled at the TV, "No. No. The *other* gun. The big one. Ouch!" Still staring intently at the screen, he asked, "What didn't go well?"

She gave him a look of intense scrutiny, but his question, no matter how stupid, seemed earnest. "I told my mom I'm pregnant," she said.

He looked away from *Bond* for a second. "*What*? You're pregnant? Fuckin' A, man!"

"I already told you, Todd."

"No way. I totally don't remember. That's fucking awesome. Kids rock." Then he turned his head back to *Live and Let Die*. "Check out this scene. Connery jumps over like 100 crocodiles."

"That's Roger Moore, son. Connery retired before this one."

Just then Maurine shattered a plate and yelled, "Ray! I need you." When Ray didn't get up immediately, she yelled again, "*Now*."

He strolled over to the kitchen with a beer in hand. Ruby heard her mom say, "Ray, stop watching TV. Your daughter. Is. Pregnant." She expelled a breath dramatically and fanned her face with a *TV Guide*.

Ruby said, "Mom, I'm not deaf. I can hear you."

"I'm talking to your father, Ruby. I'll let you know when I'm ready to speak to you." She held out Ruby's phone for Ray's inspection.

He said, "What the hell is that supposed to be?"

Before Maurine could hammer home whatever point she was making, Ruby said, "Dad, that's my phone," and she held out her hand for him to give it back to her. At the same time, she gave her mom a threatening glance. "Whatever it is, Mom, let's just eat dinner."

Ray rubbed Ruby's shoulder affectionately. "I agree. Let's eat."

Around the dinner table, Maurine had them say a prayer, a reaction to the declining morality of her daughter, apparently. Ruby never remembered saying grace at her parents' table. She looked questioningly at her mom who responded pointedly, "I think it's time we focus on living our values."

Ray looked at Todd, "So what line of work are you in, Todd?"

"Uh, I was working for Ming, but we parted ways recently."

Surprised, Ruby asked, "Really? What happened?"

"I used my lab space for" — he laughed — "*unapproved* activities, so she cut me loose." To Ray, he added, "Doesn't matter though 'cause Rubes and Ming don't charge me rent. The job was just a place to park during the day."

"Unapproved activities..." Ruby repeated, trying to wrap her mind around that.

Todd went on, "Yeah, actually, I've decided to head down to the Rez for a while. I've got a friend living in a teepee down there. He told me that if you lie still for long enough you can hear the sound of the universe."

Ray said, "Well, how you gonna make money doing that, son?"

"Money? I don't believe in possessions or paper currency. Money is fucking nuts." He took another swig of beer and added, "No offense or anything."

"How does that work? You *need* to buy things."

"Actually, Dad, Todd doesn't buy anything. He is a complete freeloader. He basically only eats questionable leftovers that Ming and I forget to throw away."

"Yeah, and I attend lectures at the University. They *always* serve pizza.

Ray set down his fork and leveled with Todd. "Do you expect Ruby to support you completely?"

"I don't expect her to. She just does. I don't try to influence anyone's behavior. It's a Buddhist thing."

Seeing that her dad was still misinformed about the baby's father, Ruby tried to cut him off.

He held up his hand. "No, Ruby. He's gotta hear this." Ray leveled with Todd. "Son, if you expect to marry our daughter and be a father to our grandbaby, you had better get yourself a real job. Freeloading just ain't gonna fly. Our family prides itself on hard work and American values." He paused to let that sink in. "I'll tell you what I'll do. I'm gonna set you up riding shotgun on a parking-lot striper. All you have to do is reload the paint when it runs low and remove obstructions from the roadway."

Ruby looked at her dad. "Todd is not the baby's father, Dad. We're just roommates. He didn't have anywhere else to be tonight." Her dad was so spacey. The hearing loss really didn't help.

Ray just looked perturbed. In his mind, he'd solved the problem. "Well, if Todd here ain't the daddy, who the hell is? Why isn't he here?"

"He and I are still working things out."

"Still working things out?" said Ray. "He finished working it out when you got pregnant."

"I didn't invite him, Dad."

"Why the hell not?"

She sighed. "Can we just take a break and eat the food. I'll tell you about him later."

"That's fine," answered Maurine. "He can't be any worse than Todd."

They finished the meal quietly. After Todd finished watching *Live and Let Die*, they collected their jackets to go home. "Thanks for dinner, Mom. It was delicious."

Maurine raised her glass to Todd and said, "Cheers. Good luck in the teepee."

On the way out the door, Todd asked Ray, "You serious about that job offer, man?"

"No."

"That's cool, just asking."

On the way home, Todd drove and Ruby noticed the photo message still open on her phone. Completely delighted, she looked at something that looked like…a butt. She couldn't be sure. It was really bad picture quality, blurry, but definitely an ass. The sexter had taken a picture of his own rear end in a bathroom mirror. She looked at the sender, assuming it was Noel. It wasn't. It was…Ned, an attorney in the DA's Office. Ned sat right above Noel in her contact list. For a full moment she sat paralyzed, staring at her phone in horror. *OH MY GOD*! She had fat-fingered the sext! It was beyond awkward. Frantically she typed in an apology, "Ned, so sorry. Meant to send boob photo to someone else. Nice ass."

• • •

Ruby rang in Christmas morning with Noel, at least on email. After deciding they would be better off avoiding abbreviations and acronyms and possibly even face-to-face contact, she sent an email. She kept it short and sweet.

Noel,

I'm not dating Eric. I'm sorry I went out with him that one time, but we are not together. Let's talk soon.

RARVAB <3 <3

Ruby

He responded:

Ruby, I'm glad to hear it. I'm out of town for the holiday, but I'll let you know when I'm back.

Noel

P.S. What's RARVAB mean?? (I hope it's dirty)

Ruby responded:

WHAT!? You RARVABed me!

Noel:

Uh, my secretary typed that in.

Ruby:

Remind me to kill your secretary. Also, I told my parents about the baby. Brace yourself.

Noel:

Just Googled RARVAB. Feeling cheated. Regarding your mother: At least my briefcase will be safe from now on.

With Noel's blessing, Ruby informed her parents that they already knew the baby's father and had in fact held his briefcase hostage. Her mom, of course, was over the moon. To be fair, she probably would have been thrilled with anyone after meeting Todd. It took Maurine every ounce of restraint she possessed not to call all of her girlfriends to announce that her daughter and Mr. Right, according to all accepted definitions, were expecting. She insisted on taking Ruby out for a shopping spree and makeover to celebrate. Ruby took the offer for what it was, a hint that she needed to freshen up the honey trap. Maurine even bought her a couple pairs of Spanx for pregnant ladies. During the shopping spree Noel happened to text Ruby a picture of a sandy beach with a palm tree with the caption, "Nice, huh?" Ruby looked at her bag full of Spanx and the icy world outside. If it was possible to click your heels and wish yourself on a tropical vacation with a sexy guy who apparently didn't hold grudges (thank you, Lord!), Ruby would have done so immediately.

Chapter Twenty

CLIENT ADVISORS

During Ruby's recent months of drama, her worldview had shrunk to that of an angsty teen brooding in a windowless basement bedroom. While she was preoccupied with the consequences of unprotected sex, social media overload, and whether leather pants worked as maternity wear, Ming made a breakthrough with her underwire compound and began talking to designers. She ruled out selling the compound to Victoria's Secret, DuPont, or any other giant underwear megacorp because she preferred to become her own giant underwear megacorp. She named her corporation LA Tits, Inc., rounded up a few investors, and located a suitable manufacturing facility in Malaysia. She accomplished this with less fanfare than most Kansas residents planning a summer vacation to Branson, Missouri.

The day after Christmas, Ruby asked Ming over

breakfast, "How's the bra design coming?"

"Great," said Ming. "I'm thinking of opening up a little boutique downtown, in addition to marketing the bras to bigger retailers, of course."

"What?" Ruby looked a little surprised. International business deals and manufacturing had no overlap with Ruby's skill set, despite the fact that the Smiddy website advertised one of her specialties as corporate law. "You mean you've already started?"

"Yep. I've got the first prototypes and the bras look pretty good. I've had the designer redo the lace trim on the Gidget Bra, but besides that, we're ready to roll. The bras are going to hit the shelves at the Biomall by spring."

"Wow. I thought you were still thinking about the…" she trailed off, unsure of what actually went into launching an underwear company.

"No. Once I figured out a stepwise process suitable for large-scale manufacture, I contacted my cousin, Jong, who designs swimsuits, and we worked out a design. I'm buying a building across from Emerald College for a storefront."

"Wow, are you sure about the location? Emerald College isn't exactly high fashion." Ruby had a point. Emerald College was an exclusive college, but a place where students pondered nihilism while treading about barefoot with unwashed hair, reading used copies of the *Communist Manifesto*. At least once a month, a contingent would make a trek across town to protest something about the Biomall: slave labor and environmental destruction being the most popular issues. "I haven't seen too many girls in push-up bras over there."

"True, but the rent is cheaper and the market is completely unexploited. There are 2,500 18-to-22-year-olds with daddy's credit card and an empty closet, and I'd guess 90 percent of them will be pretty well-groomed by grad school, so I might as well be the one to sell them lace panties." She chewed a mouthful of cereal and said, "Also, I wanted to tell you, there is a small office space upstairs that I can't use for sales. I thought maybe you would like to rent it." Ming glanced meaningfully at Ruby. "I'm not really sure what you want to do with it, but it might be a good start. I'd charge you a couple hundred a month for rent just to cover the utilities."

"Ming! Are you serious?" Ruby suddenly felt the giddy lightness of unexpected salvation. "That would be great! I was thinking I'd get a job at Starbucks, but a law firm would be cool if it was affordable. I would love to rent your space. Plus, we could hang out every day at work."

"Actually, Ruby, it's just good business for me. I have to do something with the space." Seeing Ruby's nearly crestfallen look she added, "But, it'll be fun. Wanna go have a look?"

· · ·

Ming's shop looked good: brick walls, high ceilings, crown molding, and huge windows that allowed sunlight to stream in and gave the place a cheery, welcoming feel. It had the perfect vibe for a high-end boutique, except for the dingy neighboring shops, but if Ming's instincts were functioning like normal, an Anthropologie and Cold Stone Creamery would move in across the street within a year.

Ming squinted into the sunny windows and shaded her eyes dramatically. "Ugh. I'm going to have to put some black-out shades up. The freaking sun is giving me a migraine."

"I think it's nice," said Ruby.

A tiny staircase at the back of the store led up to an old office with a Sam Spade vibe to it—door with a frosted glass window, exposed brick walls, and mounds of dust. Ruby pushed open the door to her office. Light streamed through the windows at oblique angles creating broad sunbeams through the dust motes. A beat-up desk the size of a barge, circa 1940s probably, sat with its back to the window, the kind of desk Spade could have banged his secretary on comfortably. A pile of old post-it notes and papers still littered its surface, many of them coffee-stained. The plaster was chipped and the room was a mess. Lettering across the windows spelled out "Client Advisors," something just vague enough to work with. On the spot, she decided to keep the name.

Ruby loved it. She didn't know what she was going to do exactly, but she knew she was going to do it in this space. If she still had to work at Starbucks, she could do that too, but she wanted this space.

"I'll take it, Ming. It's Bea–u–ti–ful!"

"Perfect. I'll need one month's rent as a deposit and one month's rent in advance. Why don't you draw up the contract? Actually, I'll give you the first month free if you take care of the legal stuff. I can be your first client."

"Great!" Ruby had no clue how to draw up a lease, but she figured it had to be simple. People downloaded that shit all the time from lawyer123.com. She would pretty much just be an intermediary.

Done standing around admiring the space, Ming said, "Okay, I've had enough of this. I need to get back to the lab for the afternoon and I have a conference call about some lace panties at four. I'm returning an entire shipment because they are impossible to dislodge from between your ass cheeks—total wedgie machines." She paused to look up. "Do you want a ride home?"

"Nope. I think I'll stick around here and dream a little, if that's okay with you."

Ming shook her head and sighed, in an affectionate way and said, "Whatever. Just leave the lease on my desk when you finish, would you?" She turned on her heel and *click-clacked* out of the room in a pair of Ruby's shoes. It almost made Ruby cry. She was starting a business with her best friend.

In the center of the room, she squared her shoulders and inhaled deeply, totally at peace with her situation now that she had been relieved of the specter of traditional employment. She went over to the desk and sat down in the office chair. It creaked and she sank down a good three inches. She swiveled and took in the view from her new office. From her window she could see Auntie Em's, a hookah shop, and a hardware store. Not exactly her element, but she liked coffee and the hookahs were displayed nicely.

She'd never had much use for a hardware store before, but she took a look at her new office and decided it was time to become acquainted. At the store, she picked up trash bags, a broom and dustpan, some random cleaning supplies, and a trash bin. She asked the kid working there about plaster-repair work and bought a basketful of supplies that he suggested. Next trip, primer and paint. She envisioned turquoise walls and a honey-colored oriental rug. On her way back up to the office she picked up a latte and a sandwich from Em's. She had always loved Em's, even though she didn't go often. It was the type of place where baristas made little heart designs on the top of your coffee and used ceramic mugs as a first option. It also reminded her of Estelle, their first and last lunch date.

Fortified with a hearty artisan-crafted sandwich, Ruby got back to work at the office. She filled trash bags with all the junk, swept the floors and dusted off the light fixtures and desk. She wheeled the decrepit chair down the stairs one *thunk* at a time, figuring it would be perfect for a college freegan. First thing tomorrow she'd pick up something better, probably from a sidewalk in her parents' neighborhood.

Based on the store clerk's advice, she used a trowel and spackle to fill in some cracks in the wall. Because she'd never done anything like this before and no one would ever believe her, she snapped a photo of herself with her iPhone. The first photo captured more of her body than her face. Looking at the image, Ruby saw her baby bump. It made her feel like she was looking at a photo of a stranger. Sure, she knew she was pregnant, but she still didn't think of herself as a "Pregnant Lady." Focusing in on her face and trowel, she snapped another photo minus the toaster-sized lump in her middle. She also took care to keep the partially unpacked boxes of bras and spare mannequins out of the picture. All she needed was to post a picture of herself at work with naked mannequins photo-bombing her! This time around, she was gonna keep things professional.

With the intent of announcing her new professional self to the world, she opened up a couple of social media accounts under her new business name. Thinking it would help people locate her business, she used a photo of the storefront as her profile pic. The LA Tits sign was significantly more noticeable than the lettering that spelled Client Advisors across her window, but she figured people could sort it out on their own. Finally she posted her first status update, "Client Advisors is open for business." She'd figure out what she was doing once the first client walked through the door. Most likely it would be legal. Well, definitely legal. Beyond that, she was open to pretty much anything.

With her adrenaline officially gone, Ruby stared at evidence of her budding business. It struck her that she would be more comfortable acting in a QVC advertisement for cellulite cream, including a close-up on her thighs, than drafting a will for her first customer. Looking away from her new office, she turned toward the window. The angle of the sun obscured her vision a little, but she could have sworn that Eric just drove by in a police cruiser with—she had to be wrong—but it looked like Todd in the back.

Chapter Twenty-One

OUT OF BODY EXPERIENCES

Turns out, it was Todd. Not long after Ruby observed the Todd look-alike riding around in a police cruiser, the phone rang. In a casual wanna-grab-a-pizza tone, Todd asked, "Yo, Rubes, can you do me a solid?"

"What kind of favor?"

"Wanna bail me out of the slammer?" His attitude didn't seem to be the least bit dampened by whatever predicament he'd gotten himself into.

"What? I thought you were out of town?"

"I came back for a Super America run. They don't sell Frito fun packs at the gas station down on the Rez." Ruby didn't choose this moment to remind him Fritos didn't really jive with his purported goal of retreating from city life to seek profound stillness and "listen for the sound of the universe"—whatever that meant. Fritos just made her think of crunching. Todd went on, "Eric busted me. I guess I forgot to pay for the chips. I don't know. Could you come get me?"

"Do you have money to pay me back?" She tried to remember if she'd ever seen Todd with money and couldn't.

"Uh, I can probably Craigslist that Yakima rack."

"You don't have a car. Why do you have a Yakima?"

"Exaaaaactly." After pausing to let the profundity of that idea sink in, he added, "Even better yet, I could just give it to you."

With a sigh, she said, "Give me half an hour." It figured that her first job would be bailing Todd out of jail and that he'd pay her with a used roof rack for her convertible.

She stomped down the stairs, thinking it would be nice to have Todd back at least. Ming had been so busy, it had been quiet around the house. At the front door, she paused to lock up. While she was fiddling with the keys, someone yelled her name from across the street.

Standing in front of Auntie Em's was Noel, looking handsomer than ever. Like the model in a Ralph Lauren ad, his crisp white shirt contrasted with his glowing vacation tan. He was the vision of a relaxed businessman. All the municipal secretaries were probably falling over themselves for this man. Ruby sighed. This was their first face-to-face meeting since the RARVAB drama and the narrowly-missed sexting debacle. The emailing had been going pretty well, but Ruby wanted to be more than pen pals with the father of her child.

With a broad smile, he loped across the street and said, "Ruby! How was your Christm—" He paused, probably not wanting to assume she celebrated Christmas and corrected sheepishly, "How was your holiday?"

She fired off a little shotgun smattering of nervous

laughter. "Christmas." She nodded. "Yep. We do Christmas. You too?"

He nodded.

And a promising reunion had turned to awkward in less than a minute. She looked behind him and noticed for the first time the statues in front of the LA Tits building. A bronze statue of a munchkin-sized bride and groom stood staring into each other's eyes. Bronze butterflies danced around them. As she and Noel stared awkwardly at each other nodding like bobble heads, the statues stared blissfully at one another, locked in endless mutual admiration. Ruby glared at the bride, who was wearing a halo of butterflies and looked to have an eleven-inch waist, "I do," trembling on her lips.

Standing in front of LA Tits with a bun in the oven, Noel unsure of whether she celebrated Christmas, Ruby had the distinct feeling things weren't going as planned. There was her dream, encased in bronze just to the left, and most likely, permanently out of reach. Here she was renting space and hanging out a shingle, riding into the sunset on the tasseled fringes of Ming's underwear empire.

"How 'bout we go to lunch?" Noel said, oblivious to the statues.

She nodded. "How about later? I have to run a quick errand." Sure, she could let Todd sit in jail, but it seemed inhumane. There was no way the police had actually detained him for stealing Fritos. Whatever they had him on, he could probably use a lawyer.

"I'll tag along? We can talk and walk," he suggested.

Ruby considered her task, filling out paperwork at jail… It wasn't really the kind of thing she envisioned doing with

Noel, but they were already miles away from saying "I do" in butterfly halos. "I guess—"

"Great. You lead the way," he said. He clearly thought she was taking him on an errand to buy staples, after which they could grab a sandwich and become a more accurate reflection of the vision in bronze. "Where're we going?"

"Well…right now we're going to walk into the jail and bail out Todd."

To his credit, he rolled with it, asking only, "Todd? As in Ski Patrol Todd? What's he in for?"

She nodded. "He thinks he was arrested for stealing a Frito Lay fun pack. I'm guessing that was just the reason the police stopped him. It'll probably turn out to be a possession charge. After we bail him out, I think we should grab a pizza and make jokes at his expense."

Ruby walked up to the jailer, explained that she wanted to bail out Todd, and started filling out the required paperwork. When the clerk saw Noel he stopped her. "Your money's no good here. This one is on the house."

Ruby looked at Noel and tried to process what had just happened. "Seriously? They won't take your money."

He shrugged. "Ozcorp. Everyone bows down whether I want them to or not."

She didn't argue because it was saving her a thousand bucks that she didn't have, but it didn't sit right.

• • •

An hour later, Noel and Ruby pulled out of the jail with Todd in the backseat. "Todd, put on your seatbelt," Ruby said.

"What?" he said staring into space.

"Put. On. Your. Seatbelt," Ruby repeated.

He responded by rolling down the window.

Ruby turned around and looked at him. She was used to him being spacey, but this was beyond his normal. "Todd, *what* are you on?"

"Blackout, baby!"

"What?" Ruby had never heard of this drug before, but she remembered hearing him sing along to "Blacked Out, Cracked Out!" recently. Naively, she had assumed that the lyrics weren't based on a real life scenario, but as she recalled the words—"Blacked out and forgot my own name. Wondering which pimps to blame"—realization dawned and she asked, "Have I ever taken Blackout?"

"Duh," he said, looking at Noel. "You both did. I asked you if you wanted a Pepsi or a *Pepsi Special*. I bet it was *aaaawwwesome!*"

Ruby and Noel looked at each other and Ruby said, "Sorry about that, Noel. I probably thought special meant diet."

Noel shook his head in astonishment. "It's not your fault."

Noel looked at Todd. "Aren't you going to apologize even?"

Todd stopped trying to touch his tongue to his nose long enough to say, "Whoa. Can you do that?"

Ruby put her hand on Noel's and quietly said, "There's no point."

Noel took a deep breath and nodded.

Later that night, Noel, Ruby, and Todd sat on the couch watching some bad TV and chowing down on pizza. Todd, unfortunately, sat in the middle of them like a child. Debbie and Charmaine were flopped at their feet. It was like they were practicing for the real thing, but with a menagerie of adopted creatures, including one overgrown surfer dude. Ruby wondered why Todd even did drugs. Given his regular level of consciousness, it seemed like a redundancy.

Noel looked over Todd's head with an amused smile. It was so sweet of Noel to spend the whole day putting up with Todd, especially after finding out about the Blackout. For the moment, her uncharted reality seemed even better than her dreams, even if less worthy of a bronze casting.

Chapter Twenty-Two

Pastor Rick

Ruby pulled her pink settee up to her office window. She meant to read her e-mail, but she was mesmerized by the way the morning sun shone on the buildings across the street making their copper-colored roofs shine bright as new pennies in sharp contrast to the dingy January streets. It looked cold outside. She was thinking of… She forgot whatever it was when a nice-looking man with a briefcase and a cashmere scarf walked by. Just as she was admiring his overall look, he casually tossed his coffee cup into the gutter. *Pig!* He didn't even look back.

She looked down at the paper in her lap, which she had been holding without really reading. Her gaze strayed to the top of the page. Staring back at her with a beauty pageant smile was none other than Destinee, giving the cameras a saucy sideways pose with a lot of leg thanks to a deep side slit. The article was about Elysian Fields.

Destinee described Elysian Fields as "Green like Seattle. Luxurious like Dubai." She emphasized that Ozcorp was cleaning up contaminated soil before building and including a variety of ecologically-minded features. "Elysian Fields will feature a LEED-certified gas station and golf course." Ruby wondered if she was missing something. *Could you get a LEED certification and sell gas?* At any rate, just for living there, residents would automatically receive a fifty-point jump in their Biomall green credit scores. Noel needed to put his sustainability training to use stat. Even without a degree, she could see things to fix everywhere.

When she looked at the picture again she realized that Destinee, in her thigh-high slit and construction helmet, was standing in front of the site. Behind her Ruby could see some guys driving backhoes, the clean-up crew she assumed. When she looked a little closer she laughed. *Is that Jermaine driving the backhoe?* Another read-through of the article added to her suspicions, "Ozcorp hired an expert in land rehabilitation, well-versed in hazardous waste disposal and soil remediation to clean up the site." She looked again at the picture of Jermaine. She wondered if Jermaine was "the expert," squeezing in a little land rehab while he was out on bail before trial. Somehow, it seemed likely.

She logged on to her computer and looked up Elysian fields. Before long, she found an EPA press release announcing that it had awarded Ozcorp $250,000 to clean up a former appliance landfill. She stared at the computer for a minute, but couldn't find anything really wrong with that scenario. Still, she couldn't kick the image of the businessman tossing his garbage in the street.

Ruby had been intending to call her mother's friends and see if anyone needed a new will, but she scrapped that task. The Elysian Fields business reeked of insider dealings and it brought back all her suspicions about Estelle's death. The trail might be cold by now, but she never did anything the easy way. She owed it to her friend to investigate. If nothing else, she would talk to the biggest suspects. Pastor Rick had been named in the will, so he was up first. Estelle had disinherited Jermaine because of Rick, so he would be second.

Only too glad to give up her estate planning goals for the day, Ruby did a quick Google search on Pastor Rick before heading out to question the man in person. Meeting Pastor Rick meant a trip to the Chapel Mall, the Biomall's biggest satellite shopping center, and location of the Glass Chapel. The Chapel took up one of the anchor store spots for the Chapel Mall as if it was Macy's or something.

For whatever reason, deep religiosity or contrition, Oswald Rancka signed over a twenty-year lease on some of Emerald's prime retail space to the Chapel for a pittance. Or, maybe he was just smart. It had produced the most profitable symbiotic relationship in retail history: Sunday had turned into Emerald's biggest shopping day, while church attendance skyrocketed. Teenagers who long ago told God to piss off began attending church in throngs because church meant a ride to the mall, no questions asked. The people who did make it to the service often purchased outfits modeled by Pastor Rick or the choir, both of whom always wore something provided by one of the neighboring stores. Sometime during service, he would find a moment to say, "And, thank you, Enzo's, for providing me with these fine khaki trousers, which are on special today for $49.99." Last month, some kids had sneaked into the chapel and taken Jesus off the cross. Before they hung him back up, they dressed him in a leather jacket and a bunch of clothes from the Gap. Strangely enough, Rick completely missed the implied criticism and said, "My, my, doesn't Jesus looks fine in those aviators?"

Everyone loved it. Trips to the Chapel had become a right-of-passage for fundamentalist Christians (of a certain type) the world over. The waiting list for weddings was purportedly seven years long. Emerald's fertility doctors were flourishing as most brides were on the downslide of their fertile years by the time they managed a Glass Chapel wedding.

Lucky for Ruby, she could walk to the Chapel Mall from her office. She grabbed her purse and hit the road. Within five minutes she was inhaling the scent of Enzo's, her favorite department store. It was named for Debbie and Charmaine's sire, Enzo, the prototypical OzDog. She sprayed on a few new fragrances and walked to Chapel Coffee in a cloud of perfumed air.

Feeling the spirit fill her, she decided to stop for a coffee. "Could I have the vanilla latte with angel foam please?" she asked a perky blonde barista whose nametag read, "Juniper."

"Sure. Did you notice that you get a discount if you can answer the trivia question?"

"No." Ruby looked at the chalkboard behind the barista. The question was: "Which saint is Pastor Rick named for?"

"I don't know."

"Saint Richard," answered Juniper in a Valley Girl accent. "He was a vegetarian." She punctuated the statement with a hair toss.

"Oh. That's cool," said Ruby. "I tried to be a vegetarian once. My mom wouldn't make two meals, though, and my dad hates vegetables." Ruby's vegetarian effort had been pretty weak. She'd only tried briefly after reading an article about Alicia Silverstone's diet in *Self*.

"Oh," said Juniper dramatically, completely simpatico with Ruby's vegetarian strife. "I couldn't make it work either after I found out there is meat in burritos." She handed Ruby her vanilla latte with angel foam, "Hope you enjoy your coffee. This is Pastor Rick's *favorite*."

"Thanks!" said Ruby and she set off for the Chapel.

Ruby stepped into the octagonal glass elevator behind a group of tourists and rode it to the top, all the way to heaven, it seemed. To hammer the heavenly effect home with blunt force, the Mall had dangled glittering angels from I-beams, creating a vortex of flying cherubs. Ruby alighted in a lobby overflowing with bouquets of roses and a gleaming marble floor. A large marble statue of Pastor Rick looking skyward greeted her. As she looked around, understanding dawned with the brilliance of a prairie sunrise. Between the vanilla latte, the scent of Chanel No. Five, and the penthouse view, she felt like she was communing with God.

Then she heard the sound of cowboy boots (Italian leather) on marble tile. It was Rick. He strode in with his fingers through his belt loops. His crisp white shirt accented his perfect tan, spray-on.

"Ah. Jermaine's friend." He nodded his head in greeting. "So glad to see you've found your way to the Chapel. We love to welcome new *families* to the Glass Chapel," he stressed the word family while nodding to Ruby's belly.

"Thanks. I'm actually here about something else, though."

"Our line of devotional jewelry?" he guessed. "It's for sale in the case outside of the elevator bank."

This man had her number. "Now that you mention it, yes. There's something else, too, though."

"Really. What might that be?"

"I'm a lawyer," she confided as if this would be a shock to him. Ruby had trouble *owning* her profession the way Oprah recommended, but she was trying, so she handed him one of her Client Advisors business cards.

He raised his eyebrows quizzically and said, "Oh, *I see*," as if the business card answered all his questions. When he looked up at her again, something had shifted, as if he'd decided to turn off the charm. Ruby couldn't help but wonder if he knew about her connection to Estelle.

Ruby continued, "One of my clients named you as a beneficiary in her will. She left you her house. Her name was Estelle Harris."

"No, Unfortunately I don't remember her."

"But I met you at her funeral," Ruby protested. "You must have known her."

"I attend a lot of funerals. They blur together." He paused and explained, "Many of my flock never attend services, especially elderly members. She probably watched the services on TV at home. We've inspired quite a few older folks with our message and many of them make note of that in their wills. I wish I was able to meet them all personally." At this point he was simply giving her canned answers from the FAQ list.

"Is there some sort of promotion, though? Didn't I hear about a promotion where the person gets something in return for leaving you an estate?" Ruby was just thinking on the fly now. She thought she remembered hearing something in a TV commercial, probably at Estelle's house.

"Yes. We provide a voucher for a free funeral in the Glass Chapel. There is nothing like a funeral in the chapel. The journey to Heaven is only a short flight for an angel. We have beautiful funerals here."

"Estelle's funeral wasn't here, though." Ruby took a deep breath. The man was starting to frustrate her. She knew he was popular, but could he really remember as little as he claimed?

"Perhaps she made another arrangement. You could check with my secretary if you'd like. What did you say your name was?"

"O'Deare, Ruby O'Deare."

"That's right. I would love to keep talking," he said smoothly "but, I have several other things to do to this afternoon. If you would like to continue our conversation, please call and make an appointment. I would love to welcome you and yours to the Glass Chapel." Pastor Rick had definitely turned off the charm in favor of the canned voice he broke out for busloads of Japanese tourists, a group he had publicly derided for trivializing the Lord's work, mainly because they sandwiched the Glass Chapel tour between Silver Dollar City and the World's Largest Ball of Twine. How Ruby went from honored visitor to Japanese, she wasn't exactly sure, but he certainly didn't like her business cards. At any rate, she was no longer going to earn a Glass Chapel baby shower.

"Well, thanks for your time," said Ruby.

"Thank you, too. I would love to see you at one of our services. There is also a regular three o'clock tour every day for visitors."

"Thanks," said Ruby. She watched Pastor Rick walk into the church offices. As she watched him go, she thought about waiting for a tour, but on impulse, she opened up the doors to Chapel and walked in alone. What she found frightened her. Instead of shafts of light striking through the clouds directly onto her anointed head, she found herself standing alone in the middle of a dark gray cloud with an undulating belly. Little shivers of freezing rain began to pelt the glass roof. It looked to her like the Glass Chapel had front row seats to a truly frightening sky, a sky that didn't look anything like the heaven it promised. She felt better about Estelle losing out on her free funeral. The place just wasn't really her style. Ruby turned on her heel, all thoughts of the tour gone.

She didn't forget the jewelry, though.

Just like Rick said, there was a glass jewelry case. All jewelry was celebrity designed and 10 percent of the profits went to tricking out the worship center.

She asked the person working the counter, "Can I see that pink rhinestone cross with the rhinestone? It's fabulous."

"Good choice."

As the girl handed her the necklace, someone called out, "Hey, hot stuff. You up here finding God or just bling-ing out?" Eric stared intently at the pink rhinestone cross. It plunged into her cleavage in a way that could only be described as sacrilegious. He made a cat growling noise and said, "Praise be, baby."

"*Eric*? What are you doing here?" She hadn't seen him since he'd driven Todd to the police station.

"Reporting for duty. I'm doing security for His Highness."

"Oh." Ruby furrowed her brows. In all of the time she'd

spent at the mall, which was considerable, she'd never seen Eric. "What kind of jobs does he have you do?"

"This and that."

Eric sauntered into the Chapel office. "Gotta get to work. Later, babe."

She stared after him. Mall security had never been sexier or so poorly miscast.

The Chapel sales woman interrupted Ruby's reverie. "Are you gonna buy that thing or what?"

Oh, yeah. Ruby handed over her Biomall credit card.

A second later, the lady said, "I'm sorry, but your card was declined."

"*What*? But I have top smart shopper rankings."

"The smart shopper rankings only help you earn rewards. They don't save you from having to pay your bill," the girl explained. The Biomall credit system ranked shoppers in categories like Green Buyer, Fair Trade Shopper, and Trend Spotter. Eight hundred points was the top score in each category. Just like the SATs. Top scores earned prizes like valet parking and monogrammed bathrobes. This year, the top green shoppers were going to earn bamboo fabric pajamas. Ruby had totally bought into the Biomall's propaganda—"The dollar is your greatest vote in a democracy! Buy green! Buy fair! Buy Biomall!"

Standing at the counter offering her worthless card, Ruby felt like an idiot. She had officially gone broke buying fair-trade soy candles. The complimentary valet parking and trend spotter score were nothing but the emperor's new clothes. She might as well have been standing there naked. Looking at her cowboy boots, she realized that she'd probably never pay them off.

Chapter Twenty-Three

Convo with Jermaine about Backhoe Driving

After dressing in head-to-toe Juicy Couture velour, which she had found to be the perfect pregnancy uniform, and drinking a ginormous coffee at Em's, Ruby hopped in her Mustang with Debbie and Charmaine and pointed it toward the Big House, which was about forty minutes outside of Emerald. Jermaine had finally pled out to some lesser charges and was serving a short sentence in the State Pen. The dogs moved around the front seat like eels in a bucket, crawling over each other and circling, each angling for the coveted spot on Ruby's lap. Ruby ignored them and sang along to a bubble-gum pop song.

After checking in at the prison, Ruby made her way to a large cafeteria-like room. Jermaine was waiting for her at a table by himself wearing the standard orange jumpsuit and a studied look of boredom. She said, "Nice to see you again,

Mr. Harris."

"Like hell it is. You trash-talked me to my grandmother. Tried to turn her against me."

"Um, no. I was your grandmother's attorney. I was just doing my best to keep her out of trouble."

"Like hell you were."

"Well, would you answer a couple of questions since I came all the way down here?"

"Ask away." He leaned back in his chair and crossed his arms in front of his chest like a bouncer.

"I saw a photo of you working in Elysian Fields. I'm wondering who hired you and what you were doing."

"The big PR hooked me up with that gig."

"Pastor Rick?"

"Yep. He's hires lots of ex-cons. Dude's big into second chances."

"So you were working for Pastor Rick?"

"Rick hooked us up with the gig. He didn't pay us, though."

"Did you have any prior experience cleaning up contaminated soils?"

"What would I need that for?"

"Well, it's a dump. It's filled with refuse. Some of the old appliances actually contain federally-regulated, toxic chemicals that probably leaked into the soil." Ruby remembered this from the newspaper article.

"It's not like we were making sandwiches out of it."

"Did anyone supervise your work?"

"No. What for?"

"What did you do with the soil? Did you dig up the soil and move it off site?"

"No, we kind of moved some of the appliances around

and covered 'em in dirt. Driving a backhoe is fucking awe-some. Hell, I do business from that site all the time anyway, so I was really just getting paid extra waiting for customers to show up."

Ruby was putting it all together. Rick sent a bunch of ex-cons Destinee's way. She paid them to drive backhoes aimlessly for a couple of days. Then, she must have collected the money from the EPA for cleaning up the place. *Classy.* She bet Food Hollow would love to know that it was being built on top of a bunch of old air conditioners, not to men-tion anyone who planned to put in a garden. Ozcorp was guilty of defrauding the U.S. government. She couldn't wait to tell Noel about this. There's no way he'd stand for a sham clean-up.

"It was awesome. I'd do it for free."

"One more question, Jermaine. Did your grandma know that you didn't really clean anything up over there?"

"Yeah, she watched us spinning cookies on those things all day long. Then, she made us lemonade and sandwiches for lunch."

"Did Destinee or Pastor Rick know your grandma was watching?"

"Everyone did. Rick and Dee had lunch with us all the time. My grandma kept asking him what the digging was about." Ruby filed this info away. Estelle could have cost Ozcorp $250,000 if she'd reported the shoddy work, not to mention fines and possible criminal penalties. That could be motive.

"One more thing Jermaine. Are you and Trudi getting married soon?"

He laughed. "That's what she tells me."

"Where's the wedding?"

"What do you care? Trying to pick out your outfit? I can save you the trouble now because you ain't invited." He laughed at his humor.

"I was just wondering."

"Well, you asking the wrong person, woman. She'll tell me where to show up and who the check goes to."

"Thanks, Jermaine. That was a real help. If you don't mind, tell Trudi I'm going to give her a call next time you talk to her."

"That's fine. If you talk to her, tell her to keep the fucking wedding costs down. I just got a bill for a fucking $1,000 tiara. Who the hell does she think she's marrying, P Diddy? How the hell am I supposed to pay for that shit from jail anyway? What the hell kind of fool sells a woman a diamond crown and then mails the bill to prison?" He paused for effect. "I tell you who—a fucking moron. I'm not paying for a bunch of diamonds, especially from some idiot who takes the time to address the envelope in some fancy-ass cursive writing to the Kansas State Pen. I would have gotten fucking raped if anyone saw that shit."

Ruby laughed as if it were a really cute story, something her mom might share at a lady's luncheon. "Will do. Cut her some slack on the tiara, though. That's really not a negotiable part of the wedding ensemble and $1,000 is really reasonable."

He didn't yell, "Where the fuck you come from lady?" but the look on his face clearly said it.

Ruby smiled back and said, "It was nice to chat with you. I've heard so much about you from your grandma. She just loved you."

Like a sulky teen, he said, "I know. Too bad she wouldn't go to bat for me in the courtroom."

Ruby was flabbergasted. "Your grandma could have gone to jail for that."

"You're shittin' me. They'd never put an old lady in here."

Ruby had to leave. She had nothing more to say to that jerk. *What an ungrateful ass.* "I've gotta go, Jermaine. Thanks for your help."

Ruby was pretty sure that hiring Marcus and Jermaine to deal dope from a backhoe didn't qualify as soil rehabilitation. If Ozcorp got caught, someone would be in trouble for fraud and it'd be criminal considering the amount of money. The development might go belly-up after the scandal.

· · ·

"Hey, Ming," Ruby called on the way through LA Tits. Ming had the place looking amazing, all the more evident after her day at the Kansas Pen. It was sultry boudoir times ten, deep pink velvet paneled walls so soft and sumptuous she wanted to rub against them naked, sort of the point, she guessed. Ornate full-length mirrors that definitely made you look five pounds slimmer. The back wall was an over-sized black-and-white mural of Betty Grable posing in relief against a sci-fi backdrop and wearing a shiny metallic bra. Ming sat on a barstool at a raised desk in a skirt that barely covered her ass. She was flipping through a magazine and listening intently to an NPR report on Prada choosing to list on the Hong Kong Stock exchange rather than New York or London. More to herself than Ruby, Ming murmured, "New York is so twentieth century."

"What's with the glasses, Ming?"

"I think people can relate to me better with them."

"Oh." Ruby saw nothing wrong with this explanation.

Without looking up from her reading, Ming said, "By the way, your man is upstairs waiting for you."

"Noel?"

"Yep. For a pregnant chick, you have a lot of boyfriends." She stopped to think for a minute and commented, "It's probably an evolutionary thing—something about a mate with proven ability to bear young."

Ruby cringed. "Eww. You might want to work on your lines. You're supposed to be selling romance."

"Romance is biology, Ruby."

Ruby opened up the glass door to her office. There he was, leaning back in her chair with his feet propped up on her desk. When he saw her, he gave her one of his adorable half smiles.

"I was just going to call you," she said. "I have a permit violation to report."

"Is that right?" He didn't look like he cared in the least. He confirmed this when he asked, "I was wondering if you want to go out to dinner tonight? Or maybe right now?" He raised his eyebrows and said, "Maybe we can leave Todd at home this time?"

"Hmm. That sounds really nice."

He pointed to a pair of cups on the table by the door. "I brought coffees."

She picked them up and sat down next to him on her settee. "Thank you!" One of the cups said VL and the other C. "Is VL for me?" asked Ruby, suddenly feeling a little weak in the knees.

"I thought you ordered that last time we were together."

She almost swooned, but she managed to say, "Thanks." If Noel accidentally kneeled down to tie his shoe or accidentally started a sentence with, "Will you…" Ruby would jump out of her chair and scream "Yes!"

He picked up a discarded negligee that was slung over the side of the settee. "Did you lose this?"

Ruby smiled slyly. Ruby pointed to the mannequin Ming had been dressing. "I think it belongs to her. But if you're good, I'll wear it for you later."

He ran his hand across her bare leg. "I think I'll hold you to that, Miss O'Deare."

The sun slanted across his face, highlighting the amber flecks in his eyes and his outdoorsy tan. She imagined touring his vineyard sometime soon—walking through the grape arbor in dappled sunlight, a light breeze ruffling her skirt. She admired his eyes again, coffee brown with amber spots. God. How had she thought they were blue? She would be the worst eyewitness, to her own life no less.

He tapped his lap and said, "Put your feet up."

"Really?" She stretched out, kicked off her boots, and he pulled her feet into his lap. When he began to rub them, she forgot the vanilla latte on the floor beside her and basked in the attention like a sun worshiper on the beach.

He looked meaningfully at her belly. "That little thing is now the size of an apple."

"Really?"

He gave her a funny look, as if everyone knew fetal development. "Am I wrong? I think it was WebMD—it said you might even be able to feel it move by now?"

"Uh…no." She couldn't believe her ears. *He* was reading

about the baby. A baby-loving, gorgeous, wine connoisseur. She shut her eyes and cozied up into the feeling of security. She wasn't in this alone.

"What'd you do today so far?"

All she wanted to do was cozy up to him and maybe unbutton her blouse a few notches, but she managed to answer. "Uh. I went to the prison to talk to Jermaine."

"Really?"

She caught the surprise in his tone. He had clearly expected her to say she was at the mall picking out a new shade of eye shadow, so she acted like she went to the prison every morning, "Yeah, I needed to ask Jermaine a few questions about a job he did for Destinee." She was starting to lose focus, though, because his hands were turning her feet into butter.

"Oh my god. You could be a masseur," Ruby said in a drugged voice as she sank deeper into the sofa.

"Tell me more."

"Are you sure? This is the part about the permit violation. I'm not sure if I want to distract you from the direction you're headed. You're gonna get so mad when you hear this one."

He smiled knowingly.

"Try me. I won't care."

"Destinee hired Jermaine and a friend to do a sham clean-up job at the Elysian Fields site."

He took a deep breath and nodded. He didn't look surprised at all.

"You don't look upset."

"I didn't think you wanted me to be upset."

"But I figured you would be." Realization dawned and

she sat bolt upright. "You already knew, didn't you?"

He nodded. "Yes."

With knit brows she said, "I don't get it. You're letting Ozcorp slide."

He made a waffling gesture with his hands. "I don't feel like I have much choice. I mean—"

She cut him off. "What? You're the municipal authority. Ozcorp is the applicant. Make them do the right thing."

"Ozcorp always gets what it wants. I don't want to rock the boat with the city or Ozcorp."

She thought about it for a second. "You shouldn't even be allowed to make the decision. You're too biased." Getting madder by the second, she said, "You're probably making money off the stupid development." She looked at her knees. "All that talk about Elysian Fields being a gentrified suburban blight—that was all bogus."

He started to protest. "I'm just being realistic. It doesn't mean I like it."

"I don't want to hear it. Seriously. You are such a hypocrite. What about that sustainability tour of Asia? Was that just for show?"

"No. It wasn't. I want to do what's right for everyone. I want to be the best public servant I can be, but I can't fight every battle. Eylsian Fields is the battle I decided not to fight."

"Well, that was a bad choice, buddy. Estelle probably died because of that development. People trust you. I trusted you." She threw the negligee on the floor in a fit of temper.

Noel shook his head. "I'm sorry."

He did look sorry, but Ruby was too mad to listen.

• • •

Ruby slumped over Ming's desk and let out a sigh dramatic enough for daytime television. She'd gotten a little too close to happily-ever-after, close enough to start losing perspective. It was like crying in the parking lot at Disney World. She wondered if other people did that too.

"Please don't cry, Ruby. I hate crying."

"It's the hormones. I can't help it." When Ming didn't ask about the tears, she explained anyway. "Noel is a slimy bureaucrat. He is ignoring all sorts of egregious permit violations."

Ming started laughing. "Holy fuck. Those hormones are hitting you hard!"

"He's letting Ozcorp slide through without following any of the rules. He's basically working for Ozcorp. I don't think I can trust him."

Ming looked thoughtful for a moment. "Everyone in Emerald is basically working for Ozcorp. He might not be all bad."

After a minute and a few deep breaths, Ruby felt the fight go out of her. She took a few sips of the vanilla latte Noel had brought her and said, "You're right. We are all to blame for whatever Ozcorp does. We all just let it happen." Noel was sweet and thoughtful. She rubbed her belly thinking that he would probably be a great dad. Everyone screws up now and then. She certainly did. "I started thinking about baby names, Ming. What do you think about Rosebud. Doesn't that sound cute?"

"Don't ask me to comment."

Ruby patted her belly again. "Want to go shopping for baby stuff with me? That might be fun."

"Maybe later. I have a meeting with Jong about a flirty new double-strap number in fifteen minutes." Her stomach growled. "Fuck, I'm hungry. I should have made a smoothie or something."

Ruby searched through her purse. The only thing in there was the bag of nasty peanuts she'd taken from Estelle's kitchen a few days ago. Normally Ming wouldn't accept bottom-of-the purse fare. She must have been starving, though, because she accepted Ruby's offering. When she took a bite of the nuts she grimaced and picked up the bag to inspect it. "There is something the matter with these nuts." Looking at the bag she observed, "Did you put something on them?"

"Just some salt."

"I believe you put something on there, but it wasn't salt."

"Yes it was. It was in Estelle's saltshaker. I just don't think I put enough on. I couldn't get it very salty."

"No, that is not salt, Ruby. It's too bitter. It tastes like potassium chloride."

"What's that?"

"Not salt. Throw those away."

Chapter Twenty-Four

Solves the Murder on Commercial Break

Ruby drove home and scrounged in the kitchen. There was nothing to eat or drink besides Diet Coke and Saltines. Ming had been too busy conquering the world to shop, and when it came down to it, Ming was the only one who came home with anything besides Diet Coke and Saltines. Ruby looked at the empty pantry and thought about driving to the store for food, but she picked out a pack of Saltines and a pop instead and settled in front of the TV. Probably not the best diet for a developing fetus, so she popped an extra pre-natal vitamin.

Thoughtlessly, she turned on the next episode in *Sixteen and Pregnant*, but a few minutes into it she got bored and flipped to *Law and Order: Special Victims Unit*. Watching Mariska Hargitay save children and kick ass while looking like an armed pin-up girl inspired her to work a little. It was as good a time as any to write down her thoughts about Estelle's case. Feeling virtuous, she muted the TV and picked up her notes, which were as coffee-stained and dog-eared as one of Olivia's old law books.

Looking through her notes, she wondered if it was even worth the effort. Her list of suspects included Destinee, who might have killed Estelle to keep her quiet about the Elysian Fields money. If she had to guess, Ruby would say that Destinee pocketed the money from the EPA that was supposed to be spent on a proper clean-up. She might have killed Estelle so she wouldn't be outed as an embezzler. Then, there was Trudi, because of general bitchiness and opportunity. As her beneficiary, Pastor Rick rounded out the list. Ruby sighed and set down the notebook and turned the volume back up.

Halfheartedly, she scrolled through her Twitter feed while Mariska kicked down a door and shot a bad guy. The tweets were mostly boring, blow-by-blow narration of strangers' lives, "crawling into bed!" and "eating gourmet macaroni" with the occasional picture of Neil Patrick Harris's dinner thrown in. Then, she stopped at a post from an old sorority pal, Ginny Hawkins. Ginny wrote: *"Thanks for the Glass Chapel Wedding, Granny! RIP!"*

Last time she'd talked to Ginny, Ginny had been three years out on the waiting list. Ruby wrote back, *"@ginnygin, Did Granny sleep with Pastor Rick? :O"*

Ginny responded, *"@rubyslippers Sick! I wish! She died. :(I exchanged the funeral voucher for a wedding. *wink*"*

Ruby cringed. Talk about the worst karma ever—one should not mess with their grandmother's funeral wishes, even for a dream wedding. The only worse thing would be exchanging your dead fiancée's funeral for a free wedding with the best man. That was a low blow, even for Ginny who would now most certainly get acne or spontaneously develop a recessed nipple on her wedding day. Ruby didn't know what that was, but she'd seen a pamphlet at the doctor's office on the topic. She wondered what kind of person would enjoy a wedding day they stole from their dead granny.

Then the light bulb went off: *Trudi wouldn't mind one bit.* Ruby thought of the salt. The salt on her bag of peanuts came from the shaker that Trudi had refilled and used to season Estelle's chicken. Ming had said it was poison.

If Trudi pulled a Ginny, she could have easily exchanged the funeral voucher for a fancy wedding at heaven's doorstep. On the off-chance the Chapel was still open, she called the main office to verify her hunch and see if Trudi was on the schedule. Ruby was starting to shake with excitement. She never actually believed she would get this close to figuring it out.

"Glass Chapel, Fabrizia speaking."

Distracted, Ruby gushed, "Oh! I love your name! It's so pretty."

"What are you calling about, miss?"

"Sorry. I was wondering about your wedding schedule. Can you tell me if you have a reservation for the O'Kieffe/ Harris wedding?"

"Let me check," answered the beautifully-named secretary who just *had to be* drop dead gorgeous and stick skinny. While Fabrizia checked the schedule, Ruby wondered if she should name her baby Fabrizia. She ran through a few combos:

Fabrizia O'Deare.

Fabrizia West.

Fabrizia O'Deare West.

Fabrizia Grace.

Fabrizia Amelia O'Deare.

"Ah! Here it is," Fabrizia said as she scrolled through the records. "It's set for next fall, a beautiful time of year for a wedding!"

"I was just wondering if we still owe any money?" Ruby lied. "I'm the bride's sister and I'm dotting all the i's for her."

"Oh, isn't that sweet!" There was another pause while Fabrizia looked through the records. "No, honey. The fee has been waived because of an estate donation. You have the chapel for two hours gratis. You only need to cover the fees for the cleanup crew."

Bingo!

"That's what I thought. Just out of curiosity, how much do you normally charge for a wedding?"

"It varies a bit based on the time of year, the day, that sort of thing. It generally costs about $20,000, though."

"Oh, that's not too bad," said Ruby.

Even though $20,000 sounded semi-reasonable to her, she knew it was enough to kill for, particularly if you were a "killer-type," which she imagined Trudi might be. She could barely wrap her mind around it, though. Trudi might be a bitch, but it was hard imagining anyone killing Estelle, especially someone who had known her.

A quick Google search for potassium chloride verified Ming's earlier observation about the deadly peanuts. Potassium chloride, a close relation to table salt, stopped the heart in a way that looked like a heart attack, particularly for diabetics like Estelle. No fewer than ten television shows had used potassium chloride as a murder weapon in recent years: *Law & Order*, *CSI*, a few movies, and most recently *Damages*, which she had loved. Someone knocked off the lead defendant in last season's *Damages*. It took Rose Byrne the whole season to figure it out.

Ruby called Eric and reported, "I think Trudi killed Estelle," as if she were answering a burning question.

"What?" Eric put his beer down and looked out at the river scape. "Trudi did what?"

"She killed Estelle."

"How do you know that?" asked Eric, who was catching up.

"Ming figured it out. I brought home a bag of nuts from Estelle's. Ming tasted them and said they were covered in potassium chloride instead of salt."

He said, "Uh huh. I'll be sure to put that in the file," which Ruby translated to, "I'll say whatever you want to hear you crazy woman."

"Oh, just have her blood tested. I'm sure that she'll have elevated levels of potassium chloride. Then, go to Estelle's house and get the saltshaker. Test that. It's not salt."

"I'll get right on that, Nancy Drew. Just curious. Why would Trudi kill Estelle? It's not like she stood to inherit and she was getting free rent while Estelle was alive."

"Because she's getting married at the Glass Chapel. Estelle donated her house to Pastor Rick. He normally does a free funeral for people who donate their estates. Trudi knew that and exchanged it for a free wedding. Between poisoning her dinner and scoring a free wedding, I think we have the motive and the weapon."

"Are you telling me she'd kill a woman just for the opportunity to cash in a coupon for a free wedding?"

"Yes. That's exactly what I'm saying."

After laughing for a few minutes, he began to mock her: "I heard they have an opening at the *Weekly World News* if Client Advisors goes under." His tone implied he thought it would. "I'll ask the medical examiner about Estelle's potassium levels, but I'm not promising anything."

"So will you do some more investigating?"

"I'll check out the potassium thing for you, but that's it. The Emerald PD isn't *CSI*. Our science dude has a microscope donated by the high school and a projector."

Though she felt obliged to say thanks, she didn't feel the sentiment. She couldn't put her finger on it, but there was definitely something wrong with Eric. It was like he didn't even bother to try doing his job. With frustration, she pressed "end." She didn't throw the phone across the room, but she thought about it. Instead, she picked up her Diet Coke and looked back at the TV.

She might not have been able to solve her case within an hour, but at least *SVU* didn't disappoint. Ruby watched Mariska with a touch of jealousy as she hauled a bad guy into lock-up. It would have been awesome if she solved the case by the end of the second commercial break. But the *Law & Order* crew never wraps things up that early. They don't reveal the real killer until ten minutes before the end. That's like six commercial breaks, not one. She needed to be patient.

Too tired to walk the dogs before bed, she just let them out in the front yard. The streetlights illuminated her block in cozy light and she sat down to watch the dogs. She could tell it was almost spring because a hint of GreenLawn chemical wafted across the street from Mr. and Mrs. Cuttings' yard.

Then she noticed a cat framed in their window. Funny. She never knew they had a cat. With its distended belly and gray stripes, it looked just like Vera Wang, except a little fatter.

She yelled in the open front door to Ming who had just gotten home from a late night at the store. "Have you seen the cats anywhere?"

Ming laughed. "They've been living at the neighbors for about a month."

"Really?" Ruby looked again at Vera. Mrs. Cutting had always doted on them. "Did you give them away?"

"I didn't have to. They just moved out."

Ruby bit her lip. She'd check in on Tom and Vera tomorrow. Looking out at the world, she rubbed her belly. Hopefully she would do better with kids.

Chapter Twenty-Five

Ruby v. Ozcorp

The thing about pro bono clients, especially deceased pro bono clients, is they don't pay. Even though Estelle's case was nothing but loose ends, Ruby needed to get some other work done. Ming had mentioned, not so subtly, that rent was due. The power bill was also about $50 higher than Ruby expected and Sallie Mae and her Biomall Visa wanted their monthly cut of her salary, which so far consisted of an IOU for a Yakima rack. The Biomall went so far as to put her valet parking privileges on hold. In other words, she needed to sue someone, draft a will, or maybe negotiate something fast.

Her pre-pregnancy T-shirt strained over her belly and her hair was matted down with a couple days of leftover product. All she was missing was a BBQ stain. "Ming, why do I have office space? What am I going to do?"

"I don't know. You rented it."

"Well, what am I going to do with it? I printed out business cards that say *Client Advisors*. What does that even mean?"

"Just be a lawyer. Sue someone. Isn't that what you're supposed to do?"

"Junior associate basically means glorified coffee bitch. I don't know how to sue anyone. Law school didn't teach me anything except how to minimize my accessories. It was like a $200,000 book club, except one where all the members hate each other and the hostess calls you stupid." It had been amusing enough until her first $900 monthly loan bill.

"Maybe we could get you some sort of transition counseling for chicks who are experiencing reality for the first time." Ming said between mouthfuls of Frosted Flakes.

"Whatever. I grew up in a trailer on food stamps."

"You didn't mind, though."

It was true. She and her mom went from bedazzling denim at the kitchen table to buying $500-a-pair rhinestone-encrusted jeans at the Biomall without thinking about, well, much of anything. What was there to worry about? "Whatever, Ming. Stop eating my Frosted Flakes."

. . .

At Auntie Em's, Ruby filled up with a vile brew of insecurity and a quadruple Americano that chewed at her gut like a rabid Chihuahua; she decided she would never go back to caramel, cinnamon, or vanilla lattes. No more vanilla. No more extras. No more sugar-coated reality. That's how she ended up pregnant and unemployed in the first place. She needed to taste the bitterness. She needed to stop wishing and make $50,000 a year, minimum, or face bankruptcy court. The era of wishing in fountains was over.

There weren't any other customers and Auntie Em was looking through her the mail muttering to herself. "God damn Ozcorp," she said.

Ruby drew her brows together and said, "What's your problem with the mall?"

"Well, for one, I invested in the damn company, along with everyone else in town. All the shares are worthless. Oz is worse than an Amway salesman."

Ruby had never thought of the Biomall as a company or Oz as a businessman. It was just "the mall" and Oz was the town's benefactor.

When she sat back down at her desk a few minutes later, she was still grappling with the incongruity, so she flipped open her laptop and typed "Ozcorp" into the search box. A Google search filled in some of the details on the Biomall's financial situation. Ozcorp went public and sold shares to fund expansions a while back. Expansions included the Chapel Mall, which was basically an extension of the Biomall (connected by monorail), but also several malls in neighboring states, bought up and retired to increase the Biomall's regional supremacy. About seven years ago everything had started going to pot, the same time the Ozcorp launched Funland.

Oh, Funland! That brought back memories. Funland had been an amusement park located inside the Biomall that functioned primarily as a hang-out for degenerate or bored high-school kids, basically the Biomall's answer to the Mall of America's Camp Snoopy, a traditional hang-out for

Minnesota gang members in February. Ozcorp built it when Ruby was in college, so she only loitered there on rare occasions. One notable evening in her second year of law school, she and her boyfriend had done it (as in *it*) in the pink cup on the kiddy teacup ride. It had seemed like the thing to do at the time. She could just file that one away under Ruby "before sanity," along with everything else that had occurred up until she realized she was living in a house of credit cards.

She kept reading.

Funland began its downward spiral after two deaths on the "Twister," a luge-style roller coaster that ejected several unsecured passengers into the stores below. When the Hollister storefront became nothing but a glorified splatter screen for Twister victims, the ride had to close. Following closely on the Twister deaths, a fourteen-year-old drowned after passing out drunk in the wave pool. The uncertified lifeguard failed to notice because he was making out with the victim's underage sister. For a while, this all added to Funland's cred, which the park capitalized on by posting extra warning signs (basically dares) that made teenagers and drunk cowboys shell out money for tickets to prove they had the *cajones* to ride the Twister, until finally, a couple of people caught Legionnaire's disease from the water fountain and died, making Funland not only dangerous, but gross. After the insurance skyrocketed and people stopped visiting, Oz ripped out the rides and installed koi ponds and a reflective pool in honor of the Twister victims, but only after he'd shelled out millions in personal injury suits and attorney's fees.

Funland might have been the crown jewel of Oz's epic failures. There was also a failed men's fragrance line. The company had recruited the *Jersey Shore* star, "The Situation" to be the face of Cut and overpaid him by millions. Seriously bad idea. Fame is ephemeral and even more so when your talent is based on abs alone. Ruby glanced down at her own belly. Abs could not be counted on.

Ruby flashed back to the news the other night and the report about the Biomall endorsing Elysian Fields. It looked like Ozcorp's profits were about to sink deeper into the muck with another dumb idea. No wonder Em was pissed. She was probably horrified to have played a part in the development of Cut or Funland.

Ruby flashed back to law school and Professor Feldman droning on… *"A shareholders' derivative suit is appropriate when the managers of a publicly held corporation put their own interests above those of the shareholders. Enron is a famous example."* Maybe she could file a lawsuit against Ozcorp on Em's behalf. It wouldn't be hard to find other investors, too. It appeared that several mutual funds had purchased big chunks of Ozcorp stock.

Because she had never filed a lawsuit by herself, she Googled "how to file a lawsuit." Ehow.com explained it in three easy steps. Step One advised, "Hire a lawyer," but she forged on. Luckily, her gifted inner workings, which had been clogged with facts about celebrities and make-up tips, started to sputter and kick into gear. She managed to type the entire complaint without taking a coffee break, staring into space, or inventing an urgent need to clip her nails. She alleged violations of his duties of care, loyalty, and dereliction of duties. Then, she drafted a client agreement for Em to sign.

With the freshly printed papers in hand, she trotted

across the street to Em's with the dogs on her heels and asked, "Em, are you busy? I have an idea."

"I've got some time. Bring in Charmaine and Debbie. We just baked dog treats. They're gluten-free." Em considered Charmaine to be gluten intolerant because of some excessive barking and a runny dog turd that had required a hose for removal a week ago.

"Thanks! I think you might be right about Charmaine and her gluten intolerance. Her fur has been so much shinier since I changed her diet. She just loves eating those things you've been baking. So does Todd." To be fair, they were really good dog biscuits. Todd hadn't made it back to the reservation after his arrest. "I'm going to need to get a few more actually."

Em gave her an odd look, but handed over another bag of dog biscuits. "They're on the house." Em loved dogs. She was one of those people who cried at all those commercials featuring one-eyed dogs and Sarah McLachlan.

"Hey, Em, after you mentioned Ozcorp this morning, I started thinking. You might have a strong case against Ozcorp, strong enough to file a decent shareholder's derivative suit."

Em started laughing. "You cut me up, Ruby O'Deare."

Ruby said, "I totally understand if you don't want to. It's a really big company and we probably wouldn't win."

Em stopped laughing and said, "It's not that. I'm just surprised. I thought you were just trying on bras over there or something." After a few seconds pause, she said, "Sure, go ahead and sue 'em. Put my name on it. I don't care."

"Really?" Ruby felt the excitement surge. It was probably a hair-brained idea and she was probably too inexperienced to manage the lawsuit, but deep down it felt like a good idea. Plus, she preferred not to think before she leaped. "I brought over a client agreement for you to sign." She pulled out the complaint and handed it over. "Do you want to read this over? You can mark any spots I need to change."

Em looked it over for a few moments and said, "Yep. Looks good to me. Do you need an envelope?"

"Sure." Ruby looked at Em skeptically. "Are you sure, Em?"

From the back room she shouted, "I'm sure. You know me, I love to raise a little hell." A moment later, Em came out of the office with a nice thick manila envelope. It was already stamped "Auntie Em's" in the left corner and someone had scrawled "receipts" across the middle. "I already wrote on it, but it's fine other than that. Reduce, reuse, you know."

"Thanks." It wasn't professional looking, but it probably didn't violate any rules, at least none that Ruby knew of, so she shoved the complaint into the envelope, crossed out "receipts," and wrote "OSWALD RANCKA" in bold letters. Meanwhile, Debbie and Charmaine ran through the store like canine vacuums, scarfing up scone crumbs.

Settled comfortably at one of Em's tables, she called up Smiddy, figuring Marvel would know a process server. "Hey, Marvel."

"Ruby!" Marvel exclaimed. "I'm so glad you called! It's been pretty dull around here since you left."

"I bet. No one sleeping with the judge lately?"

Marvel laughed, "Yep. I wish you'd come back. It was more fun."

Ruby said, "I'm calling for a favor, actually. Do you

know any process servers?"

"Sure. I've got lots of names. Is the person you want to serve in the Emerald or somewhere else?"

"Oh, I'm suing Ozcorp, so I thought I'd serve Oz."

Marvel laughed. "You're joking! I just can't imagine you suing the mall. What if they red-flag you and don't let you in anymore? What would you do?"

Ruby forced a little laugh, and repeated her question, "What's the guy's name and number?"

As Marvel pulled up the number, she advised, "You know you can't serve Oz, right? The guy skipped town years ago. He pled guilty to criminal liability in the Funland case after that last kid died on the Twister. When the court released him on bail he disappeared."

"Seriously? That must have happened while I was in college or law school." There was a seven-year gap where she basically didn't know what happened in the world. She studied for some exams and sat in Starbucks. Really, it was only recently that she had begun to develop situational awareness.

"Most people think Oz is holed up in Switzerland or Japan or something, but he could be working at a gas station in a baseball hat and shades for all anyone knows."

Ruby frowned. Estelle had lunch with him not long ago. He must be in town somewhere, even if no one else knew about it. "Oh. Thanks anyway, Marvel. I'll drop by soon."

"You do that!" said Marvel with real sincerity.

The news about Oz completely floored Ruby. Inspired, she changed her status update on her new Client Advisors Facebook page. Ruby hadn't bothered to check, but only a few people were following her page: the Emerald Police

Department, Ming, Em, Noel, her mom, the Joel Smelch for Governor Campaign, and one Destinee. Her update appeared:

Client Advisors™: Whoa!? Did anyone else know Oz went missing? If you happen to see him, let him know Client Advisors™ is looking for his address. ;-)

Chapter Twenty-Six

AT THE OFFICE PARK

At 10:40 p.m. Ruby pulled into the Bank of West call-center parking lot to wait for Trudi's shift to end. After typing up the complaint, she'd decided she'd like to talk to Trudi about the night Estelle died. Trudi worked the three to eleven p.m. shift at the call center. When Ruby processed this information, all of the evil forces in her life aligned. Estelle's assassin was one and the same as the debt collector she'd been avoiding. And for a moment, everything made sense.

Ruby didn't even mind the late hour. It was either wait for Trudi or watch infomercials with Todd. The Bank of the West call center sat in a bland-looking building within a larger office park. It was the kind of building that looked corporate formal on the outside, but was probably business casual on the inside. Ruby could imagine rows of employees clad in wrinkly khakis biding their time in rows of dusty gray cubicles. As she stared at the doors waiting for Trudi to emerge, her phone rang. *Please be Noel!* Her racing heart stilled when she saw the number. Someone from inside of the office park was calling to collect on her Bank of the West card. She hit mute, as usual. Little did they know she was sitting in the parking lot. She wondered if Noel's parents would ever notice that she was on their outstanding accounts list. That could be awkward.

About ten minutes before quitting time, Trudi walked out to her car in jeggings and hooker boots. It looked as if the debt-collection industry had a particularly relaxed definition of biz casual; i.e., if it worked on the city bus, it worked in the office. Stepping out of her car, Ruby started waving. "Trudi, Hi." She ran to catch up with her. "I was wondering if we could talk for a minute."

Trudi did a double take and said, "What are you doing here? You a paparazzi?"

Ruby laughed. "I wish! Actually, I have a question and Monette said I could find you here."

"You never heard of a phone?" Trudi lacked her usual sass. She looked genuinely tired, probably from spending the last eight hours haranguing with debtors on the phone about payment plans. "What's the question?"

"It's about Estelle."

Strangely enough, Trudi didn't shut down. With a sigh, she said, "Whadya wanna know?" It wasn't the type of behavior Ruby expected from a killer.

In a serious tone, the kind of tone a teacher would use to confront a cheating student, Ruby leveled with her. "I know you traded Estelle's free funeral in for a wedding." She paused to let that statement sink in and watch Trudi's reaction.

Trudi laughed. "Is that what you're worried about? It's not like Estelle is gonna know. Who cares?"

"That's a little harsh isn't it?"

Trudi just shrugged. "Estelle wouldn't have turned her nose up at a free wedding." Then, she added, "I don't see why it matters anyway. It's not like I killed her to get a free wedding or something. The woman died of a heart attack."

Either Trudi was a good liar or she believed her lines. In carefully measured tones, Ruby said, "I don't think so. Someone poisoned her."

Trudi snorted. "No fucking way. No one would kill Estelle."

"Just out of curiosity, I'm wondering where you bought the salt that you put in Estelle's chicken, you know that day I came over to take her out for lunch?"

The moment Trudi mentally traced the line between "Estelle was poisoned" and "Didn't you make her chicken?" her breathing went all jagged and the color drained from her face. In a high-pitched voice, she said, "I didn't—"

"Oh no. It wasn't you." Ruby said, waving her hands as if the idea was preposterous. She hated to see Trudi upset about something she did by accident. As she heard herself comforting the killer, she decided she probably needed a partner if she was going to stick with this business. "I only want to know one thing... Where did you get the special low-sodium salt you put on her food?"

Trudi looked at her like she was off her rocker. "Pastor Rick told me about it. It was supposed to be good for the heart."

Ruby's radar could be malfunctioning, but she was

almost 100 percent sure that Trudi had not poisoned Estelle intentionally. Pastor Rick, she wasn't so sure about. He certainly had motive, but killing someone by suggesting a new brand of salt to the victim's would-be daughter-in-law sounded so complicated. It wasn't one of those simple, elegant answers that smacked of truth. It was just another piece of the puzzle that didn't quite fit.

Because Ruby was of the philosophy that there is no sense feeling meaningless pain, she decided the best route was to reassure Trudi and send her on her way. She said, "Don't worry. You didn't do anything wrong." She never would have guessed it, but it didn't look like Trudi had committed an intentional crime, unless you counted bank robbery and crimes against fashion. Until she snagged a job writing for *Glamour's* "Fashion *Don'ts*" feature, Trudi was safe.

When she saw Trudi heading for the bus stop, Ruby impulsively offered, "Hey, I'll give you a ride if you want." Even though Trudi was bitchy, it seemed that she'd actually been a good friend to Estelle. "So when is Jermaine getting out of prison?"

Trudi sighed and shook her head. "Not for a while."

"Estelle was sure she could get him out earlier. It's too bad that didn't work out."

"What do you mean?" Ruby asked. Had Trudi known about Estelle's secret plan?

"Oh, she had some dirt on Oz. She was going to threaten to blab if the police didn't let Jermaine out." Trudi sighed again. "I'm so bummed it didn't work. I had the date picked out for the wedding and the flowers lined up."

Ruby stopped listening. Estelle had planned to blackmail

Oz into letting Jermaine out? It all led back to Oz. Estelle died to protect his secret. When she heard it, she knew it was the puzzle piece she'd been looking for.

She called Eric and reported her findings. He said, "Cool. Nice work, babe." He promised he'd get right on it. His tone of voice didn't convey any urgency. He sounded like he would have promised anything to get her off the phone and go back to sleep. She couldn't blame him. It was almost midnight. She'd call him again tomorrow.

Chapter Twenty-Seven

The next morning she hit the office bright and early, motivated to catch Oz. Right after she finished her coffee and called Noel. He'd tried to apologize for letting Ozcorp slide through the land reclamation process and she'd given him cold shoulder without even bothering to listen. The more she thought about it, the more she realized that she didn't want a bad land use decision to stand in the way of happiness. That was not the fight she wanted her happy ending to go down over. Before she'd even sat down, though, she heard someone coming up the stairs. Definitely not Ming. Whoever it was had a macho, I'm-coming-your-way-sugar type walk.

Eric.

"Hi, Eric." She flashed a smile forged by thousands of years of evolution, a smile filled with the promise to bear his children and fill the world with taller, even-more-strapping Erics. It wasn't just a smile. It was basically cheating.

"Nice pad, Rubes. I like the location."

"You like lingerie?"

He raised his eyebrows, wordlessly indicating his masculine approval of all things involving lace and boobs and refusing to dignify such an obvious question with a verbal response. She might as well have asked, *Do you eat food?*

He sat down at the pink settee with a grim sort of look. "So, do you plan on helping any men? How the hell is a person supposed to sit on this thing?" He sat awkwardly in the middle, not wanting to recline like a swooning maiden, as it invited.

With a tinge of excitement in her voice, she said, "What's up? Are you going to arrest Oz?" She laughed, but she was only half joking.

"Fuck no. I did get the tox-screen results back on Estelle, though."

"And?" Ruby was pleasantly surprised that he'd started taking her seriously.

"She had elevated potassium levels, so you might be right, but I can't do anything about it. Elevated potassium isn't abnormal." He let that sink in for a second, then went on, "Even if Trudi testifies that Pastor Rick gave her some low-sodium alternative to salt, which sounds crazy as shit, the tox results don't support the finding that she was poisoned." He paused to finger some lace panties Ming had left next to the pink chair. "Sweet panties."

"The tox screen results and motive support reopening the investigation at least. You should get a warrant to search…somewhere for the potassium chloride."

"Search where? Not to mention, the chain of custody on the poison is whack. You might have motive for Oz, but where's the proof that he had the poison or knew about it? Hell, no one even knows where Oz is. The dude could be living on the International Space Station wearing astronaut diapers and eating freeze-dried caviar. You have no case."

Feeling frustrated, she drummed the desk with her fingers. "I'm not asking for the moon. I've given you plenty to show that someone killed an old lady and is getting away scott-free. I don't get why you won't take that seriously."

"Even if I do find the killer, there is no usable evidence. The peanuts you took would not be admissible in court. You know that. Plus, Trudi's testimony is useless. She's a felon. The defense will tear apart anything she says."

Ruby frowned and Eric continued. "Like I said, there's no point. The department will not allocate any resources for cases that don't have a high likelihood of a win. Too broke for goose chases, especially when Ozcorp is the goose."

"You should at least question Trudi."

"There's no point. Ozcorp money paid for both the judge's and the mayor's campaigns. Without Ozcorp, none of us would have jobs and everyone knows it."

After a pause, he changed the topic, saying, "I saw your Facebook update, the one about suing Oz. Why not just be happy with that? Go all class-action on his ass, get a fat settlement, and buy yourself something nice."

He was right. She felt her spirits lifting already. Her optimism made for harder falls, but it also made for fast recoveries. Right now, she was thinking that even if the police wouldn't press criminal charges, she had her civil case to fall back on. She smiled. "Thanks, Eric. That's good advice."

Eric seemed reluctant to leave.

Ruby asked, "What else is on your mind? You seem distracted."

Eric took a deep breath and shrugged, his too-sexy attitude lost in the moment of despair. "Rick wants me to get more involved in the Chapel."

Ruby laughed and blurted out, "Has he met you?" Eric wasn't ethical enough for police work. Sure, she could see that it might be a good idea for him to pursue a career where he wasn't required to carry a side arm, a career where he didn't have access to government databases that doubled as dating websites, but religious leadership didn't seem to be the logical next step.

"He says I have the *right look* to be a 'Chapel Man.' He wants me to move off the houseboat and settle down, start acting like an upstanding citizen."

Ruby didn't say anything, unsure of the proper condolences when one is shamed out of living on a beloved, but rusted-out houseboat. The more she knew about Eric, the less she understood him. Nothing made sense—his security gig, the off-grid houseboat, his causal police work, his platonic relationship with Destinee. Something had started to seem "off" about him and his interest in her. *Maybe he's gay? Probably.* He was too perfect for a mortal woman. *But, shouldn't a gay man look more comfortable on a chaise lounge?*

Chapter Twenty-Eight

Ultrasound

Ruby took a long sip of her coffee like she was taking a drag off a cigarette and stared into space as if confronting a long and poorly lit day on a Hollywood back lot. Outside, the Kansas sun glared. She resented it and indulged in her fit of noir. The legal research for the shareholder's suit was offering a glimpse of the dark underbelly of the mall, and not the well-lit glass tile tornado shelter underneath Enzo's. For Ruby's family, the Biomall had not only represented the American dream, it had *been* the dream. Today she felt like she was waking up and realizing it had been a completely unrealistic dream, on par with her childhood fantasy of living in a castle made of marshmallows. She wanted to crawl back into bed.

Lost in reflection, Ruby didn't notice when Em, who had taken it upon herself to educate Ruby on non-Kardashian current events, tossed her the paper. "Hey, lawyer. Take this and read up. It might be relevant to my lawsuit."

The article Em pointed to was called, *Ozcorp: Too Cool to Fail*. It started, "Ozcorp is in bankruptcy and hoping that Emerald will bail it out. The mayor, who is thinking it over, commented, 'If it weren't for the Biomall, we'd still be cleaning out hog pens wearing shit kickers. The Biomall employs over half of Emerald's citizens.' Bailing out the Biomall is a no brainer. We can even make it a good investment. One of our own city officials, Noel West, is an expert on turning superstructures like the Biomal into sustainable investments."

Em huffed. "All this town does is whore itself out to shoppers."

Maybe it was just her credit card debt talking, but Ruby didn't see why the mayor had such a hard-on for the Biomall. First of all, there was Funland, Oz's $40-a-ticket deathtrap. Not to mention she was starting to think the mall had a more generalized, corrupting influence. She would probably have a healthier outlook and less debt if she hadn't grown up in the Biomall's shopping biome. After perusing the article, she said, "Can I have one more coffee to-go, Em?" She needed to drink thirty-two ounces of liquid before her doctor's appointment that afternoon. They probably didn't mean thirty-two ounces of latte, but whatever.

Em handed her the coffee and said, "Go raise some hell for me."

"Will do. As soon as I find out if this baby is a boy or a girl."

"Aww!" Em, in her butch haircut and coveralls, smiled and went as gooey as a thirteen-year-old girl in a kitten store. "You come back and let me know as soon as you find out."

Ruby smiled happily and said, "You're such a softie, Em."

"Nope. I just love babies."

"Ha! Softie."

"Hey, I forgot. I brought in my sewing machine for you to borrow."

"Thanks, Em!" Em had convinced Ruby that she could save money by sewing her own clothes.

Lugging out the twenty-five pound plastic case, she smiled and blew Em a kiss. "I'll try to make you something cute, too."

"No thanks, buttercup. I don't think I could pull off that much razzmatazz."

On her way out the door, a couple of girls pointed at her and snickered. Reflexively, she brushed some imaginary spilled food off her shirt and checked to make sure she didn't have her skirt tucked into her underwear. She had some crumbs and a coffee stain on the baby bump, but who didn't?

• • •

Ruby paused on Em's patio to call Noel. She needed a ride to the ultrasound and he was the obvious choice. She'd meant to call him and straighten out their argument over the Elysian Fields thing earlier. They'd just have to do it on the way to the ultrasound, if he could pick her up.

Noel pulled up to the stop fifteen minutes later. "Hey."

"Hey."

"So where is this appointment?" Noel asked.

"The Biosound."

He turned the car that direction. "I know you're mad at me, but I really want to be included in baby stuff. The ultrasound is a big deal. Isn't this where we find out the sex?"

"I'm not mad at you anymore, Noel. I'm sorry I flew off the handle. I don't think you made a good decision, but I understand."

He sighed. "I know I screwed up. I can see now that it was partially about my father. I didn't want to piss him off the very moment he came back into my life. You were right." He took her hand and said, "Will you accept my apology?"

Feeling her last ounce of frost melt, she said, "Of course." Squeezing his hand in return, she said, "I'm sorry I didn't tell you about the ultrasound earlier." Truthfully, she had balked because she didn't know what to expect from baby doctor appointments. She could never be sure when the doctor would pull out the stirrups and rubber gloves. It just didn't seem like somewhere she wanted to go with someone who had only seen her without lipstick once by accident.

He smiled. "Good. I want to be at everything from now on." Looking at the gigantic box he had loaded into the backseat for her, he said, "What's that?"

"Em loaned me her sewing machine. I'm gonna learn how to sew."

"Really?" He looked at her skeptically.

"Yeah, why not? I can make stuff for the baby. Maybe even something for myself."

He nodded. "That's a great idea."

Ruby stared out the window and watched the world pass by. It was sweet that he hadn't assumed she could learn to sew. Most everyone else got a good laugh out of the idea.

The Biosound, as it called itself, was a typical Emerald building, that is, completely over-the-top, basically the Lady Gaga of all ultrasound facilities. The front of the building sported a lenticular image of an Anne Geddes-style flower bloom opening to reveal a pink-cheeked baby that winked as you passed by the building like one of those 3D book marks for kids. It meshed poorly with the marble and fountains.

The whole facility looked like it had been designed by a group of people with no unifying design concept except "Fabulous!" The lenticular, winking baby had turned into a mild sensation with the pro-life community and had inspired a slew of winking baby billboards along I-86. You could actually gauge your distance from Emerald by the number of winking billboards per mile.

As befit Emerald, the Biosound felt more like an exclusive spa than a clinic. The receptionist greeted Ruby cheerfully, offered her a cup of green tea and a complimentary massage after the ultrasound before ushering her to a little waiting room with modern chairs made of clear plastic. Unfortunately, all the luxury touches and Anne Geddes photos in the world couldn't change the fact that a kid was sitting on her bladder, which was now filled with twenty-four ounces of vanilla latte, not to mention the fact that she was wearing a short skirt (because her pants didn't fit) and her thighs were sticking uncomfortably to the clear plastic chair. Every time she moved, it sounded like she was peeling scotch tape off of a window.

Oblivious to her discomfort, Noel flipped through the numerous pamphlets on birthing classes until, finally, a woman with a chart called, "O'Deare, Ruby."

"Thank God," said Ruby.

In the examination room the tech introduced herself. For a second she stared at Ruby, as if trying to place her. When she did, her eyes grew silver-dollar big. Then, her attention shifted to Noel and her lower lip began to quiver with mirth.

"What is it?" asked Ruby. "Have we met before?" Something was going on. This was the second time people had gotten all wiggy around her today.

"Oh…nothing." The tech could barely get out the word "nothing" because she was trying not to giggle. "I just love your video, though. I'm so thrilled you're having a baby." Attempting to staunch her mirth, she said, "Just lie back. I'm going to put some conductive jelly on your belly."

Ruby looked at Noel to see if he understood what was so funny. He shrugged, completely clueless.

Back to business, the tech perfunctorily rubbed the receiver onto Ruby's belly while Ruby and Noel stared at the screen anticipating the first look with anticipation and more than a little dread. The troublemaker was about to show its face. Or make that its feet. The tech refocused the camera and assessed a few baby parts. Ruby watched without feeling much until a pair of tiny feet came into view. She wasn't expecting the force of emotion that hit her. Prior to this moment Janet Jackson had been as real to her as the peach-sized human growing in her belly. But seeing a picture of her child—it made pregnancy one-hundred times more real than it had been. She suddenly imagined the tiny baby in her arms, a little person all her own, a person she would love unconditionally.

Noel saw the feet too. "Hey, a foot," he said. Oblivious to Ruby's wide-eyed amazement, he went on. "Big feet. I bet it's a boy."

"Nope, make that a girl," said the technician. As she stared at the screen clicking away, counting ventricles, she remarked, "Looks like a healthy baby girl. From her size, I

guess she'll be fully cooked right around June twentieth."
She looked at Ruby and Noel, "Is that what you were
expecting?"

"Sounds about right. Can I pee now?" she asked eagerly.

"Sure. Right over there," the tech said pointing towards
an attached bathroom.

When she walked back into the room, Noel was looking
at a calendar on his iPad. He blocked off a few days around
the tenth, which made Ruby happy.

The tech asked them, "Would you like to augment your
baby photo with any touch-ups before we print it?"

"What?" asked Noel, confused.

"Many parents are disappointed with the quality of their
baby photos, so we offer a photo enhancement service." She
showed a before and after photo of a baby with a misshapen
schnoz, followed by a Gerberized photo touch-up. This made
Ruby remember the description of Destinee's father's job:
"plastic surgery for children, but not the charitable kind."
The meaning finally became clear and she shuddered. For
the first time ever she felt bad for Destinee. Living with that
kind of pressure to be perfect couldn't be helpful for a kid's
development.

"It looks fine to me," he said. "What do people expect,
a Gerber ad?"

The tech laughed. "Basically. You'd be surprised how
many people upgrade."

A $50 upgrade to the Gerber baby didn't sound as offen-
sive to Ruby as it did to Noel, but she smiled and accepted
the picture. Her baby didn't look like an alien anyway. Baby
Rosebud Fabrizia O'Deare was perfect with little smoochy
lips and an upturned nose.

Noel saw Ruby's copy of the photo and spontaneously asked her, "Would you mind printing off a second photo for me? For the office," he added. "Betsy will want to see it."

She smiled at Ruby in a conspiratorial way as if to say, "Wow, what a catch!" As Ruby carefully tucked the baby photo into her pocket, she realized that she would have a baby on her hip at the Fourth of July picnic this year, at Ming's birthday, for everything. She would have a six-month-old baby next Christmas, hopefully without the James Bond marathon.

They walked in silence to the car. The air was tinged with the smell of fresh rain and Ruby inhaled the smell of damp pavement. Noel ushered her to his car and opened up the door for her, insisting on holding her bag while she buckled in.

As they drove down Biomall Promenade, Noel ventured, "Well, what do you think? A girl, huh?"

Ruby looked down at the profile picture. "I'm glad you were there."

When they pulled up to Ruby's house on Primrose, there was a huge box out front. "I bet it's the crib. My mom ordered one for the baby. Do you want to see it?"

"Sure, why don't you let me help you get it inside. You shouldn't be lifting anything that big." As he said this, he picked up the box and hoisted it through the door and into the living room like it was no bigger than a sack of flour. Ruby was impressed. She figured that box was a two or three person job.

After cutting into the box and sifting through the insane amount of packing material, which Noel found to be offensive for environmental reasons, Ruby found the coverlet. It was just as cute as she remembered, with little embroidered bees wearing tutus. She spread it over the back of the couch and carefully smoothed out the wrinkles. "What do you think? Isn't it perfect!"

Where most men would have probably said whatever she wanted to hear so that they could move on to dinner as fast as possible, Noel looked thoughtfully at the bees and said, "I like the bees. I don't want her to be scared of bugs and dirt." Then, probably taking in the tutus, he mentioned, "Good thing she turned out to be a girl."

"Good point." For some reason she just assumed the baby would be a girl. Really, even if Noel had contributed a Y chromosome, her X was bound to overwhelm it.

After a respectful moment of mock reflection, Noel interjected, "How about dinner? You still hungry?"

"I am, but I'm really excited about the crib too. I want to see it all put together."

"Cool. Let's order take-out. I'll pick up my tools and some Mai Thai. Does that sound good?"

"Are you kidding? That sounds amazing." A warm glow of contentment filled her, until logistics intervened. "You know, on second thought, we shouldn't put the crib together here. Ming doesn't want to room with me after the baby is born. I'd just have to take it apart again in a couple of months when I move." With a slightly dead voice she said, "I'll just drive it over to my parents' place later."

Noel cringed. "That sounds...bad."

Ruby looked at him hopefully. "I'm open to any suggestions."

"Well, I'm your landlord. None of the renters I've knocked up had to move back in with their parents." He flashed his adorable half smile, the one she loved.

Confessing her problem to Noel and realizing he would help felt like heaven. She smiled involuntarily. "So are you going to put me up in a dorm with all the other pregnant renters?" She laughed a little. "How many other pregnant chicks are going to be living with me in your mistress shack?"

"You're the first. Maybe I'll add a few more, though. It'd be a great political scandal. It'd knock John Edwards or Bill Clinton out of the park." He shifted to a serious tone and said, "I bought an old farm a few years back, but I haven't been able to spend much time there. I'm thinking I want to move out there, get a few animals, and plant a big garden. I read *Omnivore's Dilemma* while I was on my sustainability journey. I'm stoked to be become a locavore."

Ruby didn't know how to respond. She was just praying that he didn't want to grow all his own food and would conflict with her own diet, which mainly consisted of things that came out of a boxes that advertised facts like "sugar-free" or "diet." "What about the vineyard?" she asked.

"Vineyard?" He drew his brows together in confusion.

As she started to say, "Marvel told me about your vine-yard," she realized that Marvel was full of shit, even if she was sweet. Marvel was the same woman who called Ruby skinny at three months pregnant. Ruby looked at Noel more closely. She really didn't know the first thing about this man. Brown eyes. No vineyard. Oz's son. What was next? Noel was right in front of her, but she could barely see him through her own assumptions. Ming had called it. She had Ken Vision.

Unaware of her personal epiphany, Noel kept talking. "You'll love it. I have almost one-hundred acres of rolling pasture. There's a little creek and a big old farmhouse. The house needs fixing, but it has good bones."

Ruby had never seen Noel so excited, even the day he had left for his two-month sustainability journey. His eyes were lit up and he was talking a mile a minute. She didn't entirely understand why a person would be so excited about gardening and fixing up old houses, but she was willing to give it a shot. Picking carrots sounded fun, given the right outfit.

"So what do you say, can I put you up at the farm?"

She wanted to go to the farm, but she also didn't trust herself. No matter how cute he was. No matter how much he offered her, Ruby knew for a fact that the man before her was Oz's son and he'd been letting Ozcorp get away with murder. Maybe literally.

"Let's not make any decisions tonight." She was excited, but she was also learning to be patient. Also, Ming would tell her what to do.

Chapter Twenty-Nine

THE DOLLAR STORE SEX TAPE

After her trip to the farm with Noel, Ruby sat down on the couch to unwind. She flipped on the TV hoping to catch something mindless with pretty dresses and flirtation, preferably a reality show. The news was still on, though. Before she flipped it off—because she definitely didn't need that kind of reality—a story caught her attention. The newscaster announced, "Local politician and zoning commissioner caught in a sex scandal!"

Noel's name chimed in her head like a gong. It had to be Noel. He was being gonged off the political stage for a...*sex scandal*? Her mind filled with questions, first among them, *What did that bastard do? Doesn't he know he has a baby on the way! Why am I finding out like this? It's so cliché!*

Suddenly scared of what she might hear, she grabbed the remote to shut off the TV. Approximately two seconds later, she turned it back on to hear something she should have seen coming, but didn't.

Janine, the newscaster, explained, "An anonymous Dollar Store employee uploaded a security footage tape to YouTube after realizing that the person pictured in the tape is currently seeking Kansas state political office. You may not know him yet, but he is running for lieutenant governor with gubernatorial candidate Joel Smelch. His name…Noel West."

Ruby knew what was coming next, so she gripped the armrest and braced herself.

"Also pictured in the tape is a local attorney, Ruby O'Deare. O'Deare is a former attorney of Smith, Dworkin, & LeBlue, and has recently opened her own law practice on Emerald's Grand Ave." Even though she knew it was coming, hearing her name on the news in association with an unknown sex tape made her hyperventilate. While she struggled to process the first part of the story, the WKOZ news team continued impugning her character, which they made look all too easy.

The reporter had the cameraman cut to a full frontal of LA Tits and explained, "Ms. O'Deare *operates* out of Client Advisors. You might also remember Ms. O'Deare from a recent sex scandal with Officer Eric Peterson." They cut to a photo of him grabbing her ass. Between the look on the reporter's face and her inflection, she might as well have said, "Ms. O'Deare operates out of a whorehouse." The camera zoomed in on LA Tits suggestively, stopping just short of zooming in and out.

In the interest of milking every last second out of this story, they included an interview with the Dollar Store employee who had uploaded the footage to YouTube. He said, "Yeah, these two people in business suits, kinda classy looking except for her hair." *What's the matter with my hair?* "They came in totally high. She was giggling and he was all over her."

At this moment, Ming walked in. Ruby looked at her fearfully, hoping Ming wasn't upset about potentially bad publicity. LA Tits figured prominently in the news story. Hesitantly, Ruby asked, "Have you seen this?"

Ming said, "Sure have."

"Are you upset?"

"No." She laughed. "It's free advertising! I'm delighted you made a sex tape. I should give you an even bigger discount on rent."

"I didn't make a sex tape, Ming!"

"Maybe you didn't know it, but you did. Business is going to freaking explode tomorrow. It's going to be awesome. You're probably going to get hit, too. You better wake up and get there on time ready to draft a bunch of wills for horny old geezers." Casually, Ming started dinner, collecting a cutting board and vegetables from the fridge to make dinner. "Have you talked to Noel yet? He's totally going to get elected now."

"I should call him."

"Damn right you should. You guys are *good* together and I totally want your asses parked front and center at the shop all weekend. It'll be like having Santa Claus at Macy's. People are going to want to have their pictures taken with you two and then they'll probably buy some underwear. They're definitely going to want to sit on your laps."

Ruby said, "Uh, I'm going to go find Noel. I think we

need to talk."

"You do that, sweetie. Don't forget the Kool-Aid."

"What?" Ruby asked.

"Watch the tape. You'll figure it out."

It only took Ruby a few minutes to get to Noel's. She parked and ran up to his doorstep in her slippers, ignoring the damp cold air and wet sidewalk. Before she could knock twice, Noel looked out of the long window to the side of the door. When he saw her, he looked almost relieved.

With a quick smile, he said, "I'm glad to see you. I thought you might be a reporter. My phone has been ringing off the hook for the last hour."

Now that she was there, she was at a loss for words. What do you say to someone in this situation? Unable to come up with an appropriate intro, she said, "So…I guess…we, uh, made a…sex tape." She could feel her cheeks burning.

"Sounds like," he said, nodding a little too much. He looked about as awkward and uncomfortable as was humanly possible for someone that good-looking. After taking her coat, getting her a water, and standing around awkwardly a bit longer, he asked, "Have you seen it yet?"

Ruby shook her head no.

"Me neither. I think everyone at work has, judging from the looks I was getting today. I don't know if you want to, but I was just going to check YouTube. Do you maybe want to watch it together? Or would that be weird?"

She could tell from his expression that he wanted to watch it, so she said, "I think we're beyond awkward." Of that much, she was sure.

"I wish we could have a stiff drink or something first at least. I'm sorry, Rubes. I feel responsible for this."

"It's not your fault."

"Well, it might not have made the news without the governor thing."

"If we're going to blame anyone, we should blame Todd and his drugs. What did he say he gave us? Blackout?"

"That works for me. We'll blame Todd." As he went to his laptop and pulled it up, he asked, "Are you sure you want to watch it?"

"Yep. 100 percent sure. We should know what we're dealing with, right?"

"That's what I think." He nodded with approval, like it was the responsible thing to do. He was beginning to treat the sex tape viewing as a business matter, something that had to be done in order to effectively manage the story. He sat down on the couch and pulled up YouTube. "What do you think I should search for?"

"I think Noel West Dollar Store Sex Tape or any combination thereof oughta bring it up."

He laughed as he typed in the search terms. "I never thought I'd be doing this."

"It might be a good thing. Ming thinks we're all going to be more popular and successful." The closer they got to watching the thing, the sweatier she felt.

"Must be a good tape." Despite the joke, Noel looked a little nervous too.

"Maybe." She laughed. As they chatted, it struck her that they hadn't really had a date without Todd or Ming yet. Here they were sitting together on Noel's couch. Alone. It felt a little cozy if you could ignore the part about watching their accidental sex tape.

"Okay, here we go. Dollar Store Sex Tape. Holy fuck,

Rubes, 31,000 hits… It already has an ad."

"Just hit play. I don't want to know."

"You never know, maybe it's all the same person."

Noel settled onto the couch and set the laptop on the coffee table. The video was black and white, but surprisingly clear. The Dollar Store had apparently invested in some high-tech surveillance equipment. It started out with a shot of the empty store. No one was there except for the store clerk sitting behind the desk. He was flipping through a magazine. The rolling time stamp read 10:55, five minutes before closing time.

A few seconds into the tape, Ruby saw herself burst through the door with Noel. They were laughing and pointing and falling all over each other like people caught at the pinnacle of the everything-is-hilarious stage of inebriation. They wandered through a couple of toy aisles and examined various squeaky toys and Pez dispensers. Ruby seriously examined a Hello Kitty purse for a minute, even going so far as to see if its small size could accommodate her wallet. In the frozen foods section, they stopped and stared at the frozen meat products. Noel pulled out a box of fish sticks and they belly laughed like complete fools before putting them back. Ruby thought, *So far so good. No nudity.*

Noel said, "Thank God I put those back. Seafood from the Dollar Store would have been worse than…"

He stopped as things began to heat up on the tape. Ruby wrapped her arms around herself and acted as if she might be cold, as if they were on a chilly nighttime stroll instead of standing in front an open freezer. Instead of shutting the freezer door, Noel gallantly wrapped his arm around her. As he shielded her from the chill of the frozen food section, he began vigorously rubbing her arms. First, he did this in an "I'm gonna warm you up" way. Then, the mood changed and the rubbing slowed down and they turned toward each other. There was a clear shift to, "Ooh, you're heating me up, baby" rubbing.

From her perch on the couch, Ruby prayed they moved away from the freezer section. For one, the camera angle was too good. And two, a sex tape in front of the fish sticks was just too ridiculous. Maybe if they just moved over to the cereal aisle or toys.

But she wasn't so lucky. With Noel's arm wrapped around her, Ruby watched as she tilted her face up to his. From the tape, it seemed that Noel was already looking down at her intensely. She could just imagine the look in his eyes. It must have been terribly inviting because she stood up on her tiptoes and wrapped her arms around his neck. The make-out session commenced. It was hot and heavy, lots of free roaming hands. Noel's hands appeared to be under her shirt and she was standing on her tiptoes egging him on.

Noel looked over at her and said, "So far so good. We haven't gotten into too much trouble yet."

Ruby looked over at him. What she saw completely shocked her. Instead of looking appalled, he was enjoying himself. She said, "Oh my God, stop looking so proud of yourself!"

"Well, I hate to admit it, but—"

"It's a Dollar Store security tape! Everyone we know is watching this, Noel!"

"I know, but still. Look. It's a pretty good sex tape." He scooted over to her and put his arm around her. "Just relax. The tape ends in two minutes. How much trouble could we get into in three minutes? It's probably just some more kissing."

She laughed. "Is that right? You don't think two minutes is enough?" His warm hand on her arm felt very nice. On the screen she watched that same hand rubbing one of her breasts and she half wished he'd do that again.

As she said this, the onscreen make-out session took a turn as they stumbled into a cardboard Kool-Aid display stacked with a random assortment Kool-Aid packets. Ruby watched her onscreen self trip and clutch Mr. Kool-Aid's handle for stability. Because it was cardboard, it gave way and she crashed to the floor in a pile of individual packets of Kool-Aid. Instead of giving her a hand up, Noel looked around with darting eyes like someone pretending to be a spy. Clearly he was high out of his mind. Just as she was thinking this, she watched him drop to the floor with her. The two of them were acting as if they thought the cardboard display was hiding them from any other shoppers or the clerk, like no one would ever see them behind Mr. Kool-Aid. Apparently Blackout gave them the hide-and-seek skills of two-year-olds.

Then it got serious, as in steamy serious. He started unbuttoning her shirt and Ruby watched as she arched her back and pulled Noel closer to her.

She covered her eyes in complete and utter shame. "Oh my god. This is so embarrassing."

Noel pulled her in a little tighter on the couch, and in a slightly husky voice, said, "I hate to admit it, but so far, I kind of like it."

She lifted her eyes to his and noted his heavy-lidded gaze. "Aren't you embarrassed?"

He said, "Maybe later, but right now I'm wondering why we haven't done that since September."

Are we going to make out while watching our own sex tape? Is that wrong? She decided that she didn't care. She started to blurt out, "You mean…"

"What are you going to ask?"

"It's just that I wasn't sure I still looked all that sexy, you know." She gestured to the bump.

Earnestly, he said, "Are you serious? You're even more beautiful."

She wasn't sure whether he was feeding her a line, but she didn't care. Just like she had at the Dollar Store exactly eighteen weeks ago, according to her pregnancy calendar, she tilted her face up and Noel leaned down and kissed her. When she looked over at the computer screen, she saw that her Dorothy Gale blouse was completely undone, exposing her Victoria's Secret *Barely There* bra. On the flip side, she was lying down, which always made her look skinny. Then, as if it couldn't get worse, Noel ripped open a packet of Kool-Aid with his teeth and poured it in a trail from Ruby's boobs to the top of her panties. Luckily, the tape was just about over, but it was clear where things were heading when he started to lick it out of her navel.

With a grimace Ruby asked, "Isn't that the kind of flavor packet without sugar added?"

Noel remarked, "I guess you were all the sweetener I needed."

Somewhere between the fall and the Kool-Aid trail (which now explained why she woke up so sticky and purple), Ruby's viewing experience morphed. Sure, she was totally ashamed, but it was also heartening that Noel seemed to like the tape so much. For the moment, she decided to focus on that. It seemed like a winning strategy. Plus, she couldn't erase the image of Noel and the Kool-Aid. In the last frame, Noel was pulling her bra down with his teeth and she was gripping the Cheerios shelf for stability.

Looking at Noel, there was zero question what he was thinking. He flipped the laptop lid down, shut off his cell phone, and pulled her close. "Too bad I don't have any Kool-Aid."

Chapter Thirty

WHERE BLUEBIRDS SANG

Noel dropped her off at Em's the next morning. Ruby pulled out her bills and decided to take care of business at Em's. As she ripped open an envelope she thought of Noel. For the second time, he'd suggested they move in together in the farmhouse he loved so dearly. The more he described it, the more she suspected it was about to fall into the ground and fill with termites. The amateur psychologist in her guessed he was punishing himself for growing up rich and being Oz's son. Whenever Ozcorp came up in conversation, he looked pinched. She hoped it was random guilt about being related to the dude rather than guilt about doing his dirty work. She suspected it was a mix of both.

This morning, though, she needed to figure out her own business. She looked over her bank statement with despair.

Starbucks…$4.56, Starbucks…$4.56, Starbucks…$7.87,

Zappos…$189.87, Auntie Em's…$10.55, Starbucks…$4.56, Starbucks…$4.56, Starbucks…$7.87, Zappos…$59.99, Auntie Em's…$10.55, Starbucks…$9.00, Starbucks…$4.56, Auntie Em's…$7.87, Etsy…$77.99, Auntie Em's…$10.55, Auntie Em's…$4.56, Pump&Munch …$59.18, Starbucks…$4.56, Starbucks…$7.96, Starbucks…$7.87, TJ Maxx…$56.88, Auntie Em's…$10.55, Auntie Em's…$4.56,

Here was the hard evidence: she had spent her entire income on peep-toe shoes and vanilla lattes, tragically ironic since she no longer wore peep toes and tossed half of the lattes in the trash.

She walked up to the counter and ordered a double vanilla latte. Yeah, she was out of money, but she needed a seven-dollar drink today. When she ordered, Em grimaced in horror and refused to make it. After Ruby insisted, Em relented, but made Ruby add her own shots of syrup so she could "understand the amount of sugar she was ingesting and be accountable for her own health."

Ruby responded, "Em, I'm so accountable it hurts," which barely made sense to Ruby, but made Em tear up because the sentiment actually resonated with her. Em raised and butchered her own hogs to satisfy her personal code of ethics.

Ruby looked at her bank statement again, but she was looking for something that wasn't there: money. In a desperate call for help, she dialed her dad and asked him to meet her at the office. Her mom had already called about twenty times since the sex tape broke, so she might as well kill two birds with one stone: 1. Provide an explanation for her deviance, and 2. Get help with her finances.

Fifteen minutes later Ray O'Deare called from the

street. "Ruby, where's the door for your office? I can't find it."

"Oh, you have to walk through Ming's store. There's a stairway to my office at the back." She just couldn't call it LA Tits when speaking with her dad.

"The underwear store?" he asked, also declining to use the word "tits."

"Yep. That's the one. My door is right behind the rack of clearance bras." Somehow saying this sounded so much worse after a sex scandal.

Ray O'Deare walked into the office looking very uncomfortable. Entering Ming's shop violated his lifelong boycott of lingerie shops. Maurine made a damn fine macaroni casserole and bought her own underwear.

Today, like every day, Ray wore a pair of work pants and an old flannel shirt, probably from 1987. He only spent money at the John Deere store. Like a small boy, he still loved any machine with a shovel attached and gladly smashed the piggy bank for the chance to park a shiny yellow machine with lots of levers and extendable parts.

He sat down across from Ruby. "Hi, Rubik's Cube. How are you doing?" Ray was also the king of awkward nicknames. They came into being as a lame attempt to bond with his teenage daughter and never went away. In that way, they were kind of cute.

"Good, Dad, but I'm stuck on some of these business things, like all of them. Want me to order some lunch and look it over?"

"How 'bout some Philly cheese steaks?"

"Okay." Ruby actually didn't eat those, but she feigned enthusiasm for her dad's sake. Her mom had put him on a diet last month. Maurine switched the dog to Canine Weight Loss dry food and Ray to salads.

Ruby moved the stack of financial documents to his side of the desk and ordered the food. "I got you extra onions and cheese," she said.

He murmured his approval and began to sort through the bills methodically and, incredibly, without judgment. "Your mom made me promise to talk to you about this… uh… tape…" He trailed off, obviously not wanting to say any details out loud.

"I'm sorry about that one. I didn't know anything about it until I saw it on the news. I wasn't in my right state of mind." She paused trying to think of something else to say, but what do you say to your dad about a sex tape? "You're going to love Noel, the guy, you know, the one in the tape with me."

Her dad cringed and sucked air through his teeth.

"He's a zoning commissioner," Ruby said, as if that made the sex tape classier.

Railroad tracks formed between her dad's eyebrows. He shook his head. "I don't know, honey."

"No, really. You'll love him. You already met him once. I really, really like this one."

Her dad raised his hands in a dismissive gesture. "Just let me know if you need any sort of help."

"Just with finances, I think."

He breathed a sigh of relief. "I can do that." After looking at her bank statements he said, "First of all, I'm wondering what you eat? Do you buy food at the coffee shop?"

"I guess I eat Ming's groceries. I contribute to the household expenses in other ways." She looked at the statement for some evidence of that, but decided to let the point drop.

"Okay," he nodded. "Well, you have no money, but I like what you've started here," he said gesturing to her business. "I think you need a good business plan, though."

Ruby steeled herself for the news that she had run the well dry and needed to sell the farm, move into her car, and live off food samples at Costco.

Instead, he said, "First things first, you have a trust fund."

"For real? I knew you and mom were doing okay, but I had *no* idea!" She remembered that moment a few months ago standing in front of the fountain and wishing for a trust fund. Someone had heard!

"You're right. Your mom and I are only doing okay. We have enough, but most of our money is tied up in the house and the business. The trust is from—this is going to come as a surprise—your trust is from Oz."

Ruby stared back with confusion. "Why?" She had never met Oz, couldn't pick him out of line-up, and didn't even know the guy hightailed it to France, or wherever, after he got busted for running a deadly amusement park.

"Sit down for a second, honey. It's sort of a long story."

Ruby sat.

"You remember before the Biomall and before Emerald turned into…well, what it is now?"

She nodded.

"Your mom was going through this naturalist phase and she spent tons of time bird watching."

Ruby couldn't imagine her mom going through a naturalist phase, but she said, "And?"

"When Oswald proposed building the mall, your mom and I attended all the local meetings, mainly because the mall was going in right across the road from us, right smack in the middle of the wetland where all the birds lived. We figured the Biomall would kill all those birds. Your mom just loved the bluebirds, the western speckled ones. Not only that, the place is right in a migratory bird path so a lot of the birds would fly smack into the mall and die. We had just watched some *Nightline* specials on that, you know. Your mom and I were real worried about bird kill so we sued the bastard. We got your Uncle Frank to draft the complaint one night." He smiled fondly. "We were drunk."

She tried not to laugh.

"Your mom doesn't like to talk about it. It's still a sore spot. The day they filled in the wetland and plowed through all those bird nests, well, it was like something died inside her. She didn't really have any interests for a while after that, until she got you into pageants."

"Well, the lawsuit with Uncle Frank sounds like it was fun," said Ruby, imagining her aunt and uncle and parents huddled around the kitchen table with a six-pack of beer in the old double-wide. Big dreams always seem that much more impressive in a little trailer over a card table, fueled by hunger and drive. In her sheltered, diamante-studded existence, she could yell out her dreams at the top of her lungs, but no matter how gusty her yell, the sound didn't reverberate and nothing was left but a tiny voice in the overwhelming space of the mall atrium. She felt jealous of her parents in that little trailer. "Did Oz take you seriously? Bird-kill suits generally don't get much traction." Every now and then she shocked herself by remembering something like this. Bird-kill suits—who knew she had that tid-bit filed away!

"Yeah, it doesn't sound like much, but the Kansas

Supreme Court had just placed an injunction on a radio tower near Topeka, which was also proposed in a wetland in a migratory path. And, we hit a real nerve for Oz. You see, he knew he was building on a nesting site of an endangered bird. We didn't know, didn't even think to look it up, but Oswald knew that if the suit made it to court, the EPA would get wind of it and there'd be a big to-do about endangered species. It probably would have stopped the mall completely."

Ruby nodded. "Why didn't you win, then? What did he give you?"

"He came over late one night with a pizza, all friendly, and sat down at the kitchen table with us. Your mom was real pregnant with you at the time and really happy about the pizza. We should have called Uncle Frank, but we didn't think to. Oz is a charming bastard and he made us an offer we couldn't refuse. He promised me exclusive rights to all the parking lot contracts in Emerald. Then he offered you a trust fund to be funded by 5 percent of the profits from the food court. Then, your mom got creative and insisted that she get to name the parking lots after her favorite birds. That's why the parking lots have all those fruity bird names."

"What happened to the birds?" she asked, suddenly sad about the Biomall's ugly side. Up until last week she had considered it an unassailable parent.

"They died. Haven't seen a one since they dug up that wetland."

Now, the question—should she feel guilty about the fact that her trust was paid for with a metric crap-ton of dead bluebirds? Best to know how much she was dealing with before making that call. She asked, "How much do I have?"

"Millions. Mostly from Pretzel King and Fritter Queen."

"That makes me a…" Ruby trailed off without saying the word "princess" but it hung in the air like a cloud of heady perfume. Practically giddy with relief and delight, she felt all of her concerns evaporate. No more worrying about paying the bills, finding clients, covering daycare costs. No more worries! She suddenly felt flushed and excited, too excited to sit still. Shot full of adrenaline, she wanted to stand up and move, go for a run even. Noticing her dad's serious stare, she tried not to act like a lottery winner and said, "That is really nice to hear."

With a little too much satisfaction for Ruby's tastes, he said, "There's a catch, though. You don't have access until you're thirty."

"*What*? That's two years from now. I don't think the business can make it that long."

"You'll be fine. I can lend you a few thousand for business expenses, but you'll have to get serious about budgeting. I'll help you work it out. Should have taught you about money a long time ago. I guess now is as good a time as any. We'll need to get those credit cards paid off. You can't use them anymore."

"That's all I have, Dad."

"I can help. I wish you could get a business loan, but you're not going to qualify. I think we should start with a business credit card. In fact, let's just do that today. I'll cosign." He put in an application for a Visa for Client Advisors. With emphasis he said, "I'm tying myself to the fate of Client Advisors. We're gonna sink or swim together, honey bun."

With that, it became apparent where Ruby's business sense came from—it was genetic.

While he was at it, he decided to shore up Ruby's housing

situation as well. Ray asked, "Also, have you decided where you are going to live after the baby comes?"

With a sigh, she said, "I'm not sure yet." Hopefully, she'd be living with Noel.

Hopefully.

"If you need to, your mom and I would be happy to have you come back home."

Ruby said, "Thanks, Dad," but she didn't think it would come to that. She couldn't imagine anything more depressing than moving back into her old room. Imagining putting a bassinet next to her old pink canopy bed and boy band posters—she would rather move into the office.

When her dad left, Ruby thanked him, then fell into a reflective silence. Being a trust funder might have been her dream, but waiting two years to become a trust funder had suddenly become Ruby's nightmare. On a purely cerebral level she knew it was silly, but she wasn't sure that she could make it. Not to mention, she'd never imagined that the road to fortune would be paved with dead bluebirds.

Chapter Thirty-One

PEANUTS

The next morning, Ruby sat at her desk with her feet kicked up and the Magic 8 Ball resting on The Bump. Food court royalty or not, she still found herself squinting at the thing, wondering what to do for the day. The viewing window was a mess of foamy blue liquid. Underneath the churning froth, she could only see the edge of the rubber thing with the answers on it. Even though she knew it would make more froth, she shook it again. If she was three months more pregnant, she might have thrown it.

Before she could resort to such dire actions, Ming came up the stairs, all stilettos on hardwood. She said, "Ruby, put the 8 Ball down and back away slowly. I've got plans for you today."

More than ready to take direction, Ruby set the ball down.

"We are going to the Glass Chapel. Destinee is going to be there all day, so you could serve her with those papers. It's some sort of Ozcorp PR thing she's obligated to be at, a million prayers to raise money for epilepsy or some shtick like that." Ming's career as a cancer researcher had less to do with a desire to cure cancer and more to do with her observation that the National Institute of Health had a lot of grant money available for cancer research. Unfortunately for cancer, there was even more money in underwear sales.

Ruby gave a blank look.

Ming said it again slower. "You need to serve Ozcorp with those papers, right?" She treated Ruby like a rusted-out Buick that needed a few kicks to get started.

"Yeah. I guess so. I just wasn't thinking about that." Mostly, she had been thinking about meeting Noel for lunch. She imagined them on the patio at Em's. She'd put her feet up. He'd loosen his tie. Or maybe they could meet in her office, lock the door, and pull the shade on that frosted window. So many options!

Ming rolled her eyes. "Seriously, Ruby. You have to serve someone, so you might as well serve Destinee. And, I need to do some recon at Gemima's Closet. They're launching a new line of bras I need to check out."

The prospect of shopping got her moving, and she put on her cowboy boots. As she stood, the boots pinched. Seemingly overnight, her feet had ballooned out to fill up all the space in the foot box. Hoping it was a passing phenomenon, she tried a few steps, but she could only move her legs enough to manage a stiff, hospital-corridor-shuffling-behind-your-walker gait, so she sat back down. "My shoes don't fit. Do you think they shrank?"

Impatient to leave, Ming cut to the chase. "It's pregnancy. I heard that some women go up two shoe sizes. Do you have anything else to wear?"

"No. That can't be. That would make me like a size ten. That's like WNBA big." With more frustration than despair, she scanned the room for something else to wear. She settled on the red sequined slippers she'd taken from Estelle's house. She had no money to buy new shoes, so they would have to do the job.

Ming scoffed at the red slippers. "All right, Dorothy, let's go to the mall and serve Oz."

Ruby picked up her envelope, shoved it in her handbag, and followed Ming out the door.

At the mall, Ruby and Ming each ordered a vanilla latte with angel foam because Ruby insisted. "My treat. Pastor Rick loves them."

While they were waiting, Ruby wandered over to the glass elevator. Next to the elevator she noticed a dispenser with a vacuum tube system attached, the same type you see at bank drive-throughs. The vacuum tube went from the box all the way up into the belly of the glass chapel, running parallel to the glass elevator. The sign on the box advertised it as the Glass Chapel donation box and said, "Beam your money to Heaven! All donations accepted."

Ruby pressed the red button and pulled out one of the "donation canisters." She didn't have any cash, but she did have lip gloss, a couple of business cards, and a hazelnut Ritter Sport candy bar. On impulse, she stuffed the Ritter Sport bar into the tube and shot it up to the church. Watching it shoot up the tube turned out to be a highly satisfying experience. A bag of airline peanuts and a Client Advisors card made the second trip. At this point she ran out of things she was willing to part with.

Shooting random objects up the donation tube ran par for the course at the Chapel Mall. Since old people and tourists actually donated money via the tubes, the Chapel accepted the prank donations without comment, except for the warning, "Please do not load liquids or live animals into the donation canisters." This reminded Ruby of a story she'd heard about someone shooting a goldfish up the tube. It was probably just an urban legend, but she couldn't help but wonder. Ming handed her a latte and said, "Let's go."

When the elevator doors opened to the Chapel, Ruby sashayed into the lobby in her tube dress, fur shrug, and red house slippers. Destinee, Pastor Rick, and a hot chick in tight zebra-striped pants were congregated around what Ruby assumed was the donation canisters receptacle. They appeared to be examining the most recent donations, which Ruby assumed must be her own.

They strode up to the men. Ruby said, "Hi, nice to see you again Pastor, Destinee." Then she looked at the woman, who was an Italian bombshell in the tradition of Sophia Lauren and guessed, "Fabrizia?"

Fabrizia nodded.

Ruby explained, "We talked on the phone once. I love your name." Ruby fumbled with her handbag while the Chapel crowd looked on. Once she managed to undo the clasp, she pulled out the manila envelope labeled Oz in bold purple Sharpie letters. "Receipts" was still visible beneath the scratches. As she handed over the reused envelope, making the first act of her solo practitioner career official, she said, "Consider yourself served." This, of course, was a bold statement stolen from television, but she didn't know what else to say. The words felt unnatural on her lips, but she held her sassy pose. If nothing else, pageants had made her comfortable delivering a bold line in an ill-advised outfit. She could thank her mom for that skill.

Pastor Rick looked at her with narrowed eyes. "Are you handing that document to me?"

"No. The papers are for Destinee. It's a suit against Ozcorp, so service to Destinee, in her capacity as a designated officer of the corporation, provides legal notice to Ozcorp." Yes, she had taken civil procedure, thank you very much!

Rick looked at her skeptically. "You sent those peanuts up the tube, didn't you?" He was fixated on the peanuts.

She laughed. "I guess I'm just three ounces of peanuts closer to Heaven."

Rick looked at her critically. "It'll take more than that."

Ming, who had been ignoring the entire interaction and acting bored in the entry, said, "So where is Oz, Destinee? Do you guys talk now that you're his number one biatch?"

Before Destinee could answer, Ruby said, "You guys remember Estelle?" She looked directly at Destinee and said, "Estelle knew Oz." Ruby didn't know what possessed her to announce this. She just wanted to see Destinee's reaction and let her know she didn't hold all the cards.

Rick raised his eyebrows. "Oh did she now? Did she tell you?"

Ruby smiled cryptically.

Ming interrupted Ruby's efforts at intimidation. "Ruby, you done? I've gotta get down to Gemima's Closet before school's out. Looking at underwear with teenagers nauseates me."

Elevators can say a lot about a person's personality. Some people jab the buttons and anxiously tap their feet. Others push extra buttons for fun. Ruby often forgot to push buttons at all. If she'd lived in a town with more elevators, this may have become obvious enough for her to change her behavior, but Emerald only had a couple of elevators and they were usually filled with at least a couple of other people also going to level two. Once, though, she and Todd had climbed in together, intending to go from the food level to Ruby's office. After a minute or so, Ruby commented, "Wow, this elevator is *slooow*."

Todd responded, "Man, have you checked out those ceiling tiles? Do you think we could bust through them and climb out if we got stuck or something?" He didn't suggest they were stuck, but he was thinking about it. Running with that idea, he jumped a couple of times to see if he could reach the ceiling and push through an escape hatch.

After about five minutes, and only moments before Todd busted out the top, someone on the outside pushed the "up" button and the doors opened. Ruby and Todd exited despite never reaching the second floor.

As usual, Ruby stepped aside and allowed Ming to take charge. As the elevator descended through the swirling vortex of angels, Ruby said, "Rick looks so young, but I don't think he is. How old is he anyway?"

"God knows. The dude got a new face when he was born again. Born again physically and spiritually."

"He looks good."

"Yeah, I know. Just like Brad Pitt," Ming said. "I heard that he modeled his look after a promotional poster from *Meet Joe Black*. He liked Joe Black's unearthly glow. A lady at the nail salon told me. I don't know if she was full of it, but it's a cool story."

Ruby remembered that poster. Brad Pitt dressed in a tux with a photo-shopped halo of light. If she remembered right, he had been playing the angel of death. Pastor Rick must not have actually seen the movie.

So many things weren't what they appeared to be in Emerald.

Chapter Thirty-Two

Panty Recon

Gemima's Closet had grown to be a three-story super-structure that housed a variety of derivative stores, Gem Kids, Gem Teen, and Gem for Dudes. It served as the Chapel Mall's second anchor store, the main anchor being the Glass Chapel. The two anchors stared each other down across the brightly lit marble atrium with surprisingly little tension.

Giant posters of Lolita-esque preteens in aqua body paint wearing Gemima panties lined the walls of Gemima's Closet. Whether the underwear was blue or see-through remained unclear because of the models' blue body paint. The store was doing an homage to the *Blue Lagoon*, Brook Shield's slightly porn-y breakout role, if you didn't count the Breck commercial, which was pretty much hair porn. As part of the promotion, the store workers had changed out their normal uniforms of tight tank tops for leis made of seashells held in place with double-sided tape.

Ruby looked at the models and pointed at the leis. "My God! That should be illegal. Those models are like fourteen and they're *naked*."

"No. They have seashells covering their boobs. I'm sure their parents are fine with that."

"I thought naked teens in stores were illegal after Abercrombie." Ruby shuddered.

Ming shrugged and said, "Who cares?"

"Maybe it's just getting to me because I'm going to be a mother soon."

"Ha! I'm sure that feeling will pass. If you have a daughter, you'll probably be scheduling glamour shots wearing matching tube tops and wearing Daisy Dukes with your hoo-hahs showing by the time she's twelve."

"Maybe," Ruby acknowledged. "What are we doing here, anyway?"

"I want to shoot myself just for saying this, but I need to check out their new Gem Magic bra." Ming pointed to a special section of the store identifiable by the large number of banners proclaiming, "It's Magic!" with photos of models staring down at their glorious boobs with delighted expressions. "I'm concerned that Gemima is infringing on my underwire patent, so I'm going to buy a few of these and road test them. If they're using my technology, they're going down."

"So, this is like corporate espionage?"

"Only if Gemima stole my ideas. Will you try one of the Magic bras for a few days and let me know what you think?"

"If you pay. I'm broke," Ruby said the words with a little drama, as if she were play-acting the part of a poor person.

"Fine," said Ming. "But you're not broke in the real sense of the word you know. You're just Ivanka Trump without any mad money."

"No, I'm broke."

"No, You're Ivana. I'll buy your bra, though."

As they browsed, Ruby wandered off into a secluded alcove. As she paused to admire a display of Magic Gems in blue iridescent fabric, she started to say, "I feel like I'm eight again. These are so…" Before she could get out "Rainbow Brite" someone shoved her into the display hard and pinned her. She started to scream, but her attacker clasped a hand over her mouth and pressed her farther into the display. The cardboard shelving began to crumple beneath her.

He breathed into her neck and said, "Back off, Ruby."

She nodded, but wondered what he meant. *Back off what?*

"I'm going to take my hand off your mouth. You better not scream." As he said this, he poked her in the side with a knife.

When he removed his hand, she said, "Back off what?"

"You know."

"No, I don't."

"Leave Oz alone."

The interaction had gone on long enough that Ruby's initial panic faded. She could tell that the guy was threatening her with a small Swiss army knife, the kind with only four or five tools and a plastic toothpick that he had probably lost unless he was OCD. Also, he smelled like cheesy fries. Imagining some bozo eating cheesy fries with a tiny Swiss army knife didn't scare her, so she swiveled in his arms to face him dead-on, which would have been sexy if he hadn't been shaped like a potato and dressed like a trucker, not to mention threatening her. As she turned, she kneed him hard in the crotch. Any girl who's ever been cornered by a potato knows that this is just reflex, but he didn't see it coming, so he took it full-on, belatedly reaching for his groin and buckling into a pile of rhinestone bras.

As she high-stepped over him, the lighting, which was designed for optimum refraction to display the merchandise, picked up the shine on Estelle's slippers and made little red rainbows dance all around the alcove. While he was still down, she grabbed the bra she had selected for her road test. She thought Noel might like it. It matched his new red and blue ties.

"Rubes, what do you think of…" Ming stopped short as she took in the scene. "Jesus, Rubes. I know you got excited about the espionage thing, but you didn't have to hurt anyone."

"He pinned me against the display and threatened me."
"Why?"
"Told me to leave Oz alone. I'm not sure if he's worried about the lawsuit or the murder investigation, though."
"Oh."

Ming went back over to the guy, who was still on the floor clutching his balls and watching the women talk. Ming gave him a swift kick just to get his attention, "Hey, freak show, what's with the threat? Is Ruby here supposed to drop the lawsuit or the murder investigation?" Taking in his camo gear, she added, "If I thought you had any skills, I'd say someone is going all Tanya Harding on your ass, Rubes."

He gave her a dumb look, not taking her seriously, "Who are you supposed to be, Lucy Liu?"

Ming ignored the comment and positioned a four-inch heel over his hand. She let it fall over his left thumb and pressed down. As she depressed her heel into his thumb, she said, "Did you know that application of pressure to the nail bed is a neurological test for brain death, the theory being that anyone who's not dead will freak out because it hurts."

Upon application of the stiletto to his nail bed, Mr. Potato squealed like a pig in burning hot oil. It would have attracted the attention of other shoppers, but the store had Katy Perry cranked at nightclub volume.

"Okay. This is your last chance. If you like having an opposable thumb, you better tell me." As she looked closer at the man on the floor with his plumbers crack and camo T-shirt, she added, "Your opposable thumb might be the only thing distinguishing you from lesser mammals. Think fast."

"Fine," he said, "Ozcorp wants Ruby to stop nosing around, drop the lawsuit, and stop looking for Oz."

He started to explain more, but she cut him off, "I get it. Doesn't want to be extradited, go to jail, et cetera." She picked up her foot like a lady and said, "Thank you. That wasn't so hard now, was it?"

To Ruby she said, "All right, Rubes, you have what you needed?"

"Yep." Ruby dangled the bra in the air.

"Let's check out."

As Ruby gave the would-be assailant one last glance, she said, "Hey, Fred. I didn't even recognize you." Then to Ming she added, "Ming, that guy is Destinee's old paralegal."

Ming shrugged.

She looked at Fred with renewed civility, as if they hadn't just brawled in the middle of Gemima's, "What have you been doing since, you know..." Destinee had loudly fired Fred during Ruby's first week at Smiddy. "I can't believe Dworkin assigned me such a fat slob in the first place," she'd gone on. "You can't even properly color-code briefs to appellate courts." With finality, she'd yelled, "You're fired!"

"Tough job market," Fred replied.

"Well, good luck with that," Ruby said before waving good-bye and sashaying toward the checkout line. Even though the line wound through the store, Ruby and Ming walked right up to the front and flashed a card. As part of its first-class customer program, the malls allowed so-called elite shoppers to check out first, no matter how long the line, in addition to valet parking and yearly glamour shots, which they displayed on the wall by the food court. Most people didn't read the fine print on their elite shopper cards, but the mall let you pass them to your lineal descendants like English titles, except not as good. Transferring the right to be first in line at Orange Julius didn't quite stack up to a castle and a dukedom, depending on personal preferences of course.

On the way out of the store, the alarm went off because the clasp of one of the display bras had stuck to Ruby's bag. Ming saw it, unhooked it, and tossed over her shoulder like a grenade.

Chapter Thirty-Three

IN PLAIN SIGHT

Ruby pulled into her driveway after making a much needed stop by the grocery store. The adrenaline of fighting for her life in an underwear store had worn off. She unloaded her bag of fancy cheese and olives and contemplated a quiet evening with the Kardashians. While she looked for her keys, Debbie and Charmaine squealed on the other side of the door. She braced herself for their doggie assault and lowered her bag to prevent them from shooting out the door and running like hell in no particular direction. After spending two months with the dogs, it had become clear to her that the OzDog geneticists had culled these two from the litter for IQ reasons. It couldn't have been fur. Debbie and Charmaine were the Heather Locklears of cocker spaniels.

The grocery bag didn't hold them back, though. One of them—she still couldn't tell them apart—shot out the door and sent the olive bag flying. Sniffer to the ground, the dog ran for her favorite bush and squatted before darting across the street. An Escalade almost took her out, but the dog didn't even seem to notice.

Thinking of her lost olives and the Kardashians, Ruby stood on her front stoop and bellowed with all the desperation of Marlon Brando. "DEEEBBBIIEEE. DEEEBBBIIEEE, DEEEBBBIIEEE."

The dog paid no heed and made a beeline for the golf course. The neighbor heard, though. Mr. Cuttings stared, his hedge trimmers suspended mid-clip. With a weather-girl smile, Ruby waved. "Beautiful weather today! How're the cats?"

"The cats are just fine." He began trimming the hedge again.

Just in case the dog hadn't heard, she called again, "DEEEBBBIIEEE!"

With another friendly wave for Mr. Cuttings, she gave up and headed inside. All she wanted to do was put her pregnant cankles up on a coffee table and eat a whole thing of olives, maybe without even putting them on a plate first.

"Inside. Inside." She shooed the remaining furball into the house and tossed her purse and packages by the door. She pulled up the doggie tracker app on her phone. For a few seconds she watched Debbie, the fucking whore, tour the golf course, making a suspiciously long stop on the third fairway. Luckily, no one seemed to realize it was her dog shitting on the golf course every day. No one but Em, who thought Ruby let her do it as a political statement. Ruby suspected that the dog got away with it because she looked just like Enzo, Oz's favorite platinum-haired pooch. That platinum fur let them get away with murder.

Looking at the tracker signal and thinking of Enzo, Ruby had an idea, perhaps even an epiphany. If she was going to be threatened for knowing Oz's identity and whereabouts, she might as well know for real.

She dialed Debbie, the crazy dog lady. "Debbie, this is Ruby O'Deare. I don't know if you remember me."

Debbie cackled. "Yep. The scarf lady."

"I was just wondering about those microchips the dogs came with."

"Uh huh. What about 'em?"

"I can't hear you very well for some reason." Ruby could hear a lot of yelling in the background—if she had to guess, she'd say at least four were people yelling "Mom" at once. Plus, animal noises, barking, and maybe some braying.

After about five minutes, during which Debbie yelled *"Be. Quiet. Do you want a time out?"* multiple times, Debbie turned on a cartoon and everyone quieted down. "I have twenty-one minutes and forty-one seconds. GO."

"So I have this crazy idea."

Her voice dry as dirt, she said, "I'm shocked."

"I want to track Enzo. The dog is still in Emerald and I would bet my life savings that he's with Oz. Oz went everywhere with his dog. I figured he had the same tracker as Debbie and Charmaine since they are all from the same place."

"That sounds legit." Debbie didn't make any comment about Ruby's goal.

"Do you know how I might do that?"

"Sure. I could figure that out. Enzo is Debbie and Charmaine's father, so it makes things easy."

"Really?"

"Yup. He has to be. That platinum fur is recessive. Enzo has to be the father and there's a pattern to the assigned microchip numbers. If Enzo is the sire, his number will be the reverse derivative of Debbie and Charmaine's. Did I tell you that I designed the system?"

"No. Wow." Ruby was impressed. Debbie contracted for Facebook and Ozcorp. It now seemed extra strange that she lived in a hoarder compound in Hackamore, but there was no accounting for taste.

"Give me a second."

"Debbie and Charmaine are 1002 and 1003. That makes Enzo 666." She cackled again. "The devil dog."

"Seriously?"

"Yep. Type it in. I gotta go, though. Only seventeen minutes left on that show and I need to take a shit."

"Cool! Thanks!" It was nice that Debbie helped out. She didn't care why Ruby wanted the information or what she was going to do with it. That must be the key to success in corporate America. Keep your nose to the ground and don't ask questions. When things got too weird, Debbie just moved to the boonies with her chickens.

Ruby plugged in Enzo's number to the app and waited for him to appear. Before long Enzo's *blip* appeared in the Glass Chapel. It made sense. Pastor Rick was probably Oz's spiritual advisor, helping him rationalize his criminal activities, giving him the feeling that God was on his side. Surrounding yourself with "yes men" can wreck a person. She'd seen it happen to Eddie Murphy—all those shitty movies in the early nineties. Admittedly, Oz wasn't as talented as Eddie Murphy, but the same principle applied.

Ruby looked longingly at her Tupperware of olives, but she couldn't ignore the 666 flashing in the worship sanctuary. If she didn't track Oz down, no one would. Oz was the only one with clear motive to kill Estelle. Not to mention his reckless pursuit of profit and the lives lost at Funland. It would be like letting Lehman Brothers off or something.

• • •

Even though it was after hours, the mall security guard let her in when she explained, "I left my purse in the Chapel."

"You come right back. I'm not supposed to let anyone in after hours. I trust you, though."

After hours the mall was still brightly lit and festive, but the stores were all closed and the halls empty, sort of like some of her girlfriends from high school or Todd. She walked up to the bank of elevators and pressed "up." The elevator car announced its arrival with a *ding* that echoed through the mall's empty space. The ding made her feel as alone as she was. From everything she knew about him, Oz wasn't violent, at least not in a hand-to-hand combat way. He only killed people Rube Goldberg-style with shitty amusement parks or poison that changed hands ten times before finding its target.

When the doors to the elevator opened, a platinum-blond cocker sprang forth and greeted her with full-force doggie enthusiasm. He must have caught a whiff of Debbie and Charmaine because he sniffed every inch of her. Enzo, it seemed, was not a guard dog.

After giving Enzo a vigorous scratch behind the ears, she walked toward the Chapel office where she heard voices.

She was grateful she was still wearing Estelle's slippers because they didn't *clickety clack* on the marble tiles.

The first voice said, "Cut stinks, Dad."

Well, if that wasn't the truth. *Cut for Men* smelled like a barn.

"It smells like a manger, son."

"Exactly."

"So explain again why you aren't going to run for office."

Ruby peeked around the corner and caught sight of Noel. She gaped for a moment. There sat the father of her unborn babe discussing Ozcorp's failed products and playing cards with Pastor Rick all casual-like. It might as well have been Bingo Tuesday at the old folk's home. Rick snapped his fingers and pointed to the floor, "Enzo, come. Lie down." To Noel he said, "Must be a storm brewing. That dog can't settle down."

Noel said, "I don't want to be in politics, Dad." Even though she should have put it together already, it hit her in the gut like Brad and Jen's break-up, no warning and full impact. Noel had just called Pastor Rick "Dad." Pastor Rick was Noel's father.

Pastor Rick was Oz.

Why hadn't she seen it before? She recalled Ming's words: "Born again spiritually and physically." Rick personified the most literal interpretation of born again ever (except for the second coming, which hadn't happened yet, at least that she knew of). Oz had been hiding in plain sight the whole time.

And Estelle's murder finally made sense. This neatly solved the whole problem. *Mens rea* and *actus reas* were located in the same individual. Oz had the motive and Rick had supplied the poison.

She remembered something her mom had told her once. "People will believe anything, as long as you sell your lie with confidence." Her mom had been talking about passing as a natural blonde, but the lesson still applied. Rick told people they could have everything their hearts desired— eternal salvation, rhinestone jeans, a trendy car, and a guilt-free conscience. It would probably take more than DNA corroboration to make people see the truth.

Noel knew, though. He had lied. Noel knew where Oz was and just sat on the information. There he sat, playing cards with "his dad" and drinking a beer. They looked downright cozy. She recalled Noel's comments about "finally getting to get to know his dad." That was not a good enough reason to let the man get away with murder. That nagging suspicion that he was too good to be true had been right. Noel wasn't as good as he looked. He was dirty.

As Noel's betrayal hit her, she let out a quick sob and clapped her hand over her mouth. When he looked over his shoulder and caught sight of her, she shook her head and gave him a look of scorn. "How could you?"

"Ruby?" Noel stood. "What are you—"

"How could you?" she repeated in an accusatory tone.

"I…" Noel was caught speechless.

Ruby turned and headed for the elevator. Just as the door shut, Noel reached her. She glared at him through the glass elevator. As she slipped below the floor, he mouthed, "I'm sorry." Enzo pressed his nose to the glass.

She ran through the main level of the mall and to her car. Safely behind the wheel, she dialed Eric and explained everything. Because she'd finally learned not to place all her trust in one man, no matter how good looking, she called

Tyrone as well. She wasn't going to be a fool and trust Eric this time. Rick was not going to be able to sit on his secret any longer. She was sure of it, but she wasn't going to sit around and wait for the authorities to arrive. She needed to go home.

As she thought of Noel, tears welled up. She couldn't know how involved in Rick's business he was. It seemed like he had been running for office at his behest. She staunched the flow of tears and put him out of her mind as best she could. She'd figure it out tomorrow.

Before climbing into bed that night, Ruby put on her jammies and sat down in front of the tube to clear her head. She couldn't find the remote, so she had to watch local TV. Every channel had nothing but weather, as if it was some big story. She caught a few stray phrases, including "global warming" and "early extreme weather," but she thought, *Big whoop*. She'd start watching the weather when she hit fifty or sixty and things like that started to matter. Until then, if it wasn't the Biomall forecast, she didn't care.

She flipped off the power and took the dogs out to pee. Standing in her back yard, she looked up at the night sky. It was clotted with stars, not a cloud in sight. Not even the slightest whisper of wind caressed her cheek.

Chapter Thirty-Four

It's a Twister!

"We apologize for this interruption in your regularly scheduled program. There is an approaching line of thunderstorms that has already produced two confirmed tornadoes in the Salina area. Three more unconfirmed sightings have been reported along I-70 between Salina and Emerald. This system is now moving quickly toward Emerald. Please find shelter immediately, preferably in a basement or a room without windows, if you have no basement. Bring appropriate supplies and stay tuned to this station or a weather radio. If you live in a mobile home, please leave immediately and seek shelter in a permanent structure."

"Just run to the edge of the trailer park and you'll be fine," Ming said, reaching for a wine glass.

The blonde newscaster continued, "Keep tuned to this station for all developments related to this storm." She adopted her most concerned face and waited for the camera to cut out.

Ming continued opening a bottle of Shiraz, one glass for her and one for Ruby. She would accidentally drink both, of course. "Noel's an idiot and an ass, Rubes. It's better that you found out before you moved into his Precambrian mansion."

"Don't I get one?" asked Todd.

Ming pulled out a third glass and poured.

Ruby sulked. She had been refusing Noel's calls all morning. The only person she'd talked to other than Ming and Todd was Tyrone. He had taken "Pastor Rick" in for questioning last night, but they'd had to release him pending the results of a DNA analysis. He assured her that they would be able to make an arrest soon.

Ming handed Ruby an *InStyle*. "Cheer up, Rubes."

"Aren't you two going to the basement to huddle under a metal desk with water bottles or something? Should I open or shut the windows? Or, is this the kind of thing where we need to use our body heat to keep each other alive?"

"No, Todd. This is Kansas. If you can't handle a tornado and a Bible thumper, you are in the *wrong state*. And no to number three." Ming did not stop for any natural disasters. As a native of L.A., a place where you are more likely to see the local river in a big-budget action movie than in person, Mother Nature just didn't factor in. Previous battles most likely included wearing heels in a gravel drive and leaving the house without an umbrella in driving rain. "Ruby and I are going to watch *Sex in the City* in the basement. Be my guest, if you want to watch from under the desk and open a window."

Ruby took a peek outside. The sky ranged from pea-soup green to inky black. Roiling, angry clouds threaded with zigzags of lightning (reminiscent of Missoni's latest charcoal-gray sweaters) rolled onto the horizon and blocked out the sun. She'd seen worse, though. She turned and explained to Todd, "AMC is playing a Sarah Jessica Parker marathon. Both *Sex in the City* movies and *Meet the Morgans*, that one where Hugh Grant and SJP move to a ranch in Wyoming." This made her think of Noel. If SJP could move to a ranch, maybe she could too?

Between Ming's "fuck tornadoes" attitude and Ruby's inertia, they sat down to watch *Sex and the City* on full volume. Ming made Todd hook up the surround-sound speakers to drown out the noise of the wind.

The dogs huddled at the base of the stairs whimpering, while the people focused on *Sex and the City*. Ming yelled, "Shut the fuck up, Debbie!" To Ruby she said, "Those dogs are driving me nuts. Maybe you should take them out or something?"

Ruby ignored Ming's complaints and exclaimed, "OMG, Ming! Look at Carrie's dress...and that hat!" SJP was working her magic. For at least the duration of the show, Ruby could forget everything but that green feather hat.

Just as Carrie Bradshaw appeared in a haute couture strapless Vivienne Westwood gown with a whimsical green feather cap, the noise outside grew freight-train loud. Todd said, "What is that noise? Is the neighbor using a leaf blower to clean out the window wells?"

"It's just a noisy storm. Turn up the volume."

All the while, Carrie sat at the church just waiting for Mr. Big to arrive, the wind hurled twigs and leaves against the windows and the panes rattled in their frames.

"Mr. Big ain't coming," Ming announced. "Anyone want popcorn?"

"Definitely," said Todd. "I'm starving."

"Looks like the sun finally came out," said Ruby. Indeed, the clouds had disappeared, leaving a beautiful sunset behind. Ruby schlepped over to her bag to find her phone. "I don't think I'm in the mood for popcorn. You guys want Pizza Emergency? How about the eggplant anchovy pie?" Ruby was developing a strange craving for anchovies in her third trimester.

"Whatever," said Todd. As a freeloader, he knew he had no right to an opinion.

Ming would have objected, but she didn't. Earlier, she'd told Ruby, "I want Todd to suffer." Not in a torture way. She simply preferred to smoke him out of his freeloading like a hostage negotiator rather than end it with a quick shot to the head. Hence, squid for dinner twice a week and chicken feet on Thursdays. As soon as he came back from his still-unexplained stint in the town jail (he claimed to have no memory of the preceding week) she went to the Asian market for the weirdest stuff she could find. As a creature of habit, though, Todd asked for chicken feet if she forgot to make them.

Ruby dialed a couple of times, "No one is picking up. I think I'm doing something wrong."

"I'll try," said Todd, "But, is someone at the door?"

"If it's a salesman, don't answer," said Ming.

As the pounding became heavier, the knocker began to yell, "Ruby! Ruuuubbbyyy! Are you in there?"

Ruby drew her brows together. "I wasn't expecting

anyone." The yelling was a little over-the-top, so she walked to the door slowly. When she opened it, Noel was waiting with a wild look in his eye. The rain had slicked his hair flat to his skull and drenched his clothes. Ruby could barely process the scene behind him. The giant cottonwood in their front yard had come down on Ming's SUV, branches were strewn all over the yard and street, and someone's overturned patio umbrella was lying in the sidewalk in front of her house.

"Holy—" Ruby stared at the mess, shocked into a state of normal perceptual ability for at least a moment.

While thus shocked, Noel hugged her tightly and patted her belly. "I'm so glad you're okay." As he hugged her, he mumbled into the top of her head, "I was at the office when the tornado hit and I couldn't get through to you. I've never been so worried."

"Tornado?" Ruby stared at the beautiful man before her. He was her fantasy but she couldn't let herself believe it even if there had been a tornado. "Thanks for checking on me, Noel, but I don't know what you're doing here. I'm not ready to talk to you."

"Ruby, I know you don't understand, but I didn't know."

Her eyebrows snapped together. "Of course you knew. You must have known all along. You knew where Oz was and you knew the things he'd done. You must have at least suspected that he killed Estelle."

Noel looked at his shoes and shook his head. "He's my dad. I mean, I know he's not perfect, but I really didn't think he could kill someone. I know he's made some bad decisions, but he's never been violent. I thought he was really turning things around."

Her shell of anger started to crack. Noel looked sincere.

If anyone could, she should be able to understand suspension of disbelief.

"I wanted to believe him so badly. I just couldn't see through my own bullshit hopes. I'm sorry I didn't tell you. I should have."

That did it. She knew exactly how he felt. She had missed the occurrence of a natural disaster. And so much else. Her life, while she'd been window shopping and watching *The Bachelor*, had become an unnatural disaster. Seeing the real man before her, she breathed in deeply, ready to embrace him even with all of his flaws. She opened up her arms and hugged him as hard as she could. With tears in her eyes, she said, "I can't blame you for believing in someone. At least it was a person. I just believed in the mall."

"Thank you," he said and he buried his face into her hair.

A laugh rose up in Ruby's throat and she rubbed the top of her belly. "Our poor baby, though. I thought you had common sense at least."

He nodded. "The poor thing will probably believe in the Easter Bunny until she's thirty."

"We'll be for there when she finds out. It's gonna be a hard fall."

He hugged her again. "I'm just glad you're okay. Thank God you're okay."

Ruby looked at Noel with newly clear vision. Noel really cared for her, maybe even loved her. He was soaked through and wild-eyed with worry for her. She felt sort of humbled, but mostly pretty psyched. Ming wasn't going to let him off that easy, but she was.

Noel looked down at Ruby, who had tears in her eyes. "I really am sorry. I should have been honest from the beginning." He put his hands on her arms and looked into her eyes intently. With clear conviction and a broken voice, he said, "I love you, Ruby."

Her breath caught in her throat. Just when she thought it was over, he became more than she ever expected. When she looked in his eyes, she knew it was the truth. They were shining with tears and with the truth of his feelings. "I love your impulsiveness and your optimism and your sense of fun. You are everything I'm not and when I see the world through your eyes, I'm happier. I'm a better person, more generous of spirit and capable of more love than I knew was possible. I'm so grateful for you."

Ruby sighed with happiness and let the moment wash over her. "I love you, too, Noel. I love you more than I realized I could." She loved the Noel that she'd come to know, rather than the guy she assumed he was. He was so much better than the person she had imagined in her head. He was someone she could have an adventure with, a partner who could surprise her. They already were having an adventure.

He pulled her close and kissed her, a kiss worthy of AMC before it started showing new releases, the romantic ambiance worthy of Old Hollywood, back when the women's hair was perfect and the men were Cary Grant. The wind whipped at them and Noel pulled her in tighter to guard against the cold air.

He whispered into her awapuhi-scented hair, "I was almost hoping that I'd get to rescue you."

She laughed into his chest. "That would have been nice, but this is good, too."

Noel grabbed her hand tightly and they walked over the threshold together.

"How bad is the damage?" asked Ruby, still holding his hand.

"It's bad. The Biomall is destroyed. They're unsure how many people were in the mall at the time. The roof is gone and there is a lot of damage. No one is going to be shopping there for a long time."

Inside she heard Ming yell, "Ruby, get rid of your dog, would you? She's sopping wet."

Ignoring Ming's plea to remove Charmaine, Ruby explained, "Ming, there was a tornado. The Biomall is wrecked."

Ming looked at her with confusion.

"A tornado took the whole roof off."

With a sudden look of panic, Ming asked, "How about the shop? Is it okay?"

Noel answered, "It's fine. The tornado stuck to the new section of Emerald. The malls sustained the worst of it. I saw a water slide stuck in the top of Chapel Mall when I was driving over. The one from the Mall Hyatt. It's sticking right out of the top of the Chapel like a straw."

Ruby's first thought was that maybe the tornado took out her old desk at Smiddy. She hoped it had.

In a shameless act of disaster tourism, Ming, Ruby, and Noel loaded into his pick-up and drove down to the Biomall. Todd decided at the last minute to drink iced tea on the porch and wait for the pizza. There was no way anyone was going to deliver a pizza after an F5 tornado, but Todd couldn't give up the dream, so he stayed. Realistically, he'd probably end up raiding the fridge for leftover chicken feet and stare at the clouds.

As Ruby, Noel, and Ming approached the mall, more and more trees were down. It was the kind of devastation that you expect to see in black-and-white photographs of disasters long gone, not in Technicolor outside your own front door. Luckily, Noel had brought his chainsaw. Several times they stopped so that Noel could clear fallen trees from the road. He took off his suit coat, rolled up his sleeves, and cleared their way like a real pioneer, not like the Oregon-trail playing city kid he was. Ruby knew she'd found a good one.

"I want to make sure my parents are okay, too," said Ruby. "Would you mind driving over there?"

At her childhood home, just across the street from the Biomall, Ruby rushed to get out of the car. She felt genuine fear when she saw the state of her childhood home. The tornado had lifted the roof right off and the outside wall had collapsed, exposing the inside as if it were a child's dollhouse. Her pink canopy bed and French-style mirrored dresser were arranged just so around her circular braided rug. Her parents' cat was sprawled on the front lawn as if nothing had happened.

"Mom!" Ruby called. She was walking through the lawn with great trepidation, scared of what she might find. "Mom! Are you here?"

"Ruby! I'm so glad to see you!" Her mom came rushing out from the back. "I'm so glad you're okay! I've been so worried."

"Where did you go?"

"Your father and I hid in the meditation room in the basement. I put on some Enya and lit some lavender incense." Maurine was shaking with excitement as she recounted this. She paused to collect her breath and stared at Ruby with laser-like intensity. "I think I actually reached a higher plane of understanding. I guess that happens when you *almost die*." She looked back at Ruby's dad, "I think even your father was able to meditate. It was *incredible*."

Ray ignored his wife and walked over to Noel's pickup. Admiring Noel's brand new Husqvarna, he said, "Nice chainsaw, son." It looked like it was going to be love at almost first sight for Noel and Ray. Ray was pretty checked-out at their first meeting.

"Yes, I am. Nice to meet you, Mr. O'Deare."

Ruby's mom suddenly forgot her transcendental state and went straight into mother-of-the-bride DEFCON 1. "Noel! I'm so glad you were watching over Ruby during the storm. Thank you! Thank you!"

Ruby flashed Noel a worried look, but he was holding his own against Maurine.

"Nice to see you again, Mrs. O'Deare. It was quite a storm, wasn't it? We'd love to stay and talk, but we need to go check on Ruby and Ming's office. Ming's concerned about looters."

"Okay, but you hurry back here soon."

"Will do."

"Thank you," Ruby whispered to him on the way to the truck. She was thanking him for everything. She could see the path ahead of her clearly with Noel—a practical future involving home-cooked meals, some light farming, and whatever else people did in the country. There was a lot of grass to mow, she guessed. Assured of his love for her and their baby, she felt like they could tackle anything together.

• • •

At the office, the three of them got out. There wasn't too much damage, just some stray shingles and branches in the road and one broken window.

Ruby busied herself picking up branches and piling them on the sidewalk. Noel kept asking her if she was okay, as if a pregnant person couldn't walk about at all, but Ruby had never felt better. She liked cleaning up the street. She rounded up a couple of stray chairs that had blown across the road and delivered them to Auntie Em's and accepted a free coffee graciously. Em said, "We don't have power, so we're going to have to make due with cold press." At the hardware store she purchased a big push broom and started sweeping the sidewalk in front of the businesses. She felt useful.

When they finished clearing the street, she, Ming, Noel, Em, and a few others sat down and snacked on some cheese and meat trays in Auntie Em's. A warm glow filled Ruby. Not only was she useful, but she belonged to a community, and a community with an appreciation for sexy lingerie, quality pork, and fine espresso. She had found her place.

Finally, Noel offered to drop off Ming and Ruby. "Thanks, but Todd called. He's swinging by to pick me up in a minute," Ming said to Ruby.

"Call if he doesn't show up. I'm going to take off with Noel."

"Great. See you later."

Noel took Ruby's hand and they walked to the pick-up. "Would you like to come to my place tonight?"

They drove almost the whole way to Noel's, and listened to a news story about the tornado. From the news, Ruby figured the tornado hit the mall right about the time that

Carrie was giving up on Mr. Big. Like an ambitious shopper, the tornado had hit both malls and Walmart on the way out of town. Where normal tornadoes picked up trash cans, tree branches, roof tiles, and the occasional cow (if Hollywood is to be believed), the Biomall tornado contained the entire contents of a Wet Seal store, including numerous fully dressed mannequins, and the entire unsold stockpile of Oz-corp's failed cologne, Cut for Men. One female storm chaser claimed that the tornado smelled just like Cut, but skeptics pointed out that Cut smells like wood chips anyway, an entirely plausible smell for a tornado. Incidentally, this also accounted for Cut's low sales figures.

Even stranger, it appeared the Biomall had spawned the tornado that took it out. Everyone knew Emerald had been affecting the weather for some time, but no one guessed it could created an F5 tornado. Apparently, the amount of concrete had finally hit a critical threshold. When an approaching cold front hit the heat rising off the Biomall and its acres of parking—that was all it took. It seemed that her parents had paved the road to Hell for Rick, literally.

Noel pulled over the truck in a particularly pretty meadow. "Want to stop for a minute and talk? There's a beautiful view here. Noel took out a couple of chairs and set them in the back of the pick-up and offered Ruby a hand up. "It's nice to sit back here and look at the stars sometimes."

"You stargaze?"

"Well, I sit out here and have a beer pretty often. Sometimes I happen to look up and notice the view."

"Somehow I feel better about that." Staring at the night sky with beer, now that was something she could get on board with. So much better than a vineyard or a yacht. So much less work, which reminded her… "I heard you say you're not running for office anymore."

"Yep."

"Why not?"

He looked at her and her belly. "I want to move to the country and have a family. Politics was my dad's idea, not mine. I was trying to make him happy."

She smiled and took his hand. It was warm and dry and felt like home. She would have supported him if he really wanted to be a politician, but she breathed a sigh of relief at his statement. Being a politician's wife didn't sound like the life for or her wardrobe. All those drab suits would have killed her.

"I really want to try my hand at farming instead."

She squeezed his hand in a gesture of support. She liked the country. If Debbie could do it, so could she.

They sat silently for a bit. It was a bit chilly outside, but the stars were incredible and the smell of wet earth filled the air, alive and green. The tornado's devastation amplified all of the smells of nature. The broken trees smelled like freshly milled wood and the grass smelled freshly mown. If Yankee Candle company tried to capture the scent of spring, they couldn't have done half as well. Noel started to say something. Ruby thought he might propose, but she didn't want him to tonight. To her the tornado meant a fresh start and she saw no need to skip the end. She wanted to enjoy the moment without thought of the next, so she leaned over and kissed him.

Chapter Thirty-Five

IMAGE IS EVERYTHING

Ruby stood in front of the makeshift shrine for Pastor Rick and absorbed the ambiance, which was downright carnival-esque. Parishioners had erected the shrine as close to the wrecked Chapel as authorities would allow. The centerpiece of the shrine was an oversized painting of Rick that looked even more like Brad Pitt than Rick did in real life. In fact, it might have been a picture of Brad Pitt. Just beyond the shrine, the Chapel Mall loomed on the horizon like the set of a Hollywood action movie at the end of filming. Nothing was left but a pile debris.

Pastor Rick had been the only fatality of the Biomall Twister. Like a captain unwilling to leave his ship even as the waves pushed him under, Pastor Rick stayed in the glass chapel until the end. Late Saturday, workers found him in a pile of debris where the Chapel Mall used to be. There was no official report on what delivered the deathblow, but it appeared that the tornado had hurled him into the marble statue of himself pointing to the heavens. Either that, or the water slide took him out. Particularly creative speculators thought he might have shot down the water slide onto the impaling arm of his marble likeness. No one respectable endorsed that theory, but some college kid animated the scenario and it went viral on YouTube, after which, it became the accepted truth, at least for news consumers under the age of fifteen. And Todd.

Most of Emerald believed that Rick's sacrifice prevented further fatalities. More rational observers attributed the low death count to the timing of the tornado. It struck a few hours after closing time at the mall, saving shoppers and employees from certain death. This explanation didn't go very far though, except in academic circles. Emerald, it seemed, was desperate for a miracle.

Noel was pretty broken up about it, grieving more for the fact that he'd never had much of a relationship with his dad than for his dad himself. Those nightly card games had been a recent development.

Looking around the crowd, Ruby knew she was living in a moment that would be remembered. People had traveled from all over the world, but mostly from Missouri, to light votive candles in front of the shrine. She looked over at Todd and said, "This display makes me almost sad he's gone."

Todd, who had come along to visit the shrine because Ruby had promised to pick up a pizza after, said, "But what a way to go out! If I had to pick a death, that'd be number two. Or maybe three."

So there she sat, sitting on a bench in front of Oz's

shrine watching Todd get baked, because that's what Todd was doing. It seemed like a proper way to commemorate the past few months.

The whole chain of events leading to Estelle's death centered on Oz. Like so many bad ideas, it had all started at a business lunch. At Clementine's, Oz had tried to impress Estelle and awe her into selling her property to him for Elysian Fields. Instead, Estelle realized Oz had handed her the trump card—knowledge of his true identity. Being the savvy lady she was, she decided to negotiate a deal with the police—turning in Oz's identity for Jermaine's freedom.

After so many months, Ruby wanted to wallow in the catharsis. Todd, high as hell, agreed to swing by Estelle's, on the condition that they grab a pizza first.

Ruby pulled her Mustang up to Hyacinth Avenue where Estelle's house had previously rested. To her surprise, there was nothing but splintered wood jutting out of the ground, loose insulation, and a random assortment of household paraphernalia scattered about in a disorganized mess. While Todd scarfed down a Little Caesar's pepperoni pizza in the car, she climbed Estelle's front steps and stared at the void where the house used to be. Slowly turning, she took in the view of the surrounding area. The tornado had destroyed everything in an act of natural justice. For once, Elysian Fields looked like the dump it was.

Then she saw it. Right where Organic Food Hollow was set to go in, sat an overturned structure. Although the tornado had flattened the house like a cardboard box and dumped it a quarter mile away, Ruby recognized the familiar yellow paint and white trim. Ruby wasn't sure if she believed in a higher power, but she couldn't help but think that Estelle would appreciate this gesture, that is, dumping her house onto Elysian Fields. It would take weeks to clean up the bezoar made of grow lights and thirty years' worth of QVC. As far as shrines went, it was even more satisfying than an oil painting of Brad Pitt.

For a moment Ruby shut her eyes to the mess around her and savored the sensation of the wind whipping her skirt about her legs. Facing into the wind with the sun beating on her face, Ruby felt like a pioneer woman.

Chapter Thirty-Six

A Click of Her Heels

A month after the twister, Ruby sat on Noel's front porch with a glass of iced tea resting on her belly, which had turned into a convenient lap desk. Noel leaned over and kissed the babe, saying "How's Honor?"

Ruby made a face of horror, as she always did when he suggested that name. She said, "We're calling her Fabrizia. *Maybe* Estelle. I really like Fabrizia, though. She would just sound skinny." They'd spent the last month playing house at Noel's big breezy farm and preparing for the baby. Noel wanted to bring her up into a new post-consumer world wearing cloth diapers and dining on homegrown vegetables. Ruby was fine with this vision, although she harbored some hope that Noel's hardcore vision for a plot of land planted with potatoes and carrots would mellow into a casual interest in growing wine grapes.

The only fly in the ointment was Destinee. As she so often did, Destinee was escaping justice's grasp. Biomall Board of Directors had rewarded her with a position as CEO of Ozcorp. As far as Ruby was concerned, it couldn't have happened to a worse person. For the moment, Ruby was choosing to classify Destinee's windfall as a delay in justice. As for Eric, the police department suspended him after Ruby notified them that Pastor Rick had been pulling his strings. No one looked surprised. Pastor Rick had been pulling a lot of strings in Emerald.

Even though justice and the American dream weren't a click of the heels away, Ruby didn't plan on becoming a socialist or throwing her TV away. Noel did, but that was his deal. What did she care if he insisted on having chickens? To her never-ending surprise, he was the anti-Ken, side-part and broad shoulders be damned. If it wasn't that he loved her, she would call him downright un-American. He didn't watch TV, read non-fiction, and deprived himself of most refined sugars. Her dad had taken to calling him "The Communist." Her mom loved him because of the broad shoulders and side-part.

Em, who Ruby hadn't even heard pull up, interrupted their porch sitting with a surprise visit. Sidling up to the railing, she asked, "What are you two lazy bums doing?"

"Em!" Ruby greeted her with genuine pleasure. "We're just hanging out. What're you doing here?"

"Clare and I just traded shifts and I thought I'd bring this by on my way home. Some stuffy-looking dude in a three-piece suit dropped it off for you. He said he was a lawyer from Ozcorp."

"That's weird," Ruby said, still casually flipping pages

in the magazine. Apparently, everyone in town knew she was working out of Auntie Em's when she wasn't at her own place.

"I tried to get him to tell me what it was about, but he acted like a mob witness. Even turned down free coffee. I'm guessing it's a letter notifying you that Oz was your father. Clare thinks they're summoning you to a special elite shoppers' pantheon. Either that, or it's about the lawsuit."

Ruby opened up the envelope and stared for a minute.

"It's a note from Ozcorp's attorneys explaining a condition of my trust. It says that if I don't drop the shareholders suit against Ozcorp, I will lose rights to my trust. Apparently, if I file a legal action against Ozcorp or any of its key officers, my trust will dissolve before I gain access." Ruby chewed on her a lip a little. "That sucks."

"Fuck 'em," said Em. "Who cares about the money?"

Noel glanced back at the peeling paint and said, "We might want to consider the money."

"Oh, come on, you two." Em looked exasperated. "What, will you have to delay installing a lap pool and buying Lipizzaner stallions to admire from the front porch? You're made of money."

"Not really," said Noel. "I only make a token salary as a zoning commissioner and my parents cut me off after I withdrew my name from the governor's race. We're going to have to live off $25,000 a year, plus whatever rent we get from Ming unless you start making some money."

Ruby smiled at him. They might not be engaged or married (yet), but the only pronoun Noel used was "we." She reported, "I'm flush out of money. Even my parents are broke. Ozcorp cancelled all their contracts and they won't get any new ones with Destinee in charge. They're going to have to live off whatever my dad didn't spend on Kubota tractors and the new house in Elysian Fields."

"They bought a house there?" Em grimaced.

With a shrug, Ruby said, "Yeah, I couldn't talk them out of it." Secretly, she was excited to escape into her dream life for an afternoon here and there.

"So it's just you and me, baby," said Noel.

"Yep. I guess it's money or justice." Ruby knew what she wanted. Giving up the trust wasn't even a hard decision. Living off a percentage of the food-court profits would make for a posh existence, a life with European vacations, walk-in closets, and probably free soft pretzels with extra cheese sauce, but she knew it wouldn't make her happy. She would be living off of Destinee's dividends. Some people could probably live like that and be happy, but now that her eyes were open, Ruby couldn't.

If she accepted the money and dropped Em's lawsuit, she would be going right back to the old days. Ozcorp would rebuild the mall, she could go back to endless shopping, and her daughter would grow up in a plastic world with artificial weather and a credit card. Sure, she still had an unhealthy love for Pottery Barn and the Gap, but she didn't want to be dependent on Ozcorp for happiness. For now, she wanted a farm, a baby, and some justice. "Em's right. I'm not dropping the lawsuit, as long as you're still on board, Em…"

Noel said, "That's fine, but it takes money to fund a big lawsuit. Not a ton, but we're a little low on discretionary income."

Em looked thoughtful and said, "How much money you talking, Noel?"

"Thousands, probably. We could do it on a shoestring, but we'd need five or ten thousand for starters."

Em said, "I've got a little idea."

Ruby thought Em intended to write her a check like a normal client, but later that afternoon Em came back with a bunch of bright orange Home Depot buckets filled up to the tops with change. She backed her pickup up to Ruby and Noel's front porch and said, "I rounded up a little funding for the lawsuit."

"What? From where?"

Ruby looked at the pickup bed. It was nearly bottomed out from hauling the load.

Em said, "This might best be a don't-ask-don't-tell moment, if you catch my drift."

As Ruby thought through all the places where Em could have found this much change, it hit her. The fountain. The fountain next to Penney's where she had wished for a trust fund. People had been tossing change into it since Oz built the Biomall. Oz didn't think the pennies were worth fishing out of the water, so they'd been piling up since 1990. Em had loaded down her pick-up with buckets of dreams, dreams that Em had officially repossessed.

Ruby smiled at Em. With a wink, she said, "Why thank you, Em! You must have been saving up your change for quite some time."

"I'm nothing if not resourceful." Em smiled sweetly. Her black T-shirt and camo pants were dripping as she said it. Em appeared to approach fountain looting like a SEAL team operative.

Ruby looked at Noel and said, "Honey, you wanna drive down to the bank and deposit this with me?"

"Why sure, sweetie."

Ruby grabbed her purse and slipped on Estelle's sequined house slippers. "I'm ready."

Auntie Em, Noel, and Ruby crowded into Em's bottomed-out, beater pickup and drove to Bank of the West.

Em added, "Why don't we swing by and pick up some lattes and cheesecake too. I reckon it's gonna take a while for the bank to sort all this change."

While they sat in the bank lobby, Ruby raised her latte and said, "I propose a toast. To Oz, for funding his corporation's own demise."

Behind them, the fountain coins *clanked* into piles as the machine sorted them. The hollow *clanking* of unrealized dreams. Dreams that probably never came true. Most of them were probably desperate I-hope-I-win-the-lottery dreams like her own, the dreams of people who'd just about given up. Ruby sat up straighter. Then and there, she decided she would use that money to empower someone just like herself, someone with a stupid dream, someone who could probably think of a better dream if they tried. And she would take down Ozcorp for Estelle.

She sank into the bank lobby loveseat with a warm feeling of contentment. She had thrown back the corporate veil and could see that Destinee was calling the shots. Whatever Enron-style, Tanya Harding bullshit Destinee pulled—in the largest glass mall on the planet, mind you—Ruby would be watching. Even better, she had a pick-up full of money to fund her legal assault and some good friends to photocopy papers and whatnot. The shareholder's derivative suit might not be the end of the story, but it was the next battle and she didn't intend on losing.

Noel must not have been thinking about derivative suits. He leaned over and kissed Ruby deeply. It was the kind of kiss that radiated from her lips to her fingertips and filled her with desire and happiness all at once. Everything in that moment felt right, except the location.

Em yelled, "Get a room, you two! We're at the friggin' bank."

Noel gave Em the finger while still kissing Ruby.

"Better watch it, pretty boy. Politicians can't do that sort of thing."

He came up for air long enough to say, "Not running for office anymore, Em. I'm gonna be a farmer. So's Ruby."

Em began to laugh so hard that she snorted iced latte through her nose. "I can't wait to see that."

Acknowledgments

I started writing this book so long ago, the list of people I should thank is ridiculously long. Mostly, I want to thank my husband who has provided unwavering support. I wrote most of this book while he was at Home Depot with the kids, or putting them to bed without my help. Thanks to my kids. They put up with me missing bedtime countless nights and are still proud of me for writing a book, at least so far.

Thanks to my parents who provided me with a never-ending pile of books during my childhood and bottomless encouragement. I hope I can provide my kids with half as much love and support. Thanks to my sister-in-law, Katie, for reading the first draft of this book and laughing at it instead of me. Thank you to my brother, Colin, for brainstorming on all your coffee breaks.

Thanks to my writing friends who read and commented on the manuscript in all of its stages and offered support: Carol Pavliska, Roselle Kaes, Kristi Belcamino, Matt Beehr,

Cristina Pippa, Sarah Henning, Joy Callaway, Brianna Shrum, Alison Bliss, and Alice Bedard-Voorhees. The book would not be readable without your help. It wouldn't make any sense at all actually.

Thanks to Alison Wagenknecht, MD for providing a real medical consult for Ruby's fake finger injury.

Thanks to Alex Jergensen for making an awesome website.

Thanks to Liz Penney for pulling Ruby out of the slush pile and thank you to my editor, Alycia Tornetta, for making it a better book.

Last but not least, thank you to my readers.

About the Author

Shortly after graduating from law school, Samantha had three children and began writing novels. She never looked back, though she suspects her husband has. *Ruby's Misadventures with Reality* is her first book, though hopefully not her last. She lives in Minnesota with her family. Connect with her at www.sambohrman.com or on Facebook and Twitter.